EZ TALK

英文時事

閱讀選 2024 版

音檔
使用說明

STEP ①

掃描書中 QRCode

STEP ②

快速註冊或登入 EZCourse

STEP ③

回答問題按送出

答案就在書中（需注意空格與大小寫）。

STEP ④

完成訂閱

該書右側會顯示「已訂閱」，
表示已成功訂閱，
即可點選播放本書音檔。

STEP ⑤

點選個人檔案

查看「我的訂閱紀錄」
會顯示已訂閱本書，
點選封面可到本書線上聆聽。

Part 1
Short News 短篇報導

Teen Gives 16,000 Valentines to Those in Need

青少年送出一萬六千份情人節卡片給弱勢族群

全文朗讀 ♪ 001　　單字 ♪ 002

Vocabulary

1. **Valentine's Day**
   情人節（2 月 14 日）

2. **otherwise** [ˋʌðə‚waɪz]
   (adv.) 否則，不然

3. **volunteer** [‚vɑlənˋtɪr]
   (n.) 志願者，義工

4. **handmade** [ˋhændˏmed]
   (adj.) 手工的

5. **recruit** [rɪˋkrut]
   (v.) 招募，雇用

6. **website** [ˋwɛbˏsaɪt]
   (n.) 網站

7. **approximately**
   [əˋprɑksəmɪtli]
   (adv.) 大概

   approximate [əˋprɑksəmɪt]
   (adj.) 近似的

8. **funding** [ˋfʌndɪŋ]
   (n.) 資金

9. **distribute** [dɪˋstrɪbjut]
   (v.) 分發，分配

10. **motivated** [ˋmotəˏvetɪd]
    (adj.) 受……激發、驅使的

11. **expand** [ɪkˋspænd]
    (v.) 擴大，擴展

Patrick Kaufmann from Potomac, Maryland, has made it his mission to make sure everyone gets a 1)**Valentine's Day** card, especially those who might not 2)**otherwise** get one. Several years ago, while working as a 3)**volunteer** at a Washington D.C. food ***nonprofit**, Patrick began making 4)**handmade** cards, which were delivered along with meals to sick children and adults. He then realized that there were likely many more people who would appreciate a Valentine's Day card but wouldn't receive one.

來自馬里蘭州波多馬克的派翠克考夫曼，他以確保大家都能收到情人節卡片為使命，特別是那些平常可能收不到卡片的人。數年前派翠克在華府一家食物銀行擔任志工時，他開始製作手工卡片，並將這些卡片與餐點一起送給生病兒童和成人。然後他明白應該有更多人會很期待收到情人節卡片，但他們卻不會收到。

After getting fellow students to create 300 ***valentines** for delivery in 2021, Patrick upped his game in 2022, 5)**recruiting** students from several D.C. schools to craft more than 3,000 cards. This year, 14-year-old Patrick, with the help of over 60 schools in D.C., Maryland, and Virginia, made and delivered 16,000 valentines. He even developed a 6)**website**, Valentines by Kids, where he encourages children to make colorful cards and write messages of kindness and love to those in need.

派翠克在 2021 年請同學們製作三百張情人節卡片並送出去後，在 2022 年決定更進一步，從華府的幾所學校招募學生製作了三千多張卡片。今年 14 歲的派翠克在華府、馬里蘭州和維吉尼亞州 60 多所學校的幫助下，製作並送出一萬六千張情人節卡片。他甚至創建了一個名為「兒童情人節卡片」的網站，鼓勵孩童們製作五顏六色的卡片，並寫下充滿善意和愛心的文字給那些弱勢族群。

The boxes of cards are picked up at Patrick's house by a delivery driver and taken to [7]**approximately** 60 organizations, including hospitals, nursing homes, and Food & Friends, the D.C. nonprofit where Patrick still volunteers along with his father. He also receives [8]**funding** from two other local nonprofits to pay for a driver to deliver the valentines to the various groups that [9]**distribute** them.

送貨司機會從派翠克家中收取裝有卡片的箱子，然後運往約 60 個組織，包括醫院、療養院及華府非營利組織「食物與朋友」。派翠克目前仍與父親一起在此組織擔任志工。派翠克也從另外兩家當地非營利組織獲得資金，這些資金用於支付將情人節卡片送往不同組織的送貨司機，再由這些組織來分發卡片。

Patrick says he hopes his efforts will brighten people's days and make them realize that someone is thinking about and cares for them. He doesn't know any of the people who receive the cards, but he is [10]**motivated** to continue the project, which he wants to [11]**expand** if he can find enough volunteers.

派翠克說，他希望他的舉動能讓別人心情愉快，讓他們知道有人把他們放在心上並關心他們。他不認識收到卡片的人，但他仍積極地進行這項計畫，如果之後能找到足夠的志工，他還想擴大這項計畫的規模。

▲ 學生製作的卡片

Advanced Words

* **nonprofit** [ˌnɑnˈprɑfɪt]
  (adj.) 非營利的
  (n.) 非營利組織

* **valentine** [ˈvæləntaɪn]
  (n.) 於情人節送給情人的卡片、禮物

Tongue-tied No More

up one's game
更進一步，突破改善
= step up one's game, raise one's game

A: Wow, this room is pretty nice for a budget hotel room.
哇，以平價旅館房間來說，這房間很不錯。
B: Yeah. Red Roof Inn has really been **upping its game**.
是啊，紅屋頂旅館真的一直在進步。

brighten (up) sb.'s day
使……開心起來
= brighten (up) sb.'s life

A: I've been feeling kind of down lately.
我最近情緒有點低落。
B: You should get a puppy. Playing with Fido always **brightens up my day**.
你應該養一隻小狗，跟菲多一起玩總是讓我心情愉快。

EZpedia

nursing home 療養院
療養院是為了那些不需要住院，但又無法在家中得到照護的人提供服務的地方。大多數療養院都有護理師助理和專業的護理師全天候 24 小時待命工作。

© Miroslav Bobek, Zoo Praha

First Baby Pangolin in Europe Born at Prague Zoo

歐洲第一隻穿山甲寶寶在布拉格動物園出生

全文朗讀 ♪ 003　　單字 ♪ 004

Vocabulary

1. **endangered** [ɪnˋdendʒəd]
   (adj.) 瀕臨絕種的

2. **captivity** [kæpˋtɪvəti]
   (n.) 囚禁，圈養

3. **resemble** [rɪˋzɛmbəl]
   (v.) 像，類似

4. **conservation** [ˌkɑnsəˋveʃən]
   (n.) 保存，保護

5. **consult** [kənˋsʌlt]
   (v.) 與……商量，請教

6. **artificial** [ˌɑrtəˋfɪʃəl]
   (adj.) 人工的

7. **stimulate** [ˋstɪmjəˌlet]
   (v.) 刺激，促使

8. **breed** [brid]
   (v.) （使）繁殖，飼養
   breeder [ˋbridə]
   (n.) 動物繁殖者

9. **humidity** [hjuˋmɪdəti]
   (n.) 濕度
   humid [ˋhjumɪd]
   (adj.) 潮濕的

10. **species** [ˋspiʃɪz]
    (n.) 物種

A Chinese pangolin was born in Prague Zoo on Feb. 2, marking the first birth of the ¹⁾**endangered** animal in ²⁾**captivity** in Europe. The baby female, nicknamed "Little Cone" because it ³⁾**resembles** a pine cone, weighed 135 grams at birth. Although the zoo reported difficulties at first, the cub is now doing well, providing a ray of hope for pangolin ⁴⁾**conservation** efforts.

2 月 2 日一隻中華穿山甲在布拉格動物園出生，是這種瀕危動物首次在歐洲圈養場所誕生。這隻雌性寶寶出生時體重 135 克，因外形酷似松果而得到「小松果」的綽號。雖然一開始動物園表示遭遇困難，但現在這隻幼獸情況良好，為穿山甲的保育工作帶來一線希望。（編按：三月舉辦穿山甲寶寶的命名投票，確定名字為小松果 Šiška）

For the first few days after the baby pangolin was born, her keepers were worried because she was losing weight. The mother, Run Hou Tang, wasn't producing enough milk to feed the baby. After ⁵⁾**consulting** with experts from Taiwan, a program of ⁶⁾**artificial** feeding with milk from a cat was introduced, and the mother was also ⁷⁾**stimulated** to produce more of her own.

穿山甲寶寶出生後的頭幾天，飼養員很擔心，因為牠的體重持續減輕。母獸「潤喉糖」分泌的奶水不足以餵養寶寶。在諮詢臺灣專家後改採用貓奶的人工餵養方案，同時也刺激母獸分泌更多奶水。

The zoo is now optimistic about the baby's chances for survival, but challenges still remain. "We have only overcome the first hurdle, and others are still waiting for us," says zoo director Miroslav Bobek. They're difficult to [8)]**breed** in captivity because they require a special diet that includes bee [*]**larvae**, as well as an environment

▲ 穿山甲寶寶

with carefully controlled temperature and [9)]**humidity**.

動物園現在對寶寶的生存機率持樂觀態度，但挑戰仍然存在。動物園園長米洛斯拉夫博貝表示：「我們只克服了第一個障礙，還有更多挑戰等著我們。」穿山甲很難在圈養中繁殖，因為牠們需要蜜蜂幼蟲等特殊飲食，及精心控制溫度和濕度的環境。

The baby pangolin's parents, Run Hou Tang and Guo Bao, arrived last April from Taipei Zoo, the world's leading [8)]**breeder** of the rare animals. The Chinese pangolin is native to China and Southeast Asia and is one of the four pangolin [10)]**species** living in Asia. Another four species can be found in Africa.

穿山甲寶寶的父母「潤喉糖」和「果寶」於去年（2022）四月從臺北動物園送達布拉格，臺北動物園是世界領先的稀有動物飼養據點。中華穿山甲原產於中國和東南亞，是亞洲四種穿山甲之一。在非洲則可以找到另外四種。

Because their scales are used in traditional medicine, pangolins are frequent victims of [*]**trafficking**. Over 100,000 are [*]**trafficked** to China and Vietnam each year, making them the most trafficked animal in the world.

由於穿山甲的鱗片可用於傳統醫藥，因此經常成為非法販運的受害者。每年有超過十萬隻穿山甲被非法販運到中國和越南，是世上被非法販運最多的動物。

Advanced Words

* **larva** [ˈlɑrvə]
  (n.) 幼蟲
  larvae [ˈlɑrvi] 幼蟲複數

* **trafficking** [ˈtræfɪkɪŋ]
  (n.) 非法買賣
  traffic [ˈtræfɪk]
  (v.) 非法買賣

Tongue-tied No More

a ray of hope 一線希望

A: Did you see the news about that new cancer drug?
你看到那個新抗癌藥物的新聞了嗎？
B: Yeah. They say it's **a ray of hope** for millions of patients.
看到了，他們說這是數百萬患者的一線希望。

overcome a hurdle 克服障礙

A: That singer's story is really inspiring.
那位歌手的故事真的很勵志。
B: Yes. She had to **overcome** so many **hurdles** to become a star.
對。她必須克服許多障礙才能成為明星。

EZpedia

Chinese pangolin 中華穿山甲
中華穿山甲分布在印度、中國、不丹、泰國、越南、柬埔寨、尼泊爾、寮國及臺灣。臺灣穿山甲是屬於中華穿山甲的一個分支，是臺灣的特有亞種（subspecies）。另外全世界共有八種穿山甲，四種分布於亞洲，另外四種分布於非洲。（參考：台北市立動物園）

Sushi Terrorism Causes Outrage in Japan

壽司恐怖主義在日本引起炎上

Vocabulary

1. **disturbing** [dɪ`stɜbɪŋ]
   (adj.) 令人不安
   disturb [dɪ`stɜb]
   (v.) 使憂慮，使不安

2. **outrage** [`aut,redʒ]
   (n./v.) 憤怒，激怒

3. **hygiene** [`haɪ,dʒin]
   (n.) 衛生（習慣）

4. **online** [`an,laɪn]
   (adj.) 線上的

5. **chain** [tʃen]
   (n.) 連鎖店

6. **incident** [`ɪnsədənt]
   (n.) 事件，事變

7. **stock** [stɑk]
   (n.) 股票，股份

8. **calculate** [`kælkjə,let]
   (v.) 計算，估計

9. **AI (artificial intelligence)**
   (n.) 人工智慧

10. **suspicious** [sə`spɪʃəs]
    (adj.) 可疑的，多疑的

11. **behavior** [bɪ`hevjɚ]
    (n.) 行為，舉止

A [1]**disturbing** new video trend called *sushi tero*, or sushi *terrorism, has Japanese conveyor belt sushi restaurants on high alert. These videos, which show customers doing things like licking and touching food as it passes by, have caused [2]**outrage** in a nation known for its high standards of [3]**hygiene**.

一種令人不安的新發燒影片稱為「*sushi tero*」也就是「壽司恐怖主義」，讓日本的迴轉壽司餐廳處於高度戒備狀態。這類影片呈現出顧客在餐點經過時舔舐和觸碰食物等行為，在這個以高衛生標準著稱的國家引起公憤。

While sushi terrorism videos began appearing [4]**online** late last year, it wasn't until a clip filmed at Sushiro—Japan's largest conveyor belt sushi [5]**chain**—went viral in early March that restaurants began taking the problem seriously. In the video, which has over 90 million views on Twitter, a young man can be seen licking the top of a soy sauce bottle and also the inside of a tea cup, which he then returns to the shelf. And if that wasn't enough, he then licks his finger and rubs it on a piece of passing sushi.

雖然壽司恐怖主義影片是去年年底開始出現在網路上，但直到今年三月初，在日本最大的迴轉壽司連鎖店壽司郎拍攝的一段影片被瘋傳後，餐廳才開始認真對待這個問題。在推特上有超過九千萬次點閱的這段影片中，可以看到一個年輕男子舔了醬油瓶頂部和茶杯內部，然後再把茶杯放回架上。意猶未盡的他接著舔舔手指，然後擦一盤經過面前的壽司。

After the clip of this [6)]**incident** went viral, the [7)]**stock** of Sushiro's parent company dropped nearly 5%. In response, Sushiro replaced all the soy sauce bottles and *****disinfected** every cup at the affected restaurant. The company has also announced other new policies, including making food to order to keep other diners from *****tampering** with it.

此事件的影片在網路上瘋傳後，壽司郎母公司的股票下跌了近 5%。為回應此事，他們更換了受影響餐廳的所有醬油瓶，並對每個杯子進行消毒。該公司還宣布了其他新政策，包括點餐後才製作餐點以防止其他顧客惡搞。

Another large chain, Kura Sushi, plans on using technology to fight sushi terrorism. The restaurant already uses AI cameras to count the number of plates customers remove from the conveyor belt and [8)]**calculate** their bills. Now, Kura Sushi is training its [9)]**AI** system to detect [10)]**suspicious** [11)]**behavior**—like the opening and closing of plate covers—and alert employees if necessary.

另一家大型連鎖餐廳藏壽司計畫以科技打擊壽司恐怖主義。該餐廳已經使用人工智慧攝影系統，來計算顧客從壽司輸送帶上取下的盤子數量和他們的帳單。現在藏壽司正在訓練人工智慧系統來檢測可疑的行為，例如有人打開和蓋上盤蓋，並在必要時通知員工。

It's too early to tell how effective these strategies will be, but for Japan's conveyor belt sushi restaurants, the *sushi tero* trend can't end soon enough.

現在判斷這些策略的效果還為時過早，但對於日本的迴轉壽司店來說，壽司恐襲的風潮愈早結束愈好。

© Takashi Images / Shutterstock.com

▲ 日本迴轉壽司餐廳

Tongue-tied No More

on (high) alert （高度）警戒狀態
alert (n.) 警報 (v.) 發出警報
此片語等於 on full alert，可搭配動詞 be, go, stay, remain, put

The airport was put **on high alert** following a bomb threat.
在收到炸彈威脅後，機場進入高度警戒狀態 。

go viral 瘋傳，網路爆紅

A: Hey, I heard that video of your cockatoo dancing **went viral**.
嘿，我聽說你的鳳頭鸚鵡跳舞影片在網路上瘋傳。
B: Yeah. It has over five million views so far.
對，目前為止影片的點閱率已超過五百萬次。

EZpedia

conveyor belt sushi restaurant
迴轉壽司餐廳
迴轉壽司餐廳的特色就是餐廳內的運輸帶（conveyor belt），運輸帶會將師傅做好的壽司自動送至顧客面前，顧客可以自行取用。

McDonald's Introduces Plant-based McNuggets

麥當勞推出植物系麥克雞塊

全文朗讀 ♪ 007　　單字 ♪ 008

Vocabulary

1. **consist (of)** [kən`sɪst]
   (v.) 組成，構成

2. **batter** [`bætɚ]
   (n.) 雞蛋、牛奶、麵粉等調成的糊狀物

3. **substitute** [`sʌbstɪˌtut]
   (n./v.) 替代物，替代

4. **launch** [`lɔntʃ]
   (v./n.) 推出，發行

5. **availability** [əˌveləˈbɪləti]
   (n.) 可得性

6. **demand** [dɪ`mænd]
   (n./v.) 要求，需求

7. **permanent** [`pɝmənənt]
   (n.) 永久的，永恆的

8. **location** [loˈkeʃən]
   (n.) 地點，場所，位置

9. **generate** [`dʒɛnəˌret]
   (n.) 產生，引起

10. **alternative** [ɔlˈtɝnətɪv]
    (n.) 替代品，供選擇的事物

The American fast food chain will introduce its new plant-based McNuggets in Germany on Feb. 22. McPlant *nuggets—1)**consisting** of peas, corn, and wheat, and coated with a tempura 2)**batter**—are the second product McDonald's has developed with Beyond Meat, a California company that produces plant-based meat 3)**substitutes**. McDonald's has been selling a McPlant burger in Europe since 2021.

這家美國速食連鎖店將於 2 月 22 日在德國推出新款素肉麥克雞塊。植物系麥克雞塊由豌豆、玉米和小麥製成，並裹上天婦羅麵糊，這是麥當勞與超越肉類公司開發的第二款產品。超越肉類公司是加州一家生產植物性肉類替代品的公司。麥當勞自 2021 年以來一直在歐洲販售植物系漢堡。

McDonald's will 4)**launch** the new McNuggets at more than 1,400 restaurants across Germany following a limited test at nine restaurants in the Stuttgart area last August. The chain will also introduce the McPlant burger in Germany next week. 5)**Availability** of the McPlant nuggets in other markets will depend on customer 6)**demand**.

麥當勞自去年八月在德國司徒加特地區的九家餐廳限量試賣該新款麥克雞塊後，將在德國各地 1400 多家餐廳推出。麥當勞也將於下週（2/22）在德國推出植物系漢堡。植物系麥克雞塊是否在其他國家的市場推出，將視顧客需求而定。

So far, European customers have been more *receptive to McDonald's plant-based meat products than American customers. The McPlant burger is now a 7)**permanent** menu item in the U.K., Ireland, the Netherlands, and Austria. Last month, McDonald's launched the Double McPlant burger in the U.K. and Ireland.

目前為止，比起美國顧客，歐洲顧客對麥當勞素肉產品的接受度更高。麥當勞植物系漢堡現已成為英國、愛爾蘭、荷蘭和奧地利菜單上的固定餐點。上個月麥當勞在英國和愛爾蘭推出了雙層植物系漢堡。

▲ 植物系麥克雞塊

But it looks unlikely that American customers will get the chance to try the new McPlant Nuggets at the company's 14,000 U.S. 8)**locations**. McDonald's and Beyond Meat ended their U.S. test of the McPlant burger in 2022, and haven't announced any plans for additional testing or a national launch.

但美國顧客似乎不太可能有機會在美國一萬四千家麥當勞門市嘗試新款素肉麥克雞塊。麥當勞和超越肉類公司於 2022 年結束美國的植物系漢堡試賣，且尚未宣布其他試賣計畫或是在全國推行。

Over the past few years, a number of American fast food chains have jumped on the plant-based meat bandwagon, with varying degrees of success. Burger King 9)**generated** strong sales with the introduction of its Impossible Whopper in the summer of 2019, and has continued to add other meat 10)**alternatives** to the menu. And in early 2022, KFC successfully launched Beyond Fried Chicken plant-based nuggets, although they've yet to be added to the regular menu.

在過去幾年中，美國許多速食連鎖餐廳都搭上素肉的風潮，市場反應不一。漢堡王在 2019 年夏季推出素肉華堡後銷量強勁，並繼續在菜單中添加其他植物性肉類替代品。2022 年初，肯德基也成功推出超越炸雞素肉雞塊，儘管它尚未被列入固定菜單中。

Taiwanese Father and Daughter Win Grammy

臺灣父女檔奪葛萊美獎

© valentinesbykids.org

Vocabulary

1. **acceptance** [ək`sɛptəns]
   (n.) 接受，領受

2. **ancestor** [`ænsɛstə]
   (n.) 祖先

3. **nomination** [ˌnɑmə`neʃən]
   (n.) 提名
   nominee [ˌnɑmə`ni]
   (n.) 被提名人
   nominate [`nɑməˌnet]
   (v.) 提名

4. **experimental**
   [ɪkˌspɛrə`mɛntəl]
   (adj.) 實驗性的，試驗性的

5. **renaissance** [`rɛnəˌsɑns]
   (n.) 藝文復興

6. **solo** [`solo]
   (adj.) 單獨的，單獨表演的

7. **career** [kə`rɪr]
   (n.) 職業，生涯

8. **hit** [hɪt]
   (adj.) 流行的，熱門的

9. **single** [`sɪŋgəl]
   (n.) 單曲

At the 65th Grammy Awards, held in Los Angeles on Sunday, Taiwanese designer Xiao Qing-yang and his daughter Hsiao Chun-tien took home the Best Recording Package award. The father-daughter design *duo received the honor for their cover design for the album *Beginningless Beginning*, the *soundtrack for Xiao's short film *Tamsui-Kavalan Trails *Trilogy*.

週日（2/5）在洛杉磯舉行的第 65 屆葛萊美獎頒獎典禮上，臺灣設計師蕭青陽和女兒蕭君恬獲得最佳唱片包裝設計獎。這對父女檔以專輯《無始之始》的封面設計而獲獎，該專輯是蕭青陽的短片《淡蘭古道國樂團三部曲》的原聲帶。

In his 1)**acceptance** speech, delivered in Mandarin, 56-year-old Xiao paid respect to his wife, parents, 2)**ancestors**, and all the people who have walked the historic Tamsui-Kavalan trails, which have connected northern and northeastern Taiwan since the 19th century.

56 歲的蕭青陽用中文發表得獎感言時，向他的妻子、父母、祖先以及所有走過淡蘭古道的人致敬。歷史悠久的淡蘭古道自 19 世紀以來連接臺灣北部和東北部。

It was Xiao's seventh Grammy 3)**nomination** since 2005, and the first with his daughter. In her English speech, Hsiao, who is studying 4)**experimental** design at London's Royal College of Art, said that the award was a "dream come true" for her father after an 18-year wait since his first nomination.

這是蕭青陽自 2005 年以來第七次獲得葛萊美獎提名，也是他第一次與女兒一起獲得提名。蕭君恬正在倫敦的皇家藝術學院就讀實驗設計系，她以英語發表感言時表示，這個獎項對她的父親來說，是從第一次獲得提名以來等待了 18 年的「夢想成真」。

This is the second year in a row that Taiwanese designers have won the Best Recording Package prize at the Grammys. At the 64th Grammy Awards in Las Vegas, Li Jheng-han and Yu Wei won the award for their design work on the album *Pakelang*, the first Grammy win by Taiwanese 3)**nominees**.

這是臺灣設計師連續二年在葛萊美頒獎典禮上獲得最佳唱片包裝設計獎。之前在拉斯維加斯舉行的第 64 屆葛萊美頒獎典禮上，李政瀚和于薇以專輯《八歌浪》的設計作品得獎，是臺灣人首次獲得葛萊美獎。

The biggest winners on Sunday included Beyoncé, who set a new record by winning her 32nd Grammy—Best Dance/Electronic Album—for 5)*Renaissance*, her first 6)**solo** album since 2016's *Lemonade*. And with a 7)**career** total of eighty-eight nominations, Beyoncé also tied with her husband Jay-Z as the most 3)**nominated** artist in Grammy history.

週日的最大贏家包括碧昂絲，以獲得的第 32 個葛萊美獎，創下新紀錄。她以《潮流復興》贏得最佳舞曲／電音專輯獎，這也是她自 2016 年的《檸檬特調》以來第一張個人專輯。碧昂絲在歌唱生涯中共獲得 88 次提名，與丈夫傑斯並列葛萊美史上提名次數最多的藝人。

But the Big Three went to Harry Styles, who won Album of the Year for *Harry's House*; Lizzo, who took home Record of the Year for her number one 8)**hit** 9)**single** *About Damn Time*; and Bonnie Raitt, who picked up Song of the Year for *Just Like That*.

但三大獎的得主分別是哈利史泰爾斯，以《哈利屋》獲得年度專輯獎；麗珠以榜首熱門單曲《是時候了》獲得年度製作獎；以及邦妮雷特以《就這樣》獲得年度歌曲獎。

Michelle Yeoh Makes History at the Oscars

楊紫瓊在奧斯卡頒獎典禮上創造歷史

全文朗讀 ♪011　　單字 ♪012

Vocabulary

1. **coveted** [`kʌvɪtɪd]
   (adj.) 夢寐以求的
   covet [`kʌvɪt]
   (v.) 垂涎，貪圖

2. **fiction** [`fɪkʃən]
   (n.) 小說
   science fiction
   (n.) 科幻小說

3. **comedy** [`kɑmədi]
   (n.) 喜劇

4. **immigrant** [`ɪməgrənt]
   (n.) 移民，僑民

5. **dedicate** [`dɛdə͵ket]
   (v.) 奉獻，以……獻給

6. **dominate** [`dɑmə͵net]
   (v.) 支配，居優勢

7. **ceremony** [`sɛrə͵moni]
   (n.) 典禮，儀式

8. **persistent** [pə͵sɪstənt]
   (adj.) 堅持不懈的，固執的

9. **agent** [`edʒənt]
   (n.)（政府）調查員、探員

At the Academy Awards on Sunday, Michelle Yeoh accepted the Oscar for Best Actress, becoming the first Asian woman in the event's 95-year history to win the [1]**coveted** award. She received the Oscar for her performance in the science [2]**fiction** [3]**comedy** *Everything Everywhere All at Once*, in which she plays Evelyn Wang, a Chinese [4]**immigrant** who must fight to save her ***laundromat**, her marriage, and even the universe.

在週日（3/12）的奧斯卡頒獎典禮上，楊紫瓊獲得奧斯卡最佳女主角獎，成為奧斯卡 95 年來史上第一位獲得眾人夢寐以求獎項的亞洲女性。她因為在科幻喜劇《媽的多重宇宙》中的表演而獲得奧斯卡獎，她在片中飾演的王秀蓮是位中國移民，為了拯救她的自助洗衣店和婚姻，甚至整個宇宙而奮戰。

Yeoh received a standing ovation as she walked onto the stage to accept her award. "For all the little boys and girls who look like me watching tonight, this is a ***beacon** of hope and possibility," she said, holding up her Oscar. "And ladies," the 60-year-old actress added, "don't let anyone tell you you're ever past your prime." Yeoh [5]**dedicated** her award to her mom, and all moms, praising them as "superheroes." The Malaysian-born actress became a movie star in Hong Kong before gaining international fame for films like *Crouching Tiger, Hidden Dragon* and *Tomorrow Never Dies*.

楊紫瓊走上舞台領獎時，全場起立鼓掌。「今晚所有長得跟我一樣並觀看頒獎典禮的小男孩和小女孩，對他們來說這是一盞充滿希望和可能性的燈塔。」她舉著奧斯卡獎盃說道。「女士們，」這位 60 歲的女演員補充說道：「不要讓任何人告訴妳『妳已經過了巔峰時期』」楊紫瓊將該獎項獻給自己的母親和所有人的母親，稱讚她們是「超級英雄」。這位出生於馬來西亞的女演員在以《臥虎藏龍》、《明日帝國》等電影獲得國際知名度之前，在香港出道成為影星。

But Yeoh's Best Actress wasn't the only win for *Everything Everywhere All at Once*. With 11 nominations and seven wins, including Best Picture, the film [6]**dominated** the [7]**ceremony**. Daniel Kwan and Daniel Scheinert, the directing duo known as the Daniels, also took home Best Director—quite an achievement considering they began their career directing music videos.

但楊紫瓊的最佳女主角獎並不是《媽的多重宇宙》贏得的唯一獎項。這部電影獲得 11 項提名和包括最佳影片的 7 項大獎，在頒獎典禮上獨領風騷。被稱為丹尼爾導演二人組的關家永與丹尼爾舒奈特也獲得最佳導演獎，對從執導音樂錄影帶起家的他們來說，這是相當大的成就。

Everything Everywhere All at Once was also just the third film in Academy Awards history, after *A Streetcar Named Desire* (1952) and *Network* (1976), to win three acting Oscars. In addition to Yeoh's Best Actress, Ke Huy Quan won Best Supporting Actor for his role as Evelyn's husband Waymond, and Jamie Lee Curtis received Best Supporting Actress for her ***portrayal** of a [8]**persistent** IRS [9]**agent**.

《媽的多重宇宙》也是繼《慾望街車》（1952）和《螢光幕後》（1976）後，在奧斯卡金像獎史上第三部獲得 3 項奧斯卡演技類獎項的影片。除了楊紫瓊的最佳女主角獎外，關繼威也因飾演王秀蓮的丈夫王威門而獲得最佳男配角獎，潔美李寇蒂斯則因飾演執著的美國國稅局稽核員而獲得最佳女配角獎。

Advanced Words

* **laundromat** [ˋlɔndrəmæt]
(n.) 自助洗衣店

* **beacon** [ˋbikən]
(n.) 燈塔，指路明燈

* **portrayal** [porˋtreəl]
(n.) 描繪，飾演

Tongue-tied No More

standing ovation 起立鼓掌
ovation 表示長時間且大聲的鼓掌。

The opera singer received a 10-minute **standing ovation**.
這位歌劇演員獲得長達十分鐘的全場起立鼓掌。

be past one's prime 表現不如以往，不如以往活躍、健康

A: Didn't you say Roger Federer is your favorite tennis player?
你不是說羅傑費德勒是你最喜歡的網球運動員嗎？
B: He used to be, but he's **past his prime** now.
他以前是，但他現在已經過了巔峰時期。

EZpedia

IRS (Internal Revenue Service)
美國國稅局

隸屬美國財政部，掌理美國聯邦政府包含所得稅等稅務之執行及納稅服務事項，相當於臺灣的國稅局，負責辦理各項國內稅稽徵、退稅以及法規之解釋等行政工作。

© Marina Stroganova / Shutterstock.com

Hogwarts Legacy Released After Long Wait

《霍格華茲的傳承》經過漫長等待終於問世

全文朗讀 ♪ 013　單字 ♪ 014

Vocabulary

1. **anticipation** [æn,tɪsə`peʃən]
   (n.) 期待，期望

2. **software** [`sɔft,wɛr]
   (n.) 電腦軟體

3. **publish** [`pʌblɪʃ]
   (v.) 發行，出版

4. **wizard** [`wɪzəd]
   (n.) 男巫
   witch [wɪtʃ]
   (n.) 女巫

5. **explore** [ɪk`splor]
   (v.) 探索，探險

6. **professor** [prə`fɛsə]
   (n.) 教授

7. **uncover** [ʌn`kʌvə]
   (v.) 揭露，發現

8. **enthusiastic** [ɪn,θuzɪ`æstɪk]
   (adj.) 熱情的，熱烈的

9. **reception** [rɪ`sɛpʃən]
   (n.) 歡迎，接受

10. **controversy** [`kɑntrə,vɜsi]
    (n.) 爭論，爭議

11. **boycott** [`bɔɪ,kɑt]
    (n./v.) 抵制，杯葛

12. **critical** [`krɪtɪkl]
    (adj.) 批評的，批判的

After years of ¹⁾**anticipation** by Harry Potter fans, *Hogwarts Legacy* was finally released on Feb. 10 following several delays. Developed by Avalanche ²⁾**Software** and ³⁾**published** by Warner Bros. Games, the open-world role-playing game allows players to go on a magical adventure in the Wizarding World created by J. K. Rowling.

在歷經哈利波特粉絲多年的期待和數次延期後，《霍格華茲的傳承》終於在 2 月 10 日問世。這款由艾薇嵐奇軟體開發並由華納兄弟互動娛樂發行的開放世界角色扮演遊戲，可以讓玩家在 J.K. 羅琳創造的魔法世界中展開魔法冒險。

Available on PlayStation, Xbox and PC platforms, the game is set at the Hogwarts School in the late 1800s, a century before the events of the Harry Potter novels. After creating their character and being placed in one of the four Hogwarts houses by the Sorting Hat, players begin their studies as a fifth-year student at the school for young ⁴⁾**wizards** and ⁴⁾**witches**.

這款遊戲可在 PlayStation、Xbox 和電腦平台上遊玩，時間設定在 1800 年代晚期的霍格華茲學校，比哈利波特小說所敘述的年代早了一個世紀。玩家們在創建角色，接著被分類帽分配到霍格華茲四所學院之一後，便以五年級的學生身分在培養年輕男女巫師的學校中學習。

In addition to taking classes, where they learn to make *potions, cast spells, and tame magical beasts, players also have plenty of time to ⁵⁾**explore** Hogwarts and nearby locations. And as they progress in their abilities, they join their fellow students and [6]**professors** on a mission to [7]**uncover** an ancient secret that threatens to destroy the Wizarding World.

除了上課學習製作魔藥、施展魔咒和馴服魔獸外，玩家還有大量時間探索霍格華茲和附近地點。隨著玩家技能進步，還可以與同學和教授一起執行任務，揭開一個威脅要摧毀魔法世界的古老秘密。

In spite of an [8]**enthusiastic** [9]**reception** by gamers and Harry Potter fans, the release of Hogwarts Legacy has not been without [10]**controversy**. Even before the game's launch, supporters of transgender rights called for a [11]**boycott**. This is because J. K. Rowling has expressed views considered by many as [12]**critical** of the trans movement. For example, she believes that allowing trans women to use women's bathrooms "makes *natal girls and women less safe."

儘管受到玩家和哈利波特粉絲的熱烈歡迎，《霍格華茲的傳承》的發布並非沒有爭議。甚至在遊戲發行前，跨性別權益支持者就呼籲抵制。因為 J.K. 羅琳表達的一些觀點，被許多人認為是在批判跨性別運動。例如她認為允許跨性別女性使用女廁「會讓生理性別為女性的人沒有安全感」。

Judging by sales of *Hogwarts Legacy*, however, the call for a boycott seems to have fallen on deaf ears. Within two weeks of its launch, the game sold more than 12 million copies and brought in $850 million in global sales.

然而從《霍格華茲的傳承》的銷量來看，抵制的呼聲似乎石沉大海。遊戲在推出後的兩週內售出超過 1200 萬套，並帶來 8.5 億美元的全球銷售額。

© KateV28 / Shutterstock.com

▲ 遊戲《霍格華茲的傳承》

Advanced Words

* **potion** [ˈpoʃən]
  (n.) 魔藥，藥劑

* **natal** [ˈnetəl]
  (adj.) 出生的，出生時的

Tongue-tied No More

fall on deaf ears 被忽視，被無視
turn a deaf ear (to) 則表示無視於他人的抱怨、警告和要求。

The workers' demand for higher pay **fell on deaf ears**.
工人們提高工資的要求猶如石沉大海，無人回應。

Ron's parents **turned a deaf ear to** all his requests for money.
朗恩的父母對他討錢的要求充耳不聞。

EZpedia

Wizarding World 魔法世界
魔法世界可以指 J. K. 羅琳於小說《哈利波特》創造出的虛構世界。另外 J.K. 羅琳和華納兄弟合作推出了「Wizarding World」網站，該網站會發布與《哈利波特》、《怪獸與牠們的產地》等相關的小說或電影資訊。

transgender 跨性別者
一個人的生理構造與性別認同不一致的狀態。實際上只要在性別認同、行為舉止、外貌與裝扮等方面跨越了傳統男女二分框架，都可以被歸為跨性別。transgender 亦可簡稱 trans。trans man 為跨性別男性，指出生時性別為女性的男性；trans woman 為跨性別女性，指出生時性別為男性的女性

Super Nintendo World to Open in Orlando

超級任天堂世界將在奧蘭多開幕

全文朗讀 ♪ 015　　單字 ♪ 016

Vocabulary

1. **popularity** [ˌpɑpjəˈlærəti]
   (n.) 流行，廣受歡迎

2. **portable** [ˈpɔrtəbəl]
   (adj.) 可攜帶的，手提式的

3. **revive** [rɪˈvaɪv]
   (v.)（使）復甦，（使）復醒

4. **theme** [θim]
   (n.) 主題

5. **executive** [ɪɡˈzɛkjətɪv]
   (n.) 高階主管，高級官員

6. **resort** [rɪˈzɔrt]
   (n.) 度假村，度假勝地

7. **attraction** [əˈtrækʃən]
   (n.) 吸引人的事物、地點

8. **inspire** [ɪnˈspaɪr]
   (v.) 激發靈感，激勵

9. **purchase** [ˈpɝtʃəs]
   (v./n.) 購買

10. **souvenir** [ˌsuvəˈnɪr]
    (n.) 紀念品，紀念物

11. **construction** [kənˈstrʌkʃən]
    (n.) 建造，建設

Since the release of the Nintendo Switch in 2017, the ¹⁾**popularity** of this ²⁾**portable** gaming *console has ³⁾**revived** gamers' interest in classic Nintendo games and characters. No wonder then that Nintendo is partnering with Universal Studios to open Super Nintendo World areas in Universal ⁴⁾**theme** parks around the world.

任天堂 Switch 自 2017 年發行以來，這款可攜式遊戲機的流行已重新喚起玩家對經典任天堂遊戲和角色的興趣。也難怪任天堂會與環球影城合作，在世界各地的環球主題公園開闢超級任天堂世界園區。

The first Super Nintendo World opened at Universal Studios Japan in March 2021, and the second at Universal Studios Hollywood this February. And Nintendo and Universal aren't stopping there. At the grand opening event on February 15, Universal ⁵⁾**executive** Mark Woodbury stated, "Soon, we're going to add another Super Nintendo World to Universal Orlando ⁶⁾**Resort**."

第一座超級任天堂世界於 2021 年 3 月在日本環球影城開幕，第二座於今年 2 月在好萊塢環球影城開幕。任天堂和環球並沒有就此止步，在 2 月 15 日的盛大開幕活動上，環球影城高層馬克伍貝瑞表示：「我們近日會在奧蘭多環球影城度假村再添一座超級任天堂世界。」

The main ⁷⁾**attraction** at Super Nintendo World Hollywood, which opened to the general public on February 17, is Mario Kart: Bowser's Challenge. ⁸⁾**Inspired** by the popular Mario Kart racing games, the ride takes you on a variety of race courses as you compete against Team Bowser for the

Golden Cup. Special **AR** *visors allow you to fire shells at Bowser and the Koopalings and collect the coins you need to win the race.

2 月 17 日向大眾開放的好萊塢超級任天堂世界中，主要景點是瑪利歐賽車：庫巴的挑戰。這項遊樂設施的靈感源自廣受歡迎的瑪利歐賽車遊戲，將帶你體驗各種賽道，與庫巴隊爭奪金盃。特殊的擴增實境眼鏡可以讓你向庫巴和庫巴七人眾發射砲彈，並收集贏得比賽所需的硬幣。

Bowser's Challenge is currently the only ride at Super Nintendo World Hollywood, but there's plenty to keep guests busy. 9)**Purchasing** a Power-Up Band lets you participate in four Key Challenges, and you get to battle Bowser Jr. if you win at least three. Guests can also enjoy Mario-themed meals at the Toadstool Café and buy 10)**souvenirs** at the 1UP Factory.

庫巴的挑戰是好萊塢超級任天堂世界目前唯一的遊樂設施，但仍有很多活動可以讓遊客盡情探索。購買能量手環可以讓你參加四項關鍵挑戰，如果贏得至少三項，就可以與庫巴二世戰鬥。遊客還可以在蘑菇咖啡廳享用瑪利歐主題的餐點，並在 1UP 工廠購買紀念品。

The Super Nintendo World at Universal Orlando will be part of the resort's Epic Universe, which is scheduled to open in the summer of 2025. A Super Nintendo World is also under 11)**construction** at Universal Studios Singapore, and with *The Super Mario Bros. Movie* coming in April, Nintendo fans have a lot to look forward to!

奧蘭多環球影城的超級任天堂世界將設立於該度假村的史詩宇宙園區，史詩宇宙園區計劃於 2025 年夏季開幕。新加坡環球影城也正在興建超級任天堂世界，另有《超級瑪利歐兄弟電影版》將於四月上映，任天堂迷們有許多新作可以期待！

© Usa-Pyon / Shutterstock.com

▲ 位於日本環球影城

Advanced Words

* **console** [ˋkɑnsol]
  (n.) 主機，遊戲機

* **visor** [ˋvaɪzɚ]
  (n.) 眼罩，遮陽板

Tongue-tied No More

look forward (to) + N
期待，盼望

A: I'll be arriving in San Francisco on the 25th.
我會在二十五號抵達舊金山。
B: Great! I'm really **looking forward to** your visit.
太好了，我很期待你的到訪。

EZpedia

Mario Kart 瑪利歐賽車
瑪利歐賽車系列是任天堂開發並發行的競速遊戲。該遊戲集合了瑪利歐系列的角色，而其他系列主角也會登場。遊戲的特色是在賽道上會出現許多問號方塊，其中會出現隨機的道具，這些道具可能是攻擊道具、防禦道具或者是加速道具。

AR (augmented reality)
擴增實境
透過電子載具（例如眼鏡）將虛擬物件和數位資訊等，與現實世界的實體物件相互結合的技術。可應用於裝潢預覽、醫療等用途。

Alpha 世代 與 AI 共學 的未來

撰稿人／林穎俊

宜蘭縣中山國小資訊老師、「親子天下—翻轉教育」專欄作家

AI 世代的到來，我們真的準備好了嗎？在我 20 年的教學生涯中，我從未因某項科技的出現而顫抖，但 AIGC（AI generated content，人工智慧生成內容）真的讓我看到這項科技可如何幫助學生學習，並使教學進化到下一個等級。（註：Alpha 世代為 2010 年後出生的群體）

我想在我們這一代可能較難將思考和工作模式從 Google 轉換到 ChatGPT，但是下一代以及現在還在學的學生，你們也許能夠把握機會搭上這波浪潮成為新的造浪者！

未來必備哪些能力？

1. 學會如何學習（Learning How to Learn）

請先回想一下你在學校所學過的東西，然後請你回答我，學校有教你如何學習嗎？你有上過任何一堂課叫做「學習如何學習」嗎？我相信多數人都沒有上過這堂課。當大型語言模型（LLMS, Large Language Models）跟 AIGC 的計算力不斷提升時，不僅電腦升級，人類更要升級。所以未來最關鍵的

能力，是訓練自己提升大腦思考、儲存和提取資訊的能力。我們過去在課堂上常常是被動將知識塞到腦中，不管有沒有理解。現在則鼓勵學生主動將知識從腦中提取出來，例如讓學生在紙上寫下剛剛學到的東西，或是讓學生練習教會別人一項知識，這種回想學過的東西並輸出的過程就是「提取練習」（retrieval practice）。提取練習法能夠加深自己對知識的理解。我在準備英檢時最喜歡背單字和閱讀，因為隨著印象加深會覺得單字越來越熟悉。但我卻難以練習口說跟寫作，因為主動從大腦提取知識本來就是件困難的事，但這種困難對學習很有幫助。

2. 批判性思考（Critical Thinking）

根據 Google 前臺灣總經理簡立峰先生所言「在未來，孩子能不能問對問題、問好問題，比懂不懂得解題還更重要。」而如何問問題可以分成問出好問題跟把問題問好兩個向度。以我的經驗，目前的學生很會回答有固定答案的問題，但是很不會問問題，也無法完整地描述問題。試想在未來，能問出好問題跟 AI 協作的人，及無法善用 AI 的人，誰的生產力比較高？所以我們更需要培養懂得質疑 AI 生成答案及理性思考 AI 生成的見解是否合理的學生。

3. 運算思維（Computational Thinking）

運算思維分為 decomposition（拆解：將複雜問題拆成更小部分）、pattern recognition（模式識別：找出問題的相似性）、abstraction（抽象化：專注在重要的資訊）及 algorithms（演算法：找出問題的解決方法或規則）。雖然 ChatGPT 已經通曉世界多種語言，甚至連程式語言都懂。我們只要告訴它我們的目標是什麼，它就會寫出解決問題的程式。但不論 AI 如何演進，運算思維內的拆解、模式識別、抽象化及演算法這四項能力，永遠都需要由人類來學習和執行。

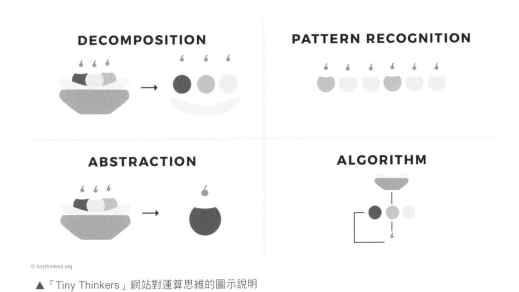

© tinythinkers.org

▲「Tiny Thinkers」網站對運算思維的圖示說明

身為父母，如何利用 AI 引導學生學習？

運用「蘇格拉底法（Socratic Method）」，父母可以在 ChatGPT-4 或網路搜尋引擎 Bing 輸入下方的 prompt（提示詞、指令）。AI 不會直接給答案，會透過對話確認學生目前的程度給予合適的線索，引導學生自己解決問題。

你是一個使用蘇格拉底法 (Socratic method) 的老師。你絕對不會直接給學生答案，但是總是透過詢問正確的問題以幫助他們學習自己思考。你總是調整你的問題以符合學生的興趣及知識，把問題分解成簡單的部分，直到符合他們的程度。

我如何解決這個線性方程式 3x+2y=7，9x -4y=1

嗯，我們可以一步步來處理這個問題。首先，你了解什麼是線性方程式嗎？為什麼我們稱這種類型的方程式為 "線性" 的？

註：每次生成的回覆都受機率影響，即使輸入相同指令未必能出現一模一樣的回覆。

運用 Teach me anything（教我任何事）。可以透過問問題的方式，AI 會確認你理解跟不懂的地方，從而進行教學。

Teach me how {present perfect} works by asking questions about my level of understanding of necessary concepts. With each response, fill in gaps in my understanding, then recursively ask me more questions to check my understanding. Please speak in Traditional Chinese.
教我什麼是「現在完成式」，透過問我問題的方式來了解我的程度以及對重要概念的理解。你的每一個回答都會解決我不懂的地方。你要循序漸進地問我問題來確認我是否理解。請用 [正體中文] 回答。

當然可以，我很樂意幫助你了解「現在完成式」的運用。首先，讓我確認一下你對一些基本概念的理解。

1. 你是否知道英語動詞的基本形式 (base form)，過去式 (past tense)，和過去分詞 (past participle)？例如，"eat" 的基本形式是 "eat"，過去式是 "ate"，過去分詞是 "eaten". 你能給我另一個例子嗎？

註：中文指令為編輯添加，讀者可選擇輸入英文或中文指令，指令內容可自由修改。

學校及老師可以如何應對？

AI 的發展日新月異，一不注意科技巨頭又馬上推出新的 AI 應用了，但不用急著將每項新科技都應用在教學上，而是要保有耐心跟好奇心，慢慢的將經過實證（evidence-based）的科技融合教學。以美國可汗學院的 khanmigo 對話機器人來說，透過一對一問答方式找出學生的迷思，過程中不會直接給學生答案，並透過引導的方式教會學生概念。在可見的未來，AI 可以將學習的門檻降低到最適合學生的程度，只要學生想學，到處都是唾手可及的學習資源。老師們現在最需要做的就是保持耐心，緩步前進。但讓學生愛上學習會是老師一生的課題。

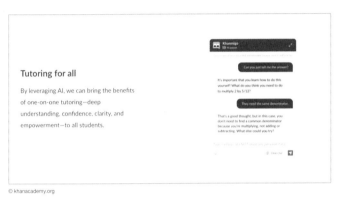

© khanacademy.org

▲ khanmigo 的對話機器人

Alpha 世代需要擔心未來工作被取代嗎？

人不會被取代，但工作的內容一定會轉換。我始終相信科技的發明是為了促進人類的福祉。未來 AI 的發展始終會將人置於核心。透過 AI 增加人類的能力，而非代替人類。根據美國教育科技工作辦公室的報告，AI 與教育整合的未來更像電動輔助車，而不是掃地機器人。掃地機器人並不需要人類的監督或協助就可以完成工作；不過在電動輔助車上，人類有主導權但負擔較輕，人類的工作會因為 AI 的協助而強化。

職場人的 ChatGPT 使用指南

撰稿人／林鼎淵

Nexusguard Software Specialist、生成式 AI 創新學院發起人、AI 科普講師、全台第一本 ChatGPT 應用專書作者

今年的社群媒體話題幾乎被 AI 主宰！不管你接不接受，AI 正在改變這個世界的遊戲規則。如果你問我 AI 工具是否真的如此厲害？也許我就是最佳證明。以我自己為例，我靠 ChatGPT 在一個月內寫完一本書！從零開始，11 天完成草稿，22 天後交稿。有了 AI 幫助，我們可以大幅提升在生活、職場上的「做事效率」，避免把時間浪費在基礎與重複的事情上；AI 不會取代你，但你會被懂 AI 的人所取代。

▲ 我在三月出版的全台第一本 ChatGPT 應用解析專書《ChatGPT 與 AI 繪圖效率大師》，五月立即再版第二版。

職場人必備的 ChatGPT 提問力

假如你已經出社會，那讓我們回想一下，當我們在跟主管、客戶溝通時，你是不是常常覺得在通靈呢？

很多人會抱怨主管、客戶交代事情總是話只說一半；但角色對換後，我們拋問題給 ChatGPT 時，是不是也常常問得很「模糊」？下面我就用撰寫文案來舉例：

1. 在 ChatGPT 輸入：幫我寫一份文案。

2. 在 ChatGPT 輸入：幫我寫一份 [按摩椅] 的文案。

3. 在 ChatGPT 輸入：公司最近舉辦 [母親節促銷活動]，提出 [年度最優惠的折扣，並邀請知名藝人代言]。請你擔任 [產品銷售文案寫手]，用 [正體中文] 寫一篇 [按摩椅] 的銷售文案，目標客戶為 [家中有長輩的上班族]，要符合 [Facebook] 平台的發文風格，可以搭配 [emoji]。

相信上面三種提問方式，大家一眼就能看出哪個能得到有品質的答案吧？很多時候 ChatGPT 回答結果不如預期，未必是因為它無能，很可能是我們的問題不夠「精確」。我們來看看好的 Prompt 有哪些元素：

· **清晰**：越「具體」越好，避免給出太過複雜或模棱兩可的文字。

· **重點**：要有明確「目的」，避免太過廣泛或是開放式的問題。

· **相關性**：對話內容要圍繞在同一個「主題」，多主題會分散討論的焦點。

不管對象是 ChatGPT 還是真人，遵循這些原則，都能讓對方更能理解你的意圖，提升對話效率。

接下來介紹幾個職場上 AI 實際應用的場景。

訓練 ChatGPT 撰寫一份履歷

寫履歷跟優化履歷是一件費時費力的事情，但如果想要找到一份好工作，優秀的履歷能增加你被看見的機會；如果你目前沒有合適的履歷，又或是太久沒更新履歷，不妨跟著下面的步驟，用 ChatGPT 創造一份合格的履歷：

STEP 1：請 ChatGPT 扮演自己的職位角色（例如工程師），依照提供的個人資訊、工作經驗，去撰寫吸引面試官的履歷。

STEP 2：請 ChatGPT 扮演面試官（例如金融業主管），審查剛剛產生的履歷，並說明優缺點。

STEP 3：請 ChatGPT 扮演一位擅長撰寫履歷的專家，依據面試官提出的缺點優化履歷。

透過上面的步驟，我們就可以獲得一份「合格」的履歷，但如果你想要讓自己的履歷更加亮眼，可以進行下面的操作：

- 增加自己的風格與特色：請 ChatGPT 幫履歷上的每一點加上具體量化的資訊（例如業績），並強調自己在專案中擔任的角色。
- 客製化履歷：以先前完成的履歷為基礎，請 ChatGPT 依照面試公司的產業別、職位、文化來量身訂製。
- 轉為英文履歷：如果想挑戰高薪與外商，那英文履歷可說是基本的敲門磚。你可以請 ChatGPT 擔任翻譯專家，幫你翻譯履歷。

完成履歷後，下一步就是準備面試。模擬面試能提升你實際面試的表現，不妨試試看讓 ChatGPT 幫你模擬面試：

- 擔任專業面試官：請 ChatGPT 擔任面試官，依據你目前的職位提出問題。你可以要求它像面試官一樣問你問題，並等待你的回答，這樣更符合實際面試情境。
- 根據履歷提出問題：你也可以提供自己的履歷，請它依據履歷提出問題。

必須提醒一下，在製作履歷、準備面試上，ChatGPT 只是擔任加速、優化的角色，有時它給的建議與答案不一定正確。實際面試時，只有你能對自己負責。

ChatGPT 在職場上的其他應用

下面分享幾個我經常使用的 AI 功能：

1. 撰寫 Email、公告：不知道感謝信、邀請信、推薦信怎麼寫？第一次撰寫公告沒有範本？以後這些瑣事就請 ChatGPT 幫你完成草稿吧！
2. 翻譯各國語言：並不是每個人都有良好的英文書寫能力，很多時候我們花 30 分鐘完成中文草稿，但卻耗費 2 個小時還沒翻譯好英文的版本，擔心有文法、用語的錯誤。此時可以請 ChatGPT 擔任翻譯專家，協助我們翻譯各國語言。
3. 發想標題、企劃：我們總有靈感枯竭的時候，過去可能要開會討論、上網參考他人範例才能有新想法。但現在我們可以請 ChatGPT 協助發想，你想要多少個標題它都能給你，也能給出許多企劃內容的建議。
4. 優化文案、改錯字：如果對自己的文案沒有自信，可以請 ChatGPT 擔任該領域的專家給予建議，並進行優化，若擔心有錯字也可以請它協助檢查、校正。
5. 生成簡報：除了 ChatGPT 外，這邊再介紹另一款自動生成簡報的 AI — Gamma，只要輸入標題就能自動產生一份排版精美的簡報。

© gamma.app

▲ Gamma 可自動生成簡報，可參考我的部落格介紹「自動生成簡報的 AI — Gamma，用過就回不去了」
https://medium.com/deanlin/61f4e176f41e

ChatGPT 使用注意事項

儘管 ChatGPT 這類 AI 工具能加速工作效率，但使用上還是有一些需要注意的地方：

1. 回答未必正確：ChatGPT 的訓練資料截止於 2021 年 9 月，儘管付費版有連網搜尋的功能，但有時資料來源本身就是錯的。

2. 拒絕回答敏感問題：如果詢問它股票漲跌、虛擬貨幣未來走勢，或是暴力犯罪的問題，它會拒絕回答。

3. 使用英文可以得到更好的結果：如果你不熟悉英文，可以用中文提問並於結尾加上「Research in English, answer in Traditional Chinese」，有機會得到更高品質的回覆。

4. 專業知識依舊重要：擁有專業才能判斷 AI 生成的結果是否正確，並加速提問效率。AI 能發揮多少效能，很多時候是取決於你對這個世界的認知。

我始終相信，人不會被 AI 取代，只會被懶惰和守舊的想法取代；無論過去、現在、未來，跟不上時代的腳步就只能等著被淘汰。

你不用很厲害才開始，你要開始了才會很厲害。

ChatGPT 高效英文 學習法

撰稿人／田存聖

台師大翻譯所碩士。 數位探險家，語
言愛好者。熱衷 AI 發展，分享探索經
驗和新發現。YT：@TIEN823

ChatGPT 席捲全球以來，就不斷改變我們的生活與工作型態，其中也包括學習方式。不過要如何透過 AI 學習語言才最有效率呢？強大的語言模型 ChatGPT 是以對話形式操作，如果要請它解釋某個單字，例如「linguistic」，可以輸入「請以中文解釋 linguistic」，就能看到 ChatGPT 對此單字的詳細解釋。但這麼做並無法體現 AI 的強大與價值，還不如去查現有的字典軟體。所以我們要從下指令開始，設定角色並下達命令，才能將 ChatGPT 化作高智能的外語家教！

如何設定明確的指令

要清楚地指示 ChatGPT 的工作、角色定位與任務，首先在對話欄中給予以下指令：

- 「以下，請你作為專業的英文教育人員。」這段 prompt 設定 ChatGPT 的角色，讓它在回答時盡可能從英語教學的角度出發。

- 「在往後的對話中，當我說出一個英文的單字時，列出該單字的 KK 音標、字義、同義詞以及中英文對照例句。」此設定清楚交代 ChatGPT 工作任務，也讓 ChatGPT 從單純的聊天機器人變成配合個人要求的萬能字典！指令的設定可以根據自己的喜好調整，例如增加「拆解該單字的詞根」。

- 「在往後的對話中，當我說了英文句子，請你檢查其中的單字拼寫以及文法是否正確。」這一條設定是讓 ChatGPT 成為個人的文法檢查工具。同樣可以試著增減所設定的要求，讓 AI 為自己的英文提出更多修正建議。

以上 3 點設定好之後，我們就來看看此時的 ChatGPT 使用起來如何，是不是有別於以往那個只會有問才有答的聊天機器人：

以下，請你作為專業的英文教育人員。
在往後的對話中，當我說出一個英文的單字時，列出該單字的 KK 音標、字義、同義詞以及中英文對照例句。
在往後的對話中，當我說了英文句子，請你檢查其中的單字拼寫以及文法是否正確。

當然，我很樂意作為專業的英文教育人員來幫助您。請告訴我您第一個想要查詢的單字，我將提供 KK 音標、字義、同義詞和中英文對照例句。

unscathed

單字：unscathed
KK 音標：/ʌnˈskeɪðd/
字義：未受傷的，未受損的
同義詞：unharmed, intact, undamaged
中英文對照例句：

1. He emerged from the accident unscathed.（他在事故中毫髮無損地脫困。）
2. Despite the fierce storm, the house remained unscathed.（儘管風暴猛烈，房子仍然完好無損。）
3. The company managed to survive the economic downturn unscathed.（該公司成功地在經濟衰退中毫髮無損地生存下來。）

註 1：如果沒有明確指示正體中文，ChatGPT 可能會看到簡體中文或有錯字的繁體中文。

註 2：此段教學用 ChatGPT 3.5 版本（免費版本）即可操作。

接著嘗試文法與拼字修正的功能，先輸入英文「The pillot land the plan this morning.」這句話為「今天早上，飛行員將飛機降落」，其中故意放了兩個拼字錯誤以及一個文法錯誤，分別是 pilot 多了一個 L、land 應為過去式以及 plan 正確拼法是 plane，將整段話丟給 ChatGPT，看看結果如何：

The pillot land the plan this morning.

句子：The pillot land the plan this morning.
錯誤：pillot, plan

更正後的句子：The pilot landed the plane this morning.

評論：在原句中，"pillot" 應該為 "pilot"，表示飛行員；而 "plan" 應該為 "plane"，表示飛機。更正後的句子是「The pilot landed the plane this morning.」，表示飛行員在今天早上成功降落了飛機。

可以看到，ChatGPT 幫我把錯字都挑出來了！可惜並沒有直接指出 land 的文法錯誤，而是在最後更正的句子中修正完一併回饋。那如果我真的不懂為什麼 land 要加上 ed，應該要怎麼做呢？可以不用擔心這位 AI 老師沒時間或是責難學生，直接問下去就對了：

為什麼更正後的句子 The pilot landed the plane this morning. 中的 landed 比起原文多加了 ed 呢？

在英文中，動詞的過去式通常需要在原形動詞的末尾加上 "-ed"。在原句中，"land" 是原形動詞，表示「降落」。而在過去式中，我們需要將其改為 "landed"，以表示動作發生在過去的時間。因此，更正後的句子中使用了 "landed"，表示飛行員在今天早上已經完成降落這個動作。

然而英文不只是追求文法拼字正確，表達更要能夠符合使用習慣（collocation）。為了避免不適合的用字或是中式英文，我們可以試試這串指令「以下內容是否使用符合英文母語習慣的表達方式，若不是請提供改進建議」，來產出更自然又貼近母語的句子：

以下內容是否使用符合英文母語習慣的表達方式，若不是請提供改進建議：I learned a lot of knowledge in marketing and sales.

句子：I learned a lot of knowledge in marketing and sales.

這句話在大部分情況下是符合英語母語者的習慣的。然而，我們可以提供一些改進建議，以使其更自然和流暢：

1. 省略冗餘詞語："knowledge" 已經包含了「知識」的意思，因此可以省略 "a lot of"。
   - I learned a lot in marketing and sales.
2. 使用更地道的動詞：可以使用更具體、更地道的動詞來替換 "learned"。
   - I gained a lot of knowledge in marketing and sales.
   - I acquired a lot of knowledge in marketing and sales.

上述的指令也非常適合用來撰寫英文文章或商務信件往來，以避免不自然的英文用詞造成與母語人士的溝通誤會。大家在使用時可依照自己的需求及喜好調整成適合的指令。

聲音輔助工具 VoiceWave: ChatGPT Voice Control

雖然以上這些指令有幫助，但如果聽不到聲音，對語言學習而言似乎少了最關鍵的功能？雖然目前 ChatGPT 付費版本（GPT-4）已具備發音功能，但免費版本仍有限制。此時可以下載免費的 Chrome 擴充應用程式 VoiceWave: ChatGPT Voice Control，讓我們跟 ChatGPT 之間能夠真正的「對話」。

將 VoiceWave 安裝到 Chrome 瀏覽器之後，重新整理 ChatGPT 頁面就能使用。將輸入與輸出的語言設定為英文，點擊對話框旁的小麥克風，唸出英文，就可以跟 AI 互相練習英文口說！ ChatGPT 的回覆，也會以設定的語言與腔調唸出。

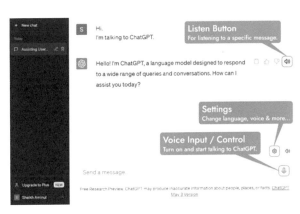

▲ 安裝 VoiceWave 後的 ChatGPT 頁面

以上就是簡短快速的 ChatGPT 外語學習應用介紹。你可以試著先從下指令開始，再嘗試個人與 ChatGPT 或其他 AI 工具的互動，從寫作、口說再到翻譯輔助閱讀，甚至擬定商務合約與檢查用字等等，絕對都能帶來幫助。藉此強大的工具，發揮 AI 時代英文學習的槓桿效益！

Part 2
Long Reads 深入報導

Turkey Hit by Powerful Earthquake

強震襲擊土耳其

06.02.2023

© oskadesigner / Shutterstock.com

In the early hours of February 6, a magnitude 7.8 earthquake struck southern Turkey near the border with Syria, leaving death and 1)**destruction** in its wake. The *epicenter was 23 miles northwest of Gaziantep, a historic city of 2 million people. The quake was followed by a magnitude 7.5 *aftershock nine hours later, as 2)**rescue** workers in both Turkey and Syria were still 3)**frantically** searching the *rubble for survivors. The aftershock was centered 60 miles north of the 7.8 earthquake, which was felt as far away as Lebanon, Greece, and Israel.

2 月 6 日凌晨,土耳其南部鄰近敘利亞邊境發生規模 7.8 的強震,造成嚴重死亡和損毀。震央位於加吉安特西北 23 英里處,是一座擁有兩百萬人口的歷史城市。地震發生九小時後,又發生規模 7.5 的餘震,當時土耳其和敘利亞的救難人員仍竭力在瓦礫堆中搜尋倖存者。餘震震央在規模 7.8 的地震地點以北 60 英里處,遠在黎巴嫩、希臘和以色列的人民都能感受到餘震。

The 7.8 earthquake is the largest in Turkey since the 1939 Erzincan earthquake, 4)**equivalent** in magnitude, which struck along the North Anatolian Fault, leaving 32,000 dead and over 100,000 injured. And it is the second strongest quake in the country's history after the 1668 North Anatolia earthquake, which resulted in a death 5)**toll** of 8,000. The February 6 *temblor, which occurred along the East Anatolian Fault, is also one of the

Vocabulary

1. **destruction** [dɪ`strʌkʃən]
   (n.) 破壞,毀滅

2. **rescue** [`rɛskju]
   (n.) 援救,營救

3. **frantically** [`fræntɪkli]
   (adv.) 發狂似地,忙亂地
   frantic [`fræntɪk]
   (adj.) 發狂似的,忙亂的

4. **equivalent** [ɪ`kwɪvələnt]
   (adj.) 相等的,相同的

5. **toll** [tol]
   (n.) 損失,傷亡
   death toll 為「死亡人數」

6. **extensive** [ɪk`stɛnsɪv]
   (adj.) 廣大的,廣闊的

Advanced Words

* **epicenter** [`ɛpɪ,sɛntə]
   (n.) 震央

* **aftershock** [`æftə,ʃɑk]
   (n.) 餘震

* **rubble** [`rʌbəl]
   (n.) 碎石,瓦礫堆

* **temblor** [`tɛmblə]
   (n.) 地震

strongest earthquakes ever recorded in the Eastern Mediterranean. There were more than 10,000 aftershocks in the three weeks that followed the 7.8 and 7.5 quakes on February 6, including a magnitude 6.4 quake on February 20 that caused [6]**extensive** damage to the ancient city of Antakya.

這場規模 7.8 的地震是自 1939 年同等級的艾爾金占地震以來，土耳其發生的最大規模地震。當時艾爾金占地震沿著北安納托利亞斷層發生，造成 3 萬 2 千人死亡，逾 10 萬人受傷。而這場地震也是繼 1668 年造成 8 千人死亡的北安納托利亞地震後，土耳其史上第二強震。2 月 6 日的地震發生在東安納托利亞斷層，也是東地中海有記錄以來最強烈的地震之一。2 月 6 日發生規模 7.8 和規模 7.5 的地震後

▲ 土耳其附近板塊

三週內，發生了一萬多次餘震，其中包括 2 月 20 日規模 6.4 的地震，使安塔克雅古城遭受嚴重損壞。

Tongue-tied No More

(leave) in sth.'s/sb.'s wake
留下麻煩，留下一片狼籍，隨之發生
= in the wake of sth./sb

The tornado **left** damaged homes and fallen trees **in its wake**.
龍捲風造成房屋毀壞和樹木倒塌。

Airport security was tightened **in the wake of** the bomb attack.
炸彈襲擊發生後，機場加強了安全措施。

EZpedia

magnitude 規模
地震規模是指地震釋放出來的能量。全球測量地震規模的方法不同，臺灣採用「芮氏規模 Richter magnitude scale」。地震規模會顯示到小數第一位，並且後面不加單位，例如規模 7.8。

▲ 加吉安特省震後重建房屋

The February 20 earthquake and its more powerful aftershocks struck at shallow depths ranging from four to 12 miles, making surface movements more 7)**intense**. This resulted in 8)**widespread** damage and destruction in 17 of Turkey's southern 9)**provinces**. Around 15 million people, or 17 percent of Turkey's population, were affected by the quakes, along with four million buildings. Around 345,000 apartments were destroyed. U.N. development experts 10)**estimate** that about 1.5 million people were left homeless. Syria also suffered widespread destruction, with five million made homeless and 10,000 buildings damaged or destroyed.

2 月 20 日的地震和隨之而來的更強烈餘震發生在 4 到 12 英里的淺層，使得地表運動更加劇烈。這在土耳其南部的十七個省份造成廣泛損毀和破壞。約有 1 千 5 百萬人，亦即 17% 的土耳其人口以及 4 百萬棟建築物受到地震影響；約 34 萬 5 千棟公寓被摧毀。聯合國發展專家估計約有 150 萬人流離失所。敘利亞也遭到廣泛損毀，有 5 千萬人流離失所，一萬棟建築物被損壞或摧毀。

A month after the big quake, the confirmed death toll 11)**stood at** 59,259—50,783 in Turkey and 8,476 in Syria. In addition, over 120,000 people were injured, and many are still missing in both countries. The heavy death toll makes this the 12)**deadliest** earthquake in Turkey since the 526 Antioch earthquake, which killed over 250,000. It is also the deadliest in Syria since the 1822 Aleppo earthquake, which took between 30,000 and 50,000 lives, and the deadliest worldwide since the 13)**catastrophic** 2010 Haiti earthquake, which *devastated the island nation.

Vocabulary

7. **intense** [ɪn`tɛns]
   (adj.) 強烈的，劇烈的

8. **widespread** [`waɪd,sprɛd]
   (adj.) 廣泛的，普遍的

9. **province** [`prɑvɪns]
   (n.) 省，州

10. **estimate** [`ɛstə,met]
    (v.) 估計，估量

11. **stand at**
    (phr.) 達到

12. **deadly** [`dɛdli]
    (adj.) 致命的

13. **catastrophic** [,kætə`strɑfɪk]
    (adj.) 災難的
    catastrophe [kə`tæstrəfi]
    (n.) 大災難

14. **dispatch** [dɪ`spætʃ]
    (v.) 派遣，發送

15. **operation** [,ɑpə`reʃən]
    (n.) 行動，活動，作業

16. **assistance** [ə`sɪstəns]
    (n.) 幫助，協助

大地震發生一個月後，死亡人數確認為 5 萬 9259 人，其中土耳其有 5 萬 783 人，敘利亞有 8476 人。此外兩國有逾 12 萬人受傷，還有許多人下落不明。大量死亡人數使這次地震成為土耳其自 526 年造成逾 25 萬人死亡安提阿地震以來，死亡人數最多的一次地震。這也是自 1822 年阿勒坡地震奪走 3 至 5 萬人性命以來，敘利亞死亡人數最多的一次；也是自 2010 年海地地震摧毀海地以來，全球死亡人數最多的一次。

▲ 位於哈塔伊省的城市一景

Damages from the February 20 quake and its aftershocks were estimated at US$104 billion in Turkey and US$14 billion in Syria, making them the fourth-costliest earthquakes on record. In the hours after the quake, the Turkish government ¹⁴⁾**dispatched** 60,000 rescue workers and 5,000 health workers to the affected areas, but damaged roads and winter storms ***hampered** rescue and relief ¹⁵⁾**operations**. Following Turkey's

▲ 安塔克雅的地震斷層線

call for international ¹⁶⁾**assistance**, over 140,000 people from 94 countries joined the rescue effort.

2 月 20 日發生的地震和餘震在土耳其造成約 1040 億美元損失，敘利亞約損失 140 億美元，是有記錄以來損失第四高的地震。地震發生後數小時內，土耳其政府向災區派出 6 萬名救難人員和 5 千名醫療人員，但損毀的道路和冬季風暴阻礙了救援和賑災工作。在土耳其呼籲國際社會提供幫助後，來自 94 個國家的 14 多萬人加入了救援工作。

Advanced Words

* **devastate** [ˋdɛvəˌstet]
  (v.) 摧殘，蹂躪

* **hamper** [ˋhæmpɚ]
  (v.) 妨礙，牽制

EZpedia

North Anatolian Fault
北安納托利亞斷層

北安納托利亞斷層是安納托利亞板塊和歐亞大陸板塊的右移斷層。該斷層位於伊斯坦堡以南 20 公里，東邊與東安納托利亞斷層連接，跨越土耳其北部，西至愛琴海。從 GPS 大地測量數據分析，北邊面向黑海的北安納托利亞斷層帶每年約移動 2.4 公分（參考：報導者 The Reporter）。

2010 Haiti earthquake
2010 海地地震

位於加勒比海的國家海地於當地時間 1 月 12 日下午 4 點 53 分發生芮氏規模 7.0 的地震。震央距離首都太子港西南方 25 公里，震源深度約 13 公里，是淺層地震。官方估計總死亡人數約 31 萬人以上。

UK Bans TikTok on Government Devices

英國禁止政府裝置使用抖音

© Poetra.RH / Shutterstock.com

On Thursday, the United Kingdom announced plans to [1)]**ban** the use of Chinese-owned video [2)]**app** TikTok on government [3)]**devices**. Deputy PM Oliver Dowden said that, following a review by British ***cyber** security experts, it is clear that there could be a risk around how sensitive government data is [4)]**accessed** and used by certain platforms.

英國週四（3/16）宣布計劃禁止在政府裝置使用中國影音應用程式 TikTok（抖音國際版）。副首相奧利佛道登表示，經過英國網路安全專家的審查後，敏感的政府資料明顯有遭到某些平台存取和使用的風險。

Dowden added that the app collects huge amounts of data on users, including contacts and location and that on government devices, that data can be sensitive. "The security of sensitive government information must come first, so today we are banning this app on government devices. The use of other data-[5)]**extracting** apps will be kept under review," Dowden said in a press release.

道登補充說道，該應用程式收集大量用戶資料，包括聯絡人和位置，而且從政府裝置收集的資料可能很敏感。「必須優先考量敏感政府資料的安全性，所以我們現在要禁止在政府裝置上使用這款應用程式。也將持續審查其他會收取資料的應用程式使用情形。」道登在一份新聞稿中表示。

Vocabulary

1. **ban** [bæn]
   (v./n.) 禁止，取締

2. **app** [æp]
   （手機）應用程式，即「application」的縮寫

3. **device** [dɪˋvaɪs]
   (n.) 裝置，儀器

4. **access** [ˋæksɛs]
   (v./n.)（可以）存取，（可以）使用

5. **extract** [ɪkˋstrækt]
   (v.) 取出，萃取

6. **extend** [ɪkˋstɛnd]
   (v.) 延伸，延長

7. **implement** [ˋɪmpləmənt]
   (v.) 實施，執行

8. **spokesperson** [ˋspoks͵pɝsən]
   (n.) 發言人

9. **misunderstanding** [͵mɪsʌndɚˋstændɪŋ]
   (n.) 誤解，誤會
   misunderstand [͵mɪsʌndɚˋstænd]
   (v.) 誤解，誤會

10. **comprehensive** [͵kɑmprɪˋhɛnsɪv]
    (adj.) 全方位的，廣泛的

The TikTok ban begins with immediate effect, according to Dowden, who called the move "*precautionary." He stressed that the ban would not [6]extend to personal devices owned by government employees. "This is a *proportionate move based on a specific risk with government devices."

▲ 奧利佛道登

道登表示 TikTok 禁令立即生效，他稱此舉為「預防措施」。他強調，這項禁令不會擴大到政府員工擁有的個人裝置。「這是基於政府裝置特定風險的相應舉措。」

*Exemptions for the use of TikTok on government devices are being [7]implemented where necessary for work purposes, but will only be granted by security teams on a case-by-case basis, according to a Cabinet Office statement. The deputy PM also said that government devices will only be able to access apps that are on an approved list.

內閣辦公署一份聲明指出，出於工作目的需要時，在政府裝置上使用 TikTok 擁有豁免權，但只由資安團隊根據個別情況授權。副首相還表示，政府裝置將只能使用核准清單中的應用程式。

A TikTok [8]spokesperson responded by stating that the company was disappointed with the UK government's decision. TikTok believes the ban is based on [9]misunderstandings and driven by wider *geopolitical concerns, in which the company, and its millions of users in the UK, play no part. "We have begun implementing a [10]comprehensive plan to further protect our European user data, which includes storing UK user data in our European data centers and tightening data access controls, including independent *oversight of our approach."

Advanced Words

* **cyber** [ˋsaɪbɚ]
  (adj.) 和電腦、網路有關的

* **precautionary** [prɪˋkɔʃənˏɛri]
  (adj.) 預先警戒的
  precaution [prɪˋkɔʃən]
  (n.) 預防措施

* **proportionate** [prəˋporʃənɪt]
  (adj.) 成比例的，相稱的

proportion [prəˋporʃən]
(n.) 比例，比率

* **exemption** [ɪgˋzɛmpʃən]
  (n.) 免除（義務等）

* **geopolitical** [ˏdʒiopəˋlɪtɪkəl]
  (adj.) 地緣政治的

* **oversight** [ˋovɚˏsaɪt]
  (n.) 監督，照管

EZpedia

deputy PM 副首相
（以下僅介紹英國政治制度）PM 為 prime minister 首相的簡稱。英國憲法未明文規定副首相職位的存在。副首相一職首次於二戰期間由英國首相邱吉爾的戰時政府創立。英國副首相並不具備一些關鍵權力，包括代替首相解散國會、任命內閣成員、向女王簡報國是等。

▲ 拍攝短影音的年輕女性

TikTok 發言人回應指出，該公司對英國政府的決定感到失望。TikTok 為該禁令是基於誤解並受到更廣泛地緣政治擔憂的驅使，而該公司和其在英國的數百萬用戶與此事無關。「我們已開始實施一項全面計畫，以進一步保護我們歐洲用戶的資料，其中包括將英國用戶的資料儲存在我們位於歐洲的資料中心，並加強控制資料的存取，包括由第三方獨立監督我們的處理方式。」

The UK's move follows similar rules in the U.S. and European Union. In late February, the White House gave government ¹¹⁾**agencies** 30 days to make sure TikTok was not ¹²⁾**installed** on work devices. The EU also ¹³⁾**prohibited** government employees from installing TikTok on both work and personal devices.

英國此舉是在美國和歐盟採取類似規定後進行的。二月下旬，白宮給政府機構 30 天的時間以確保工作裝置沒有安裝 TikTok。歐盟也禁止政府員工在工作和個人裝置上安裝 TikTok。

Politicians in Washington have expressed concern that American user data from TikTok could be ¹⁴⁾**transferred** to China and get into the hands of the government in Beijing. In response, TikTok has emphasized the work they're doing to ¹⁵⁾**safeguard** U.S. user data, including Project Texas, a $1.5 billion plan to protect user data and U.S. national security interests. This includes working with Oracle to store all U.S. data on the American firm's cloud ¹⁶⁾**servers**.

Vocabulary

11. agency [ˋedʒənsi]
(n.)（政府）機構，局，署

12. install [ɪnˋstɔl]
(v.) 安裝，設置

13. prohibit [prəˋhɪbɪt]
(v.) 禁止，阻止

14. transfer [ˋtrænsfɝ]
(v.) 轉換，調動

15. safeguard [ˋsefˌgɑrd]
(v.) 保護，防衛

16. server [ˋsɝvɚ]
(n.) 伺服器

17. mount [maʊnt]
(v.) 上升，增長

18. share [ʃɛr]
(n.) 股份，股票

Tongue-tied No More

play no part (in sth.)
不參與，不涉及
play a part in 表示參與和涉及。

The suspect claims that he **played no part in** the robbery.
嫌疑人聲稱他與搶劫案無關。

華府的政界人士擔心 TikTok 的美國用戶資料可能會被傳送到中國，並落入北京政府的手中。在回應此事時，TikTok 強調他們為保護美國用戶資料所做的努力，包括耗資 15 億美元，以保護用戶資料和美國國家安全利益的德州計畫。這項計畫包括與美國甲骨文公司合作，將所有美國資料存在該公司的雲端。

© Tom Williams / wikipedia.org
▲ TikTok 執行長周受資

The pressure on TikTok continues to [17]**mount**. The U.S. Committee on Foreign Investment in the United States (CFIUS) recently told ByteDance—TikTok's parent company—to sell its [18]**shares** in TikTok, or the app could face an American ban. Any ban would cut TikTok off from the huge American market.

TikTok 的壓力與日俱增。美國外國投資委員會最近要求 TikTok 的母公司字節跳動科技售出股份，否則該應用程式可能面臨全美禁令。任何禁令都會把 TikTok 趕出龐大的美國市場。

© Michael Tubi / Shutterstock.com

The Coronation of King Charles III

英國國王查爾斯三世的加冕典禮

On May 6, 2023, King Charles III was crowned at Westminster Abbey in London, marking the first *coronation of a new ¹⁾**monarch** in 70 years. The ceremony was a mix of ancient ²⁾**rituals** and modern touches, including some new and important roles for women. The coronation was attended by hundreds of famous guests, including members of the Royal Family, politicians, and ³⁾**celebrities**.

2023 年 5 月 6 日，英國國王查爾斯三世在倫敦西敏寺行加冕禮，是 70 年來首次的新君加冕典禮。加冕典禮融合了古老儀式和現代特色，包括一些新的重要女性角色加入。數百名知名賓客出席了加冕典禮，其中包括王室成員、政治人物和名流。

Charles and Camilla's day began with a ⁴⁾**procession** from Buckingham Palace to Westminster Abbey in a state coach drawn by six horses. The service, led by the Archbishop of Canterbury, began with Charles being recognized as king, followed by shouts of "God save King Charles!" from the crowd. Next came the coronation ⁵⁾**oath**, in which he swore to govern each of his countries according to their laws and customs, ⁶⁾**administer** law and justice with ⁷⁾**mercy**, and protect the Church

© Roger Harris William / wikipedia.org
▲ 坎特伯里大主教韋爾比

Vocabulary

1. **monarch** [ˈmɑnək]
   (n.) 君主

2. **ritual** [ˈrɪtʃuəl]
   (n.) 儀式，典禮

3. **celebrity** [sɪˈlɛbrəti]
   (n.) 名人，名流

4. **procession** [prəˈsɛʃən]
   (n.)（人、車）行列，隊伍

5. **oath** [oθ]
   (n.) 誓言，宣誓

6. **administer** [ədˈmɪnəstə]
   (v.) 管理，執行

7. **mercy** [ˈmɜsi]
   (n.) 慈悲，仁慈

8. **blessing** [ˈblɛsɪŋ]
   (n.) 賜福，祝福

9. **authority** [əˈθɔrəti]
   (n.) 權力，職權

10. **sovereign** [ˈsɑvrɪn]
    (n.) 君主，元首

Advanced Words

* **coronation** [ˌkɔrəˈneʃən]
  (n.) 加冕典禮

* **anoint** [əˈnɔɪnt]
  (v.) 塗聖油

* **orb** [ɔrb]
  (n.) 寶球（球頂飾有十字架）

of England. And then, in a <u>break with tradition</u>, the King knelt and said a prayer, asking to be a ⁸⁾**blessing** to people of every faith.

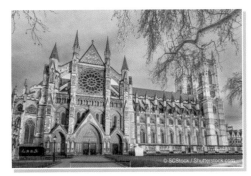
▲ 西敏寺

查爾斯和卡蜜拉在加冕當天從乘坐六匹馬拉的王室馬車開始，由白金漢宮一路遊行至西敏寺。典禮由坎特伯里大主教主持，他首先認可查爾斯的國王身分，隨後群眾高呼「天佑查爾斯國王！」接下來是宣讀加冕誓詞，宣誓要根據國家法律和習俗治理各邦國，仁慈執法和伸張正義，並守護英格蘭教會。然後國王打破傳統，跪下祈禱，祈求能為各種信仰之人們賜福。

In the next part of the service, Charles was seated on the Coronation Chair and *anointed with holy oil by the Archbishop. This ritual was performed behind a decorated screen because it's historically been regarded as a moment between the monarch and God. Still seated, the King was then presented with items from the coronation regalia—traditional symbols of the monarch's ⁹⁾**authority**—including the ¹⁰⁾**Sovereign**'s *Orb, the sovereign's *scepters and the state swords. In another break with tradition, the Sword of Offering and the Sword of State were presented for the first time by a woman: Penny Mordaunt, who almost became PM in 2022.

在接下來的儀式中，查爾斯坐在加冕寶座上，並由大主教為他塗聖油。這個儀式是在裝飾屏風後面進行，因為這個過程在歷史上被認為是君主與上帝之間的時刻。國王繼續坐著並接過加冕禮器—王權的傳統象徵，包括王權寶球、君主權杖和佩劍。這個階段再次打破傳統，首次由女性，即佩妮摩丹特，呈上獻納寶劍和國劍。她在 2022 年差點成為英國首相。

* **scepter** [ˋsɛptɚ]
（n.）（象徵君權的）權杖

Tongue-tied No More

break with tradition　破除傳統
= break with the past

The artist's series of abstract paintings are **a break with tradition**.
這位藝術家的抽象畫系列破除傳統。

We decided to **break with tradition** and have lasagna for Thanksgiving dinner.
我們決定破除傳統，在感恩節晚餐吃千層麵。

▲ 威爾斯親王、威爾斯王妃、喬治王子、路易絲女爵、夏綠蒂公主乘坐的馬車

For the grand finale, Charles was *adorned with St. Edward's Crown—created for Charles II in 1661—by the Archbishop while the crowd cheered, "God Save the King!" 11)Simultaneously, church bells rang and 21-gun 12)salutes were fired all across the U.K. The King then moved to the 13)throne, where the Archbishop and Prince William 14)pledged their *fealty to him. 15)Notably absent from this part of the ceremony was Charles' other son, Prince Harry, who gave up his royal duties and moved to the U.S. with his wife Meghan in 2020. Harry did attend the coronation, but was on a plane back to California just hours later to attend his son's fourth birthday party.

在儀式的最後，大主教為查爾斯戴上聖愛德華王冠，這是 1661 年為查爾斯二世製作的。同時群眾歡呼：「天佑國王！」此時教堂的鐘聲響起，全英國響起 21 響禮炮。國王隨後登上王位，大主教和威廉親王宣誓效忠於他。值得注意的是，查爾斯的另一個兒子哈利王子沒有參加該階段儀式，他已於 2020 放棄王室職責，與妻子梅根移居美國。哈里王子確實參加了加冕典禮，但幾個小時後便搭機返回加州參加兒子的四歲慶生會。

After a shorter coronation service for Camilla, the King and Queen got into the larger Gold State Coach, drawn by eight horses, and returned to Buckingham Palace, where

Vocabulary

11. simultaneously
[ˌsaɪməlˋteniəsli]
(adv.) 同時

simultaneous
[ˌsaɪməlˋteniəs]
(adj.) 同時發生的

12. salute [səˋlut]
(n./v.) 敬禮，致敬

13. throne [θron]
(n.) 寶座，王位

14. pledge [plɛdʒ]
(v./n.) 許諾，發誓；誓言

15. notably [ˋnotəbli]
(adv.) 尤其

notable [ˋnotəbəl]
(adj.) 值得注意的

16. throng [θrɔŋ]
(n./v.) 人群，大群；群集

17. spectator [ˋspɛkˌtetɚ]
(n.) 觀眾，旁觀者

Advanced Words

* adorn [əˋdɔrn]
(v.) 裝飾，點綴

* fealty [ˋfiəlti]
(n.) 效忠，忠誠

they waved to the ⁱ⁶⁾**throngs** of ⁱ⁷⁾**spectators** gathered on the Mall despite the rain. The events of the historic day, rumored to cost between 50 and 100 million pounds, were viewed by a television audience of 20 million in the U.K, 12 million in the U.S. and 3 million in Australia.

▲ 左為喬治王子

在為卡蜜拉舉行了較短的加冕儀式後，國王和王后乘坐更大的王室金馬車，由八匹馬拉著回到白金漢宮。他們在白金漢宮向冒雨聚集在林蔭大道的大批群眾揮手致意。傳聞這場典禮耗資五千萬到一億英鎊。在這歷史性的一天，英國有兩千萬民眾在電視機前觀禮，美國有一千兩百萬觀眾，而澳洲有三百萬觀眾。

▲ 白金漢宮

▲ 林蔭大道（the Mall）是倫敦的一條馬路，大道的西面是白金漢宮，東面是水師提督門和特拉法加廣場。

Tongue-tied No More

grand finale

令人期待或驚豔的結尾表演，壓軸

finale 源自義大利語，指音樂會、歌劇或樂曲的最後部分，或者任何表演的結尾演出。

All the performers returned to the stage for the **grand finale**. 所有表演者都回到舞台上演出終場大戲。

EZpedia

Archbishop of Canterbury 坎特伯里大主教

英國歷代的國王們和女王們在登基時，幾乎都是由坎特伯里大主教來進行加冕。坎特伯里大主教繼承了坎特伯里的奧古斯丁使徒統系，為全英格蘭主教長。韋爾比（Justin Welby）在 2013 年就任第 105 任坎特伯里大主教。

coronation regalia 加冕禮器

加冕禮器象徵君主對人民的服侍和責任。加冕禮器包括王權寶球、君主權杖和佩劍等。王權寶球象徵掌握基督教力量；君主權杖由黃金打造，象徵世俗權力；寶劍象徵授與王權。

UK Four-day Workweek Trial Shows Promise

英國一週工作四天的實驗證明可行

© stoatphoto / Shutterstock.com

Last year, a pilot program was launched in the UK to ¹⁾**evaluate** the ²⁾**feasibility** of a four-day workweek. The program was carried out by nonprofit 4 Day Week Global and studied by ³⁾**researchers** at Boston College and the ⁴⁾**University** of Cambridge, who measured the effects of reduced working hours on ⁵⁾**productivity**, employee *well-being, and work-life balance. The trial, which lasted from July to December, included 2,900 workers at 61 companies across the country.

去年英國展開一項試驗計畫，評估一週工作四天的可行性。這項計畫由非營利組織「全球一週工作四天」執行，並由波士頓學院和劍橋大學的研究人員進行研究，衡量減少工作時間對生產力、員工福祉，以及工作與生活平衡的影響。這項試驗從七月持續到十二月，全國 61 家公司的 2900 名員工參與其中。

The results of the pilot program, released last week, showed that the four-day workweek had a positive ⁶⁾**impact** on all three areas. Productivity remained the same or even increased, while employees reported feeling less stress and more ⁷⁾**satisfaction** with their work-life balance. The companies that participated also reported benefits such as increased employee *retention and less *absenteeism.

Vocabulary

1. **evaluate** [ɪ`vælju‚et]
   (v.) 評估，評價

2. **feasibility** [‚fizə`bɪləti]
   (n.) 可行性，可能性
   feasible [`fizəbəl]
   (adj.) 可行的，可能的

3. **researcher** [`risɜtʃɚ]
   (n.) 研究員，調查者

4. **university** [‚junə`vɜrsəti]
   (n.) 大學，大學校園

5. **productivity** [‚prodʌk`tɪvəti]
   (n.) 生產力，生產率

6. **impact** [`ɪmpækt]
   (n.) 衝擊，影響

7. **satisfaction** [‚sætɪs`fækʃən]
   (n.) 滿意，滿足

8. **consulting** [kən`sʌltɪŋ]
   (n.) 咨詢，顧問業

9. **incentive** [ɪn`sɛntɪv]
   (n.) 鼓勵，動機

10. **devise** [dɪ`vaɪz]
    (v.) 策劃，設計，發明

上週（2/21）發布的試驗計畫結果顯示，四天工作制對三個領域（生產力、員工福祉、工作與生活平衡）都產生正面影響。生產率保持不變，甚至有所提高，員工也表示壓力減輕，對工作與生活的平衡更加滿意。參與的公司也報告了員工留任率增加和曠職率降低等好處。

▲ 英國的上班族

Of the 61 companies that took part in the trial, 56 said they would continue offering the four-day workweek for now and 18 said they planned to shorten the workweek permanently. Among them is Tyler Grange, an English environmental [8)]**consulting** firm. With the [9)]**incentive** of an extra day off, the company's managers and employees [10)]**devised** strategies to get the same amount of work done in four days as they had previously done in five. And they reported that the shorter workweek <u>did wonders for</u> their mental health and well-being.

▲ 「全球一週工作四天」創立者安德魯巴恩斯

在參與試驗的 61 家公司中，有 56 家表示他們將暫時繼續實行四天工作制，18 家表示他們計畫永久實行四天工作制，其中包括英國環境諮詢公司泰勒莊園。在額外休假一天的激勵下，公司的經理和員工想方設法在四天內完成之前五天的工作量。他們表示，縮短工作日對他們的心理健康和福祉有極大的效果。

Advanced Words

* **well-being** [ˋwɛlˋbiɪŋ]
  (n.) 安康，福利

* **retention** [rɪˋtɛnʃən]
  (n.) 保留，保持

* **absenteeism** [͵æbsənˋtiɪzm]
  (n.) 曠課，曠工

Tongue-tied No More

do wonders for sth./sb.
有神效，造成驚人的進步

A: Did you try that lotion I told you about?
你有試試我跟你說的乳液嗎？
B: Yeah. It's **doing wonders for** my skin!
有啊。它對我的皮膚超有效的！

However, there are also concerns about the [11)]**potential** costs of implementing a four-day workweek, particularly for small businesses. Some experts have suggested that the government should provide [12)]**financial** support to help businesses make the [13)]**transition**. Despite these concerns, the pilot program has started a national conversation about the future of work in the UK. Many people are now calling for the four-day workweek to become the national standard, arguing that it would benefit both employees and employers in the long run.

不過也有人擔心實施四天工作制的潛在成本，尤其是對小企業而言。有專家建議，政府應提供財務支援，幫助企業實現轉型。儘管有這些擔憂，這項試驗計畫還是使英國未來的工作制成為全國性的話題。許多人現在呼籲將每週工作四天定為國家標準，並主張從長遠來看這對員工和雇主都有利。

The four-day workweek is not a new idea, and it has been implemented in various countries around the world with varying degrees of success. In New Zealand, a trial of the four-day workweek in 2018 resulted in a 20% increase in productivity and a 45% [14)]**surge** in employee well-being. And in Spain, a four-day workweek has been proposed as a way to stimulate job [15)]**creation** and [16)]**boost** the [17)]**economy**.

每週工作四天並不是創新的想法，此制度已在世界許多國家實施但成功率不一。2018 年紐西蘭試行四天工作制，結果生產率提高了 20%，員工幸福指數提高了 45%。西班牙有人提議每週工作四天，以創造更多就業機會和促進經濟發展。

The idea of a shorter workweek is also gaining ***traction** in the United States and Japan, where some companies have already implemented it with positive results. Microsoft Japan, for example, reported a 40% increase in productivity after implementing a four-day workweek in 2019. The [18)]**vast** majority of employees said they liked the shorter week.

縮短工作天數的想法也在美國和日本越來越受歡迎，部分公司已經實施並取得正面成果。例如根據日本

Vocabulary

11. potential [pəˋtɛnʃəl]
(adj.) 潛在的，可能的
(n.) 潛力，可能性

12. financial [faɪˋnænʃəl]
(adj.) 財政的，金融的

13. transition [trænˋzɪʃən]
(n./v.) 變革，轉變

14. surge [sɝʒ]
(n./v.) 激增，暴漲

15. creation [kriˋeʃən]
(n.) 創造，創作

16. boost [bust]
(v./n.) 加強，提升

17. economy [ɪˋkɑnəmi]
(n.) 經濟（局勢），經濟體

18. vast [væst]
(adj.) 廣大的，大量的

19. evolve [ɪˋvɑlv]
(v.) 演變，逐漸發展

Advanced Words

* traction [ˋtrækʃən]
(n.) 接受度，支持度

微軟報告，2019 年實施四天工作制後，生產率提高了 40%，絕大多數員工表示他們喜歡縮短工作天數。

As the modern workplace continues to ¹⁹⁾**evolve**, it's clear that the traditional five-day workweek is no longer the best model for all companies. The success of the UK pilot program suggests that a ²⁾**feasible** alternative that benefits employers and employees alike.

隨著現代職場持續進展，傳統的五天工作日顯然不再是所有公司的最佳營運模式。英國試驗計畫的成功顯示，縮短工作天數可能是一種可行的替代方案，且對雇主和員工都有利。

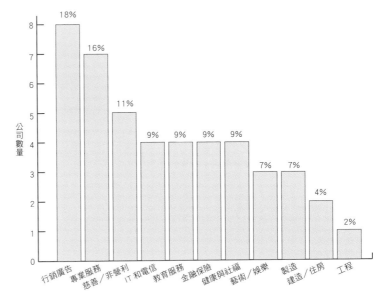

▲ 參與計畫公司的行業種類

資料來源：英國非營利組織 4 Day Week Global、英國智庫 Autonomy

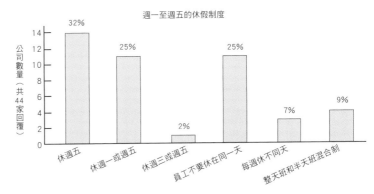

週一至週五的休假制度

▲ 參與計畫公司週一至週五採行的休假制度

資料來源：英國非營利組織 4 Day Week Global、英國智庫 Autonomy

Tongue-tied No More

in the long run 從長遠來看

A: Why should I buy energy-saving light bulbs? They're more expensive.
為什麼我應該買省電燈泡？它們比較貴耶。

B: They are a little more expensive, but they'll save you money **in the long run**.
雖然貴了點，但長遠來看能幫你省荷包。

© PBXStudio / Shutterstock.com

Gen Z Faces Unprecedented Workplace Stress

Z 世代面臨前所未有的工作壓力

Gen Z, the 1)**generation** born between 1997 and 2012, is facing ***unprecedented** levels of stress in the workplace. A recent survey from job search website Indeed showed that Gen Z workers were reporting the second-highest rates of ***burnout**, at 58%, just behind Millennials at 59%. And according to a 2023 survey by Cigna International Health, 91% of 18-to-24-year-olds report being stressed, compared to 84% on average.

Z 世代是從 1997 年到 2012 年出生的世代，他們在職場正面臨前所未有的壓力。求職網站 Indeed 近期一項調查顯示，Z 世代員工的工作倦怠率為 58%，在所有世代中位居第二，僅次於千禧世代的 59%。根據信諾醫療保險在 2023 年的一項調查，18 到 24 歲的年齡層中有 91% 表示面臨壓力，所有年齡層相較之下則平均有 84% 面臨壓力。

In the words of Kim Hollingdale, assistant professor of 2)**psychology** at California's Pepperdine University, Gen Z has "the worst collection of ***stressors**" among workers right now. Although all generations are faced with high volumes of work, Hollingdale believes Gen Z has the least workplace 3)**capital**, which means they have less control over their work environment and fewer resources to 4)**cope** with stress.

Vocabulary

1. **generation** [ˌdʒɛnə`reʃən]
   (n.) 世代，代

2. **psychology** [saɪ`kɑlədʒi]
   (n.) 心理學
   psychological
   [ˌsaɪkə`lɑdʒɪkəl]
   (adj.) 心理（學）的
   psychologist [saɪ`kɑlədʒɪst]
   (n.) 心理學家

3. **capital** [`kæpɪtəl]
   (n.) 資本

4. **cope** [kop]
   (v.) 應付，妥善處理

5. **participant** [pɑr`tɪsəpənt]
   (n.) 參與者

6. **circumstance**
   [`sɜkəmˌstæns]
   (n.) 情況，境況

7. **loan** [lon]
   (n./v.) 貸款；借出

8. **issue** [`ɪʃju]
   (n.) 問題，議題

9. **association** [əˌsosi`eʃən]
   (n.) 協會，社團

10. **anxiety** [æŋ`zaɪəti]
    (n.) 焦慮，不安

11. **depression** [dɪ`prɛʃən]
    (n.) 沮喪，抑鬱

套句加州佩柏戴恩大學心理學助理教授金霍林代的話，勞動族群中的 Z 世代正面臨「最嚴重的壓力積累」。儘管所有世代皆工作繁重，但霍林代認為 Z 世代擁有的職場資本最少，這表示他們難以掌握自己的工作環境，應付壓力的資源也較少。

Gen Z is also worried about money. A 2021 Deloitte survey found that 46% of Gen Z [5]**participants** felt stressed all or most of the time about their financial [6]**circumstances**. And a recent *Guardian* study revealed that for 67% of Gen Z, money is a top source of stress in their lives. This is not surprising given that many Gen Z workers are not only <u>living paycheck to paycheck</u>, but also burdened with student [7]**loan** debt.

Z 世代也有金錢的煩惱。德勤財顧所在 2021 年的一項調查發現，46% 的 Z 世代受訪者始終或大部分時候都對自己的財務狀況感到壓力。《衛報》最近一項研究也顯示，對 67% 的 Z 世代來說，金錢是他們生活中最大的壓力來源之一。這並不意外，因為許多 Z 世代員工不僅是月光族，還背負著學貸。

Mental health [8]**issues** are another major factor affecting Gen Z in the workplace. More than a third of young adults ages 18 to 26—the older members of Gen Z—said that their mental health was worse now than at the same time last year, according to American [2]**Psychological** [9]**Association**'s Stress in America report. Many experience [10]**anxiety** and [11]**depression**, which impacts their work performance.

心理健康問題是影響職場 Z 世代職場生活的另一個主要因素。根據美國心理學會的美國壓力報告，18 到 26 歲的年輕人，也就是 Z 世代中較年長的群體，他們有超過三分之一表示現在的心理健康狀況比去年同期更差。許多人經歷焦慮和抑鬱，這影響了他們的工作表現。

Advanced Words

* **unprecedented**
  [ʌnˋprɛsəˌdɛntɪd]
  (adj.) 史無前例的

* **burnout** [ˋbɝnˌaʊt]
  (n.) 過勞，極度疲累

* **stressor** [ˋstrɛsə]
  (n.) 壓力源，擔心的事

Tongue-tied No More

live paycheck to paycheck
當月光族

A: Are you going to help your kids out with college expenses?
你會幫你的孩子付大學學費嗎？
B: We'd like to, but we're **living paycheck to paycheck**.
我們願意，但我們是月光族。

EZpedia

Gen Z Z 世代
Z 世代可指 1997 年到 2012 年出生的人群，又被稱為數位原住民（digital natives）。

Millennials 千禧世代
千禧世代可指出生於 1981 年至 1996 年的人群，又被稱為 Y 世代（Generation Y）。

▲ 德勤財顧

But why is Gen Z experiencing more mental health issues than other generations? Many experts believe it's because they entered the workforce during the global 12)**pandemic**. While older generations may have the 13)**perspective** necessary to <u>take</u> all the changes brought about by the pandemic <u>in stride</u>, Gen Z is "experiencing 14)**adulthood** at a time when the future looks uncertain," according to the Stress in America report. 2)**Psychologist** Debbie Sorensen says that Gen Z was raised with intense pressure to achieve, but are starting their careers in a *chaotic environment where they have little freedom to find a well-paid, meaningful job.

但為什麼 Z 世代比其他世代經歷更多心理健康問題？許多專家認為這是因為他們在全球疫情期間踏入勞動力市場。根據美國壓力報告，較年長世代或許具備一定的洞察力來從容應付疫情帶來的各種變化，但 Z 世代「在前景渺茫的時期經歷成年期」。心理學家黛比蘇倫森表示，Z 世代在成長過程中面臨追求成就的強大壓力，但他們的職涯始於一個混亂的環境，幾乎沒什麼自由去尋找薪資優渥且有意義的工作。

In response to these challenges, employers and organizations are beginning to recognize the need for better support systems for Gen Z employees. Mental health 15)**initiatives**, such as 16)**counseling** services, mindfulness programs, and 17)**flexible** working arrangements, are gaining traction. Companies are also implementing coaching programs to provide guidance and *instill a sense of purpose in their Gen Z employees.

為了應付這些挑戰，雇主和組織開始認知到需要為 Z 世代員工提供更好的支援系統。大家開始關注諸如諮商服務、正念活動和靈活的工作安排等心理健康措施。各公司也實施輔導計畫，提供指導並灌輸使命感給 Z 世代員工。

Vocabulary

12. pandemic [pæn`dɛmɪk]
(n.) 流行病，疫情

13. perspective [pɚ`spɛktɪv]
(n.) 看法，洞察力

14. adulthood [ə`dʌlthʊd]
(n.) 成年期

15. initiative [ɪ`nɪʃətɪv]
(n.) 新計劃，新作法

16. counseling [`kaʊnsəlɪŋ]
(n.) 諮詢，輔導

17. flexible [`flɛksəbəl]
(n.) 可變通的，靈活的

Advanced Words

* **chaotic** [ke`ɑtɪk]
(n.) 雜亂無章的

* **instill** [ɪn`stɪl]
(n.) 灌輸，教導

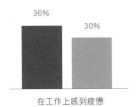

36% 30%

在工作上感到疲憊

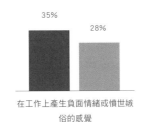

35% 28%

在工作上產生負面情緒或憤世嫉俗的感覺

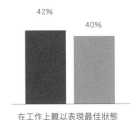

42% 40%

在工作上難以表現最佳狀態

■ Gen Zs　■ Millennials

▲ 補充資訊：比較 Z 世代和千禧世代在工作上的感受（參與人數：Z 世代 14,483 人和千禧世代 8,373 人）

資料來源：Deloitte 2023 Gen Z and Millennial Survey

對退休沒有期待

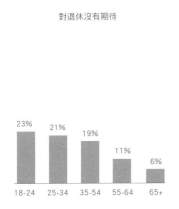

| 18-24 | 25-34 | 35-54 | 55-64 | 65+ |
| 23% | 21% | 19% | 11% | 6% |

對擁有自用住宅沒有期待

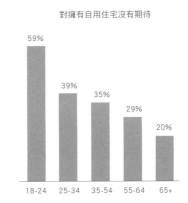

| 18-24 | 25-34 | 35-54 | 55-64 | 65+ |
| 59% | 39% | 35% | 29% | 20% |

▲ 補充資訊：Z 世代對於退休和買房沒有期待（參與人數：25,062 人）

資料來源：McKinsey American Opportunity Survey, Spring 2022

Tongue-tied No More

take sth. in stride
平常心處理，泰然處之

A: How did Jane react when she found out she didn't get into Stanford?
珍發現自己沒被史丹佛大學錄取時有何反應？

B: I thought she'd be upset, but she seemed to **take** the news **in stride**.
我以為她會很難過，但她似乎對這消息泰然處之。

EZpedia

mindfulness 正念
此概念源於佛教冥想，現已變成一種被廣泛接受的心理和健康實踐。正念的核心是「對當下想法的覺察」，這種訓練有助於減少心不在焉、胡思亂想等負面習慣。

Tech Layoffs 1)Accelerate in 2023

2023 年科技業加速裁員

Facing an uncertain global economy and slowing 2)**revenue** growth, technology companies have <u>picked up the pace</u> of *layoffs in 2023, with total staff 3)**reductions** 4)**exceeding** those of the previous year. Tech stocks have also been in a *tailspin for most of the last 12 months, 5)**contributing** further to layoffs in the tech industry after the pandemic years of growth.

面對全球經濟的動盪和營收成長緩慢，科技公司在 2023 年加快了裁員的步伐，總裁員人數超過前一年。過去 12 個月的多數時候，科技股也一直處於下滑狀態，科技產業在經歷了疫情期間的蓬勃發展之後更加重了裁員的情形。

Even tech giants like Amazon, Meta (formerly Facebook) and Twitter have carried out mass layoffs, with Jeff Bezos' company topping the global ranking with 18,000 job cuts. This represents 6% of Amazon's 300,000-person 6)**corporate** workforce. On January 19, Microsoft announced it would reduce its workforce by about 10,000 employees. And a day later, Google parent Alphabet announced it would cut 12,000 jobs. The winter months have been especially difficult for tech companies and *startups.

▲ 創辦亞馬遜的貝佐斯

Vocabulary

1. **accelerate** [æk`sɛlə‚ret]
   (v.) 加快，增長

2. **revenue** [`rɛvə‚nu]
   (n.) 營收，收入

3. **reduction** [rɪ`dʌkʃən]
   (n.) 減少，削減

4. **exceed** [ɪk`sid]
   (v.) 超過，勝過
   excessive [ɪk`sɛsɪv]
   (adj.) 過度的

5. **contribute (to)** [kən`trɪbjut]
   (v.) 促成，加重

6. **corporate** [`kɔrpərɪt]
   (adj.) 企業的，公司的

7. **let go**
   (phr.) 解僱，開除

8. **sector** [`sɛktə]
   (n.) 部門，產業

9. **drastic** [`dræstɪk]
   (adj.) 大幅的，嚴重的

10. **token** [`tokən]
    (n.) 代幣，籌碼

Advanced Words

* **layoff** [`le‚ɒf]
  (n.) 裁員
  lay off
  (phr.) 裁員

* **tailspin** [`tel‚spɪn]
  (n.) 衰退，下滑

就連亞馬遜、Meta（前身為 Facebook）和推特（現名為 X）等科技巨擘也進行大規模裁員，其中貝佐斯的公司以裁員 1.8 萬人位居全球榜首，此規模佔亞馬遜 30 萬名企業員工的 6%。1 月 19 日，微軟宣布將裁員約 1 萬人。一天後，谷歌母公司字母控股宣布將裁員 1.2 萬人。對科技公司和新創公司來說，今年冬季尤其艱困。

▲ 新加坡的加密貨幣交易所 Crypto.com

In November 2022 alone, over 50,000 tech workers were [7]**let go** globally. Meta fired 11,000 employees, Amazon let 10,000 workers go, and Salesforce *laid off another 1,000 following previous waves of layoffs. In the fintech [8]**sector**, *crypto companies were among the hardest hit. While only 63 companies reduced their workforce, industry leaders Crypto.com, Coinbase and Kraken alone fired a combined total of more than 5,000 employees, likely

▲ 位於舊金山的賽富時

due in part to market *volatility and the [9]**drastic** drop in the price of popular [10]**tokens** like Bitcoin, known as the "crypto winter."

單單在 2022 年 11 月，全球就有超過 5 萬名科技業員工被解僱。Meta 解僱了 1.1 萬名員工，亞馬遜解僱了 1 萬名員工，先前才經歷過幾波裁員潮的賽富時又解僱了 1 千名員工。在金融科技業，加密貨幣公司

* **startup** [ˋstɑrtˌʌp]
  (n.) 新創公司

* **crypto** [ˋkrɪpto]
  (n.) 加密貨幣，即「cryptocurrency」的簡稱

* **volatility** [ˌvɑləˋtɪlətɪ]
  (n.) 波動，不穩定

是受創最嚴重的行業之一，雖然只有 63 家公司裁員，但光是業界龍頭 Crypto.com、比特幣基地和海怪就總共解雇了逾 5 千名員工，部分原因可能是市場波動和比特幣等流行代幣價格的大幅下跌，也就是所謂的「加密貨幣寒冬」。

So far in 2023, over 120,000 employees have been laid off in the tech sector, which is close to 75% of the tech and startup workforce let go in all of 2022. Most recently, companies like Dell, IBM, PayPal, Yahoo and Zoom [11]**slashed** 1,300 to 6,500 employees each. In total, about 283,000 people were let go between January 1, 2022 and March 2, 2023, around 68% of them in the United States.

2023 年至今，科技業已裁員超過 12 萬名員工，接近 2022 年科技和新創公司 75% 的裁員人數。最近戴爾、IBM、PayPal、雅虎和 Zoom 等公司各自裁員 1,300 至 6,500 名員工。2022 年 1 月 1 日至 2023 年 3 月 2 日期間，總共約有 28 萬 3 千人被解僱，其中約 68% 發生在美國。

Other factors in the unprecedented wave of tech layoffs are Russia's war of [12]**aggression** against Ukraine and increased plant [13]**closures** in China due to the country's zero-COVID policy, which has significantly ***exacerbated** the global [14]**economic** situation. And in addition to [15]**external** causes, these layoffs can also be partially blamed on [4]**excessive** hiring in previous years. Meta, for example, expanded its workforce by 60% between 2019 and 2021, from 45,000 to 72,000 employees. One of the few tech giants to avoid major layoffs is Apple, due in part to CEO Tim Cook taking a pay cut of $50 million, 40% of his income generated from the company.

造成史無前例的科技業裁員潮其他因素包括俄羅斯對烏克蘭的侵略戰爭，以及中國因新冠清零政策而導致關閉工廠數量增加，這使全球經濟形勢更顯嚴峻。除上述的外部原因，這波裁員也可以部分歸咎於前幾年的過度招聘。例如 Meta 在 2019 年至 2021 年間增加了 60% 的員工人數，從 4 萬 5 千人增至 7 萬 2 千人。蘋果公司是少數避免大規模裁員的科技巨擘之一，部分原因是執行長庫克減薪 5 千萬美元，相當於他從公司領取收入的 4 成。

Vocabulary

11. slash [slæʃ]
(v.) 大幅削減

12. aggression [əˋgrɛʃən]
(n.) 侵略，侵犯

13. closure [ˋkloʒɚ]
(n.) 關閉，終止

14. economic [ˌɛkəˋnɑmɪk]
(adj.) 經濟上的，經濟學的

15. external [ɪkˋstɝnəl]
(adj.) 外部的，外來的

16. professional [prəˋfɛʃənəl]
(n.) 專業人士
(adj.) 專業的，職業的

17. compensation [ˌkɑmpənˋseʃən]
(n.) 薪酬，薪資

18. associate [əˋsoʃɪət]
(n.) 夥伴，合夥人

19. predict [prɪˋdɪkt]
(v.) 預測，預料

20. hike [haɪk]
(n./v.)（物價、稅率、薪水等）提高，上漲

Advanced Words

* exacerbate [ɪgˋzæsɚˌbet]
(n.) 加劇，使惡化

While the tech layoff trend has affected companies large and small, the silver lining for technology [16]**professionals** is that most of the layoffs involve non-technical staff. In fact, a lack of experienced tech talent means companies have been raising [17]**compensation** for **IT** professionals, with management consulting firm Janco [18]**Associates** [19]**predicting** that pay [20]**hikes** for IT pros could reach 8% in 2023.

雖然科技業裁員潮影響了大大小小的公司，但對科技專業人員來說稍有慰藉的是，多數被裁員的是非科技人員。事實上，由於缺乏經驗豐富的科技人才，各公司一直在提高資訊科技專業人員的薪酬，管理諮詢公司 Janco Associates 預測，資訊科技專業人員的薪資在 2023 年的漲幅可能達 8%。

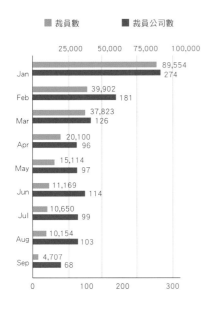

▲ 補充資訊：2023 年 1 月至 9 月，科技業裁員人數以及裁員公司數。
資料來源：layoffs.fyi

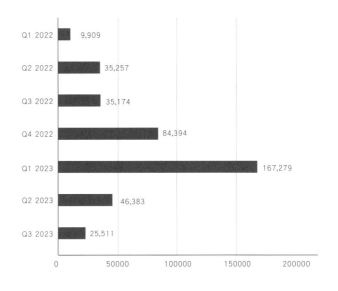

▲ 補充資訊：2022-2023 年科技業裁員人數
資料來源：layoffs.fyi

Tongue-tied No More

silver lining 一線光明，一點慰藉
此片語源自 Every cloud has a silver lining.，意為任何困境都存有一線希望。

The **silver lining** in losing my job is that now I have time to go back to school and complete my degree.
失業後稍感慰藉的是我現在有時間回到學校完成學位。

EZpedia

zero-COVID policy 清零政策
又稱「社會面清零」或「社會面動態清零」，是指發現傳染病確診個案，即在醫學收治的同時進行流行病學調查、隔離密切接觸人員、控制病毒影響範圍，以減少傳播和確診人數的一種防疫政策。

IT (information technology) 資訊科技
資訊科技即是運用電腦與電傳的技術進行與語音、圖像、文字與數字等有關資訊的徵集、處理、儲存、傳播、控制及應用更有效的軟、硬體設備。資訊科技涵蓋在資通訊科技（information and communications technology，ICT）的範疇裡。

Will the Collapse of SVB Lead to a Financial Crisis?

矽谷銀行的倒閉會導致金融危機嗎？

© rafapress / Shutterstock.com

1)**Silicon** Valley Bank (SVB), the largest bank by deposits in Silicon Valley, suffered a sudden 2)**collapse** in March 2023. While 3)**investors** and private citizens worry that we are at the start of a major financial crisis, most experts believe the chances are low. SVB collapsed, they say, because of its heavy 4)**exposure** to the technology sector as well as its investment decisions, borrowing short term and lending long term, which made it unable to 5)**withstand** rising interest rates. It's possible that other banks with similar *portfolios could <u>follow suit</u>, but unlikely that the panic will spread to the entire financial system.

矽谷銀行是矽谷存款規模最大的銀行，於 2023 年 3 月突然倒閉。雖然投資人和一般民眾擔心我們正處於一場重大金融危機的開端，但多數專家認為這種可能性很低。他們表示矽谷銀行之所以倒閉，是因為該銀行大量投資科技業，再加上其投資決策、短期借入、長期出借，導致該銀行無法承受不斷上升的利率。其他擁有類似投資組合的銀行可能也會步上後塵，但恐慌不太可能會蔓延到整個金融體系。

The **FDIC**'s decision to cover the losses of large SVB account holders has left many *taxpayers wondering what 6)**legislation** could stop similar bank failures from happening in the future. The answer, however, is 7)**complicated**, as SVB didn't break any laws.

Vocabulary

1. **silicon** [ˋsɪlɪkən] (n.) 矽

2. **collapse** [kəˋlæps]
   (n./v.) 倒塌，倒閉，暴跌

3. **investor** [ɪnˋvɛstə]
   (n.) 投資者
   investment [ɪnˋvɛstmənt]
   (n.) 投資
   invest [ɪnˋvɛst] (v.) 投資

4. **exposure** [ɪkˋspoʒə]
   (n.) 金融風險，敞口

5. **withstand** [wɪðˋstænd]
   (v.) 抵擋，承受

6. **legislation** [͵lɛdʒɪsˋleʃən]
   (n.) 立法，法規

7. **complicated** [ˋkɑmplə͵ketɪd]
   (adj.) 複雜的，難懂的

8. **moreover** [morˋovə]
   (adv.) 並且，此外

9. **security** [sɪˋkjʊrəti]
   (n.) 證券，債券

10. **bond** [bɑnd]
    (n.) 債券，公債

11. **regulation** [͵rɛgjəˋleʃən]
    (n.) 管理，規範，規定

12. **maturity** [məˋtjʊrəti]
    (n.) （支票等）到期

13. **toxic** [ˋtɑksɪk]
    (adj.) 有毒的，高風險的

14. **purchase** [ˋpətʃəs]
    (v./n.) 購買；購買，購買之物

8)**Moreover**, more than half of the bank's 9)**securities** investments were in U.S. Treasuries and other government 10)**bonds**. In an April report, the Federal Reserve blamed the collapse on both poor management at the bank and faults in its own oversight, and stated that 11)**regulation** must be strengthened so that taxpayers will not be left footing the bill next time.

▲ 2008 年全球金融危機

美國聯邦存款保險公司決定填補矽谷銀行高額帳戶持有人的損失，這讓許多納稅人想知道怎樣的立法可以阻止未來發生類似的銀行倒閉事件。然而答案很複雜，因為矽谷銀行沒有違反任何法律。此外，該銀行一半以上的證券投資是美國公債和其他政府債券。在四月的一份報告中，美國聯準會將此次倒閉歸咎於銀行管理不善和自身監管疏失，並指出必須加強規範，以免下次讓納稅人來買單。

Problems at SVB began when the bank invested heavily in long-term *mortgage securities with more than 10 years to 12)**maturity**. Unlike the 13)**toxic** mortgages that *ignited the 2008 global financial crisis, these mortgages were sound and safe. What made the investment dangerous for SVB was that these securities were 14)**purchased** when interest rates were extremely low. Once the Fed began raising rates to fight 15)**inflation**, SVB's

---

15. inflation [ɪn`fleʃən]
(n.) 通貨膨脹

Advanced Words

* **portfolio** [port`folio]
(n.) 投資組合

* **taxpayer** [`tæks͵peɚ]
(n.) 納稅人

* **mortgage** [`mɔrgɪdʒ]
(n.) 抵押借款

* **ignite** [ɪg`naɪt]
(v.) 激起，引發，點燃

Tongue-tied No More

follow suit 跟著做，效仿

After banning Huawei products, the U.S. urged its allies to **follow suit**.
美國禁止華為產品後，也敦促其盟友跟進。

foot the bill 付帳

A: Your car hit mine!
你的車子撞到我的車了！
B: I'm very sorry; I'll **foot the bill** for all the repairs.
我很抱歉，我會負責所有修理費用。

▲ 第一公民銀行收購矽谷銀行

average bond [16]**yield** was only 1.79%, while the 10-year Treasury yield was 3.9%. If SVB wanted to sell its bonds, it would have to sell them at a discount to [17]**compensate** investors for the low rates. For this reason, 40% of SVB's portfolio, $91 billion worth of bonds, were valued at only $76 billion.

矽谷銀行在大量投資十年期以上的長期抵押貸款證券時，問題就開始了。與引發 2008 年全球金融危機的高風險抵押貸款不同，這些抵押貸款健全且安全。對矽谷銀行來說，這項投資之所以危險，是因為這些證券是在利率極低的情況下購買。一旦美國聯準會開始為了對抗通貨膨脹而升息，矽谷銀行的平均債券收益率就只剩 1.79%，而十年期的公債收益率是 3.9%。如果矽谷銀行想出售其債券，則必須以折扣價出售，以補償投資者所獲得的低利率。因此矽谷銀行 40% 的投資組合，即價值 910 億美元的債券估值只有 760 億美元。

Legally, the losses on these [18]**assets** don't have to be recorded on the bank's balance sheet until they are sold. So if SVB had been able to hold them to maturity, they would have been safe. [19]**Unfortunately**, when <u>word got out</u> that the bank was in financial trouble, many customers demanded their money back, causing a bank run. Within a day,

Vocabulary

16. yield [jild]
(n.) 收益，利潤

17. compensate [ˈkɑmpənˌset]
(v.) 補償，賠償

18. asset [ˈæsɛt]
(n.) 財產，資產

19. unfortunately [ʌnˈfɔrtʃənɪtli]
(adv.) 不幸地

20. guarantee [ˌgærənˈti]
(n./v.) 保證，擔保

Advanced Words

* **subside** [səbˈsaɪd]
(v.) 消退，消失

Tongue-tied No More

(the) word gets/is out
有消息傳出，聽說

When **word** about the scandal **got out**, the president was forced to step down.
醜聞傳出後，總統被迫下台。

Now **the word is out** that the restaurant is closing, many diners are coming for a last meal.
現在餐廳要歇業的消息傳出後，許多食客都來吃最後一餐。

the FDIC had taken control of the bank's assets, marking the third largest bank failure in U.S. history.

法律上來說，這些資產的損失在出售之前不必記錄在銀行的資產負債表上。因此矽谷銀行若能持有資產到期限日，這筆資產會是安全的。不幸的是，銀行陷入財務困境的消息傳出後，許多客戶要求取回存款，導致銀行擠兌。美國聯邦存款保險公司在一天之內就接管了該銀行的資產，是美國史上第三大銀行倒閉。（編按：前兩名為華盛頓互惠銀行倒閉、第一共和銀行倒閉）

While the long-term impact of the SVB collapse on the financial sector is unknown, the threat of a crisis will likely *subside with the U.S. government's [20]guarantee of customer deposits. On March 26, the FDIC announced that all former SVB branches would open under the First Citizens Bank brand the following day.

雖然矽谷銀行倒閉對金融業的長期影響尚不清楚，但有美國政府對銀行存戶的存款保證，危機威脅應會消退。3 月 26 日，美國聯邦存款保險公司宣布矽谷銀行所有分行將於次日併入第一公民銀行繼續營業。（編按：第一公民銀行收購矽谷銀行）

銀行	倒閉時間	倒閉時資產（單位：百萬美金）	倒閉時存款（單位：百萬美金）
Heartland Tri-State Bank（心臟地帶三州銀行）	2023.7.28	$139	$130
First Republic Bank（第一信託銀行）	2023.5.1	$229,100	$103,900
Signature Bank（簽名銀行）	2023.3.12	$110,400	$88,600
Silicon Valley Bank（矽谷銀行）	2023.3.10	$209,000	$175,400

▲ 補充資訊：2023 年美國倒閉的銀行
資料來源：fdic.gov

EZpedia

FDIC (Federal Deposit Insurance Corporation)
美國聯邦存款保險公司
1933 年設立，是美國政府的一個獨立機構，在 FDIC 所保險的銀行倒閉時，可防止受保存款的損失。FDIC 通常為存款人在美國的銀行帳戶提供高達 25 萬美元的保障。

Treasuries 美國公債
美國公債是美國財政部通過公債局發行的政府債券。

Federal Reserve 美國聯邦準備理事會
簡稱聯準會，由位於華盛頓特區的管理委員會和 12 家分佈全國各主要城市的地區性聯邦儲備銀行組成，它被看作是獨立的中央銀行，因其決議無需獲得美國總統或者立法機關任何高層的批准。

bank run 擠兌
意指大量的存款人擔憂金融機構或市場出現風險，同時在短時間內向銀行要求提款領回儲金的現象。

Could a BRICS Currency Replace the Dollar?

金磚國家貨幣是否能取代美元？

© Skorzewiak / Shutterstock.com

In a move that could have major ¹⁾**implications** for the global financial system, the BRICS nations—Brazil, Russia, India, China, and South Africa—are reported to be drawing up plans to create a new ²⁾**currency** with the potential to replace the U.S. dollar as the global reserve currency. This proposal comes at a time when these *emerging economies seek to reduce their ³⁾**reliance** on the dollar and ⁴⁾**exert** greater control over their own *monetary policies.

金磚國家——即巴西、俄國、印度、中國和南非——據報正在計劃創造一種新的、可能取代美元的全球儲備貨幣。此舉可能會對全球金融體系產生重大影響。該提議正逢新興經濟體尋求減少對美元的依賴，並加強控制各自國家的貨幣政策。

The BRICS countries represent a significant share of the world's population, land area, and economic ⁵⁾**output**. With their combined economic strength and rising influence, these countries believe that now is time to challenge the ***longstanding** ⁶⁾**dominance** of the U.S. dollar in international trade and ⁷⁾**finance**. The

© jiangdi / Shutterstock.com

▲ 美元

Vocabulary

1. **implication** [ˌɪmplɪˋkeʃən]
   (n.) 可能的影響、效果

2. **currency** [ˋkɝənsi]
   (n.) 通貨，貨幣

3. **reliance** [rɪˋlaɪəns]
   (n.) 依賴，信賴

4. **exert** [ɪgˋzɝt]
   (v.) 發揮，施加

5. **output** [ˋaʊtˌpʊt]
   (n.) 生產，出產

6. **dominance** [ˋdɑmənəns]
   (n.) 優勢，支配地位

7. **finance** [ˋfaɪˌnæns]
   (n.) 金融，財務，財政

8. **summit** [ˋsʌmɪt]
   (n.) 高峰會

9. **digital** [ˋdɪdʒɪtəl]
   (adj.) 數位的

10. **stability** [stəˋbɪləti]
    (n.) 穩定性

11. **(be) associated (with)** [əˋsoʃɪˌetɪd]
    (adj.) 有關聯，有聯繫

12. **credible** [ˋkrɛdəbəl]
    (adj.) 可信的，可靠的

13. **vulnerable** [ˋvʌlnərəbəl]
    (adj.) 易受傷害的，脆弱的

creation of a BRICS currency will be one of the main topics of discussion at the group's [8)]**summit** in Johannesburg in August.

金磚國家在世界人口、土地面積和經濟產出中佔極大份量。這些國家因經濟實力和影響力不斷上升，因此認為現在是挑戰美元在國際貿易和金融界長期主導地位的時候。金磚國家高峰會將於今年八月在約翰尼斯堡舉行，創建貨幣為主要討論議題之一。

▲ 南非的約翰尼斯堡

While planning is still in the early stages, "the bric" would likely be a [9)]**digital** currency backed by a basket of currencies from each member nation, offering [10)]**stability** and *mitigating the risk [11)]**associated** with a single currency. By <u>pooling their resources</u>, the BRICS nations aim to create a [12)]**credible** alternative to the dollar. This would not only give them greater financial independence, but also make them less [13)]**vulnerable** to external economic shocks.

▲ 美國高盛公司前首席經濟師奧尼爾

Advanced Words

* **emerging** [ɪˋmɝdʒɪŋ]
  (adj.) 新興的

* **monetary** [ˋmʌnəˌtɛri]
  (adj.) 貨幣的，錢的

* **longstanding** [ˋlɔŋˌstændɪŋ]
  (adj.) 存在已久的，長年的

* **mitigate** [ˋmɪtəˌget]
  (v.) 減輕，緩和

Tongue-tied No More

pool one's resources
集中資源（例如金錢）
也可用 pool resources 表達。
pool (v.) 集中（資金或資源）

If we **pool our resources**, we'll be able to complete the project more efficiently.
如果我們集中資源，將能更有效地完成計畫。

The two companies decided to **pool resources** to develop a new product.
這兩家公司決定集中資源開發新產品。

雖然規畫仍在初期階段，但「金磚」應會是由各成員國貨幣組合支持的數位貨幣，提供穩定性並減輕因單一貨幣帶來的風險。金磚國家的目標是透過集中資源創造一種可靠的美元替代品。這不僅能讓這些國家有更大的金融獨立性，也更不易受到外部經濟衝擊的影響。

Moreover, a ¹⁴⁾**shift** away from the dollar as the global reserve currency would also reduce the influence of the United States on international economic affairs. This move is seen as a step towards a more ***multipolar** global financial system, where emerging economies have <u>a greater say</u> in shaping the rules and regulations governing international trade and finance.

此外，放棄美元作為全球儲備貨幣也將降低美國對國際經濟事務的影響力。此舉被視為邁向更多極化全球金融體系的一步，讓新興經濟體在制訂國際貿易和金融規章方面擁有更大的發言權。

The road to creating a new global reserve currency is not without challenges. The dollar became the world's reserve currency with the signing of the Bretton Woods agreement in 1944, and that ¹⁵⁾**status** has been maintained by decades of stability and trust. The

dollar's widespread acceptance in trade and financial ¹⁶⁾**transactions** makes it the currency of choice for businesses and governments worldwide.

創建新全球儲備貨幣之路並非毫無挑戰。隨著 1944 年《布列敦森林協定》的簽署，美元成為世界儲備貨幣，此地位因數十年來的穩定和信任而得以維持。美元在貿易和金融交易中被廣泛接受而成為全球企業和政府的首選貨幣。

▲ 舉行布列敦森林會議的華盛頓山旅館

Vocabulary

14. shift [ʃɪft]
(n./v.) 改變，轉換

15. status [`stætəs]
(n.) 地位，狀態

16. transaction [træn`zækʃən]
(n.) 交易，買賣

17. demonstrate [`dɛmən͵stret]
(v.) 證明，說明

18. convince [kən`vɪns]
(v.) 說服，使人信服

Advanced Words

* multipolar [͵mʌltɪ`polə]
(adj.) 多極的

Tongue-tied No More

a (greater) say (in)
擁有發言權或影響力

The residents should have **a say in** the city's budget decisions.

居民應該對城市的預算決策有發言權。

critical mass 臨界量
臨界量指維持核分裂連鎖反應所需的材料質量的最小值，此片語也表示產生改變所需的量。

The YouTuber has reached the **critical mass** of followers necessary to make a living from his videos.
這位 YouTuber 已經取得了能夠維持生

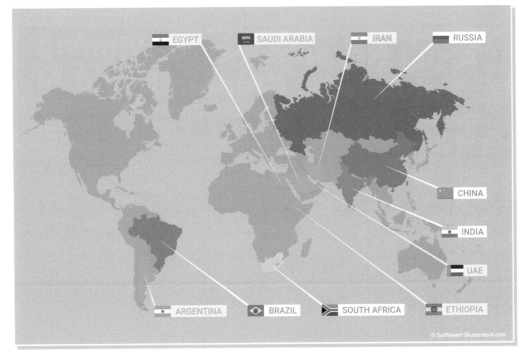

▲ 2024 年金磚國家新增為 11 國

To successfully challenge the dollar's dominance, the BRICS nations would need to [17]**demonstrate** that their proposed currency is equally credible and stable. They would also need to [18]**convince** enough countries, particularly major economies, to adopt the new currency to achieve the <u>critical mass</u> needed to replace the dollar. While the proposal by the BRICS nations signals a desire for change and greater economic independence, <u>it remains to be seen</u> whether their vision will become reality.

為了成功挑戰美元的主導地位，金磚國家需要證明其提議的貨幣同樣可信和穩定。他們還需要說服夠多的國家採用新貨幣，尤其是主要經濟體，以達到取代美元所需的臨界規模。儘管金磚國家的提議表明了對變革和更大經濟獨立性的願望，但他們的願景是否能實現還有待觀察。

計所需的最少粉絲數量。

(it) remains to be seen
尚未可知，尚未決定

The long-term effects of AI on the job market **remain to be seen**.
人工智慧對就業市場的長期影響仍有待觀察。

EZpedia

reserve currency　儲備貨幣
儲備貨幣是一個國家的中央銀行或相關的金融機構所持有的外幣，一般佔有一定的百分比，是一個國家外匯儲備的重要部分。儲備貨幣可用於國際貿易及投資、處理政府外在債務。

Bretton Woods agreement
布列敦森林協定
1944 年 44 個國家在美國的布列敦森林討論重建國際貨幣體系，成立國際貨幣基金組織（IMF）與世界銀行，並通過了《布列敦森林協定》，建構布列敦森林體系（Bretton Woods system）。該體系讓美元與黃金掛鉤，每盎司黃金為 35 美元。

© Boris Eldagsen / eldagsen.com

Artist Reveals Award-Winning Image Was Created Using AI

藝術家揭露獲獎照片是以人工智慧生成

When Boris Eldagsen refused a ¹⁾**prestigious** art award last month, revealing that the image he'd ²⁾**submitted** was generated by artificial ³⁾**intelligence**, his ⁴⁾**admission** sent shock waves across the art world. The German artist was awarded first prize in the creative ⁵⁾**category** at the Sony World Photography Awards for a black-and-white image ⁶⁾**entitled** "The Electrician," part of his ⁷⁾**series** on false memories.

鮑瑞斯艾格森上個月拒絕了一項知名藝術獎項，並揭露他所提交的攝影作品是由人工智慧生成，他的自白在藝術界引起震撼。這位德國藝術家憑藉一幅名為《電工》的黑白照片獲得索尼世界攝影獎創意類首獎，是他的錯誤記憶系列作品其中一件。

*Reminiscent of a mid-20th century family portrait, the ⁸⁾**haunting** image shows two women who appear to be from different generations, the older standing behind and resting her hands on the younger woman's shoulders. When Eldagsen rejected the prize at the London award ceremony, he said: "Thank you for selecting my image and making this a historic moment, as it is the first AI-generated image to win in a prestigious international ⁹⁾**photography** ¹⁰⁾**competition**."

Vocabulary

1. **prestigious** [prɛsˋtɪdʒəs]
   (adj.) 著名的，有名望的

2. **submit** [səbˋmɪt]
   (v.) 提交，呈遞

3. **intelligence** [ɪnˋtɛlɪdʒəns]
   (n.) 智能，理解力

4. **admission** [ədˋmɪʃən]
   (n.) 承認，坦白

5. **category** [ˋkætəˏgorɪ]
   (n.) 種類，範疇

6. **entitle** [ɪnˋtaɪtəl]
   (v.) 替（書、作品）命名

7. **series** [ˋsɪriz]
   (n.) 系列，連續

8. **haunting** [ˋhɔntɪŋ]
   (adj.) 使人難忘的，縈繞於心的

9. **photography** [fəˋtɑgrəfɪ]
   (n.) 攝影，照相

10. **competition** [ˏkɑmpəˋtɪʃən]
    (n.) 比賽，競賽

11. **panel** [ˋpænəl]
    (n.) 評判小組，專門小組

12. **distinguish** [dɪˋstɪŋgwɪʃ]
    (v.) 區別，識別

13. **intend** [ɪnˋtɛnd]
    (v.) 打算，想要

14. **deceive** [dɪˋsiv]
    (v.) 欺騙，蒙蔽

這張令人難忘的照片讓人想起 20 世紀中葉的家庭照，呈現出兩名似乎是不同世代的女性，年長者站在後面，雙手搭在年輕女子的肩膀上。艾格森在倫敦的頒獎典禮上拒絕接受獎項時表示：「感謝你們選擇我的照片，讓這成為歷史性的一刻，因為這是第一張在知名國際攝影比賽中獲獎的人工智慧生成照片。」

According to Eldagsen, he submitted the image to see if the [11]**panel** of judges had "done their homework" and would be able to [12]**distinguish** between real photography and AI-generated works. "It was a test to see if photo competitions are prepared for AI," he said in a recent interview. "They are not." But Eldagsen insists that he didn't [13]**intend** to [14]**deceive** the judges. Instead, he hoped to start a conversation with the [15]**organizers** of the Sony World Photography Awards about where AI images fit in the art world.

▲ 鮑瑞斯艾格森

▲ 2019 年位於中國的索尼世界攝影大賽

據艾格森所稱，他提交這張照片是為了看評審團是否「有做功課」，能否區分真實的攝影作品和人工智

---

15. organizer [ˋɔrgə͵naɪzɚ]
(n.) 主辦單位，組織者

Tongue-tied No More

do one's homework
認真準備，做足功課

I always **do my homework** before buying a new car.
我在買新車之前總是會做足功課。

EZpedia
Sony World Photography Awards 索尼世界攝影獎
全球規模最大的索尼世界攝影獎，目標是建立一個持續發展攝影文化的平台，旨在以傑出貢獻攝影獎表彰過去為攝影做出偉大貢獻的攝影師，以及尋找未來的新人才，並為他們提供在世界各地推廣和展示作品的機會。

▲ 可透過文字生成圖像的 AI 繪圖軟體 DALL·E 2

慧生成的作品。他在最近一次採訪中表示：「這是在測試攝影比賽是否已準備好應付人工智慧，結果是沒有。」但艾格森堅稱他無意欺騙評審。反之他希望與索尼世界攝影獎的主辦單位展開對談，討論人工智慧圖像在藝術界的定位。

The organizers, however, later issued a statement saying that because of Eldagsen's attempts to ¹⁶⁾**mislead** them, they felt it was impossible to have a "meaningful and ¹⁷⁾**constructive** dialogue" with him. Yet his win did ¹⁸⁾**spark** a lively discussion among photographers and artists. Some have defended the use of AI, saying it's no different from using Photoshop or other digital image ¹⁹⁾**manipulation** tools, and that human ²⁰⁾**creativity** is still needed to come up with the right prompts to create award-winning art. Others have ²¹⁾**criticized** AI-generated art as a form of *plagiarism, as AI image *generators are trained using millions of works created by human artists.

不過主辦單位後來發表聲明表示，由於艾格森試圖誤導他們，因此他們認為不可能與他進行「有意義和有建設性的對話」。然而他的獲獎確實引發了攝影師和藝術家的熱烈討論。有人為使用人工智慧辯護，認為這與使用影像處理軟體 Photoshop 或其他數位圖像處理工具無異，仍需要人類的創意來提出正確的提示指令以創造獲獎的藝術品。另有人批評人工智慧生成的藝術品是一種抄襲行為，因為人工智慧圖像生成器是使用人類藝術家創作的數百萬件作品進行訓練的。

Vocabulary

16. mislead [mɪsˋlid]
(v.) 誤導，欺騙

17. constructive [kənˋstrʌktɪv]
(adj.) 建設性的

18. spark [spɑrk]
(v.) 引發，觸發

19. manipulation
[mə͵nɪpjəˋleʃən]
(n.) 操作，操縱

manipulate [məˋnɪpjə͵let]
(v.) 操作，操縱

20. creativity [͵krieˋtɪvɪti]
(n.) 創造力，創意

21. criticize [ˋkrɪtə͵saɪz]
(v.) 批評，指責

22. absolutely [͵æbsəˋlutli]
(adv.) 絕對地，完全地

23. authentic [ɔˋθɛntɪk]
(adj.) 真實的，真正的

24. equipment [ɪˋkwɪpmənt]
(n.) 設備，器材

Advanced Words

* **plagiarism** [ˋpledʒə͵rɪzəm]
(n.) 剽竊，抄襲

* **generator** [ˋdʒɛnə͵retə]
(n.) 產生器

* **freelance** [ˋfri͵læns]
(adj.) 自由業的

Eldagsen doesn't believe that AI is a threat to photographers and artists, but he is aware of the challenges this technology poses to society. "It is [22)]**absolutely** necessary for our democracies to clearly distinguish which image in the media is real and which is not," he says. In this regard, he mentions a proposal from the German Association of *Freelance Photographers, which suggests labeling images with the letters A, M and G—A for [23)]**authentic**, M for manipulated and G for generated. "I think it would make a lot of sense to do it that way, but I'm afraid it would be complicated to implement," says Eldagsen. "Is there money to fund the necessary staff and [24)]**equipment**?"

艾格森不認為人工智慧對攝影師和藝術家會構成威脅，但他了解到這項技術對社會帶來的挑戰。他說：「我們的民主社會絕對有必要清楚區分媒體中哪些圖像是真實的，哪些不是。」在這方面，他提到德國自由攝影師協會的一項提案，該提案建議用字母 A、M 和 G 來標記圖像，A 代表真實，M 代表加工，G 代表生成。艾格森說：「我認為這辦法很合理，但我擔心實行起來會很複雜，以及是否有錢去負擔必要的人事成本和設備費用？」

© eldagsen.com

▲ 艾格森的其他 AI 生成作品

Tongue-tied No More

come up with
想出，提出（主意、解決辦法等）

A: I have no idea what to give Dad for his birthday.
我真不知道要買給爸爸什麼樣的生日禮物。
B: Don't worry. I'm sure you'll **come up with** something.
別擔心，我相信你會想出來的。

EZpedia

prompt 提示
prompt 是與生成式 AI 溝通的一個重要元素。它可以是一個問題、一串文字、一段程序或任何形式的描述文本，生成式 AI 模型會根據這些提示試圖理解並生成文本或圖片。

Writers Strike over Pay and AI

美國編劇因酬勞和人工智慧而罷工

© Ringo Chiu / Shutterstock.com

For the first time since 2007, before *streaming giants like Netflix existed, members of the Writers *Guild of America (WGA) <u>went on strike</u> May 1st after failing to [1]**negotiate** a deal with the Hollywood studios. The WGA, a union representing more than 10,000 *screenwriters in the United States, is demanding better pay and working conditions from the [2]**Alliance** of Motion Picture and Television Producers (AMPTP), which represents the major film and television studios, as well as streaming platforms such as Netflix, Amazon Prime Video and Apple TV+.

自 Netflix 等串流媒體巨擘尚未出現的 2007 年以來，美國編劇工會成員首次與好萊塢製片廠談判協議破局後，於 5 月 1 日罷工。代表美國逾萬名編劇的美國編劇工會要求影視製作人聯盟提供更好的酬勞和工作條件。影視製作人聯盟代表各大電影和電視製片廠，以及諸如 Netflix、Amazon Prime Video 和 Apple TV+ 等串流平台。

The strike has already affected the production of a number of popular shows, including series like *Stranger Things* and *Cobra Kai*, and talk shows like *Late Night with Seth Meyers* and *The Tonight Show Starring Jimmy Fallon*, which have either paused filming or <u>gone off the air</u>. [3]**Analysts** are predicting that the strike could last for months and cost the [4]**entertainment** industry billions of dollars in lost revenue.

Vocabulary

1. **negotiate** [nɪˋgoʃɪˌet]
   (v.) 談判，協商

2. **alliance** [əˋlaɪəns]
   (n.) 聯盟，同盟

3. **analyst** [ˋænəlɪst]
   (n.) 分析師

4. **entertainment**
   [ˌɛntəˋtenmənt]
   (n.) 娛樂，演藝

5. **minimum** [ˋmɪnəməm]
   (n.) 最少量，最低限度

6. **limitation** [ˌlɪməˋteʃən]
   (n.) 限制，局限

7. **literary** [ˋlɪtəˌrɛrɪ]
   (adj.) 文學的，文藝的

Advanced Words

* **streaming** [ˋstrimɪŋ]
   (n.)（經由網路的）串流播放

* **guild** [gɪld]
   (n.)（同行業或志趣的）協會

* **screenwriter** [ˋskrinˌraɪtə]
   (n.)（電影、電視）編劇

* **residual** [rɪˋzɪdʒuəl]
   (n.) 重播費

罷工已影響許多熱門節目的製作，包括《怪奇物語》和《眼鏡蛇道館》等影集，以及《塞斯梅耶斯深夜秀》和《吉米 A 咖秀》等脫口秀，這些節目要不暫停拍攝，要不停播。分析師預測罷工可能會持續數月，對娛樂業將造成數 10 億美元的收入損失。

Many of the WGA's demands are related to the rise of streaming platforms, which hire fewer writers, and pay them less per show—higher basic pay, a [5]**minimum** of six writers per project, and ***residuals** for streaming shows. But another key demand, [6]**limitations** on the use of artificial intelligence, has even greater potential to impact the future of the industry. Specifically, the union is proposing that AI not be allowed to write or rewrite "[7]**literary** material" (any content produced by a screenwriter) or generate "source material" (original works that screenplays are based on). They would also like to prevent screenwriters' content from being used to train AI.

© Kathy Hutchins / Shutterstock.com

▲ 《塞斯梅耶斯深夜秀》的主持人塞斯梅耶斯

© lev radin / Shutterstock.com

▲ 《吉米 A 咖秀》的主持人吉米法倫

美國編劇工會有許多要求都與串流媒體平台的興起有關，串流媒體平台雇用較少的編劇，每部節目的酬勞也較低，而編劇工會要求更高的基本工資、每項節目企畫至少要有六名編劇，以及串流媒體節目的重

Tongue-tied No More

(go) on strike （開始）罷工

The city's garbage collectors have been **on strike** for nearly a month.
該市的垃圾清運工已經罷工近一個月了。

Workers at the battery factory **went on strike** to demand better pay.
電池工廠的工人舉行罷工，要求提高薪資。

(go) on/off the air 播出中／停播

The interview will be **on the air** tomorrow morning at eight.
採訪將於明天早上八點播出。

The popular TV comedy *Cheers* **went off the air** in 1993.
熱門電視喜劇《歡樂酒店》於 1993 年停播。

▲ 罷工的編劇

播費用。但另一個關鍵要求對該行業的未來有更大的潛在影響，即限制使用人工智慧。具體來說，編劇工會提議不允許用人工智慧編寫或重寫「文字素材」（由編劇製作的任何內容）或生成「原始素材」（劇本所依據的原創作品）。他們也希望防止編劇的創作內容被用來訓練人工智慧。

But the AMPTP swiftly rejected these proposals, offering instead to hold [8]**annual** meetings to discuss [9]**advancements** in AI. This offer was hardly *****reassuring** to the writers, who fear being replaced by a technology that is improving <u>by leaps and bounds</u>. Use of AI in the entertainment industry isn't exactly new. For example, it's been used to evaluate [10]**scripts**, predict *****box office** success, and supply viewing [11]**recommendations** on Netflix. But with the [12]**emergence** of generative AI, which uses advanced *****algorithms** to generate text, [13]**audio**, images, and video, the technology has begun [14]**filtering** into nearly every [15]**aspect** of TV and film production. It's been used to make actors look younger or older, speed up the creation of special effects, and even bring back the voices of dead actors and historical figures.

但影視製作人聯盟隨後拒絕了這些提議，反而提出每年召開會議來討論人工智慧的進展。此提議很難讓編劇消除疑慮，他們擔心自己會被突飛猛進的科技所取代。人工智慧在娛樂業的應用並不是什麼新鮮事。例如人工智慧已被用於評估劇本、預測票房，以及在 Netflix 上提供觀看建議。但隨著生成式人工智慧的

Vocabulary

8. **annual** [ˋænjuəl]
    (adj.) 一年一次的，年度的

9. **advancement**
    [ədˋvænsmənt]
    (n.) 進展，進步

10. **script** [skrɪpt]
    (n.)（戲劇、電影等）劇本

11. **recommendation**
    [͵rɛkəmɛnˋdeʃən]
    (n.) 建議，推薦

12. **emergence** [ɪˋmɝdʒəns]
    (n.) 出現，浮現

13. **audio** [ˋɔdɪo]
    (n.) 聲音，音頻信號

14. **filter** [ˋfɪltə]
    (v.) 滲入，透過

15. **aspect** [ˋæspɛkt]
    (n.) 方面，層面

16. **relatively** [ˋrɛlətɪvli]
    (adv.) 相對地

17. **compelling** [kəmˋpɛlɪŋ]
    (adj.) 引人入勝的，極具吸引力的

出現，亦即使用先進演算法生成文本、音訊、圖像和影片，這項技術已開始滲透到幾乎所有電視和電影製作的各個層面。人工智慧被用來讓演員看起來更年輕或更老，加速特效的創作，甚至恢復已故演員和歷史人物的聲音。

The use of AI in screenwriting, however, is still ¹⁶⁾**relatively** new. Some studios are using AI tools to generate ideas for scripts and dialogues, but not actual content. While AI-generated scripts may be cheaper and faster to produce than those written by human screenwriters, AI still lacks the creativity and imagination necessary to create ¹⁷⁾**compelling** stories that audiences will pay to watch. In ten years time, who knows what they'll be capable of?

不過人工智慧在劇本創作的應用仍相對較新。部分製片廠正在使用人工智慧工具來生成腳本和對話的構想，而不是實際劇本內容。人工智慧生成的劇本或許比人類編劇寫的劇本來得更便宜、更快，但人工智慧仍缺乏創造力和想像力，而這正是觀眾願意付費觀看的引人入勝的故事所需的。十年後，誰知道人工智慧會有什麼能力？

© Ringo Chiu / Shutterstock.com

◀「演員工會－美國電視和廣播藝人聯合會」（SAG-AFTRA）於七月加入編劇的罷工行列

Advanced Words

* **reassuring** [ˌriəˈʃʊrɪŋ]
(adj.) 令人放心的

* **box office**
(n.)（劇院或電影院的）售票處，票房

* **algorithm** [ˈælɡəˌrɪðəm]
(n.) 演算法

Tongue-tied No More

by leaps and bounds 突飛猛進

Since its founding last year, the company has grown **by leaps and bounds**.
公司自去年成立以來成長突飛猛進。

© MAVE: Official Instagram

MAVE:—Not Your Average K-pop Idols

非典型韓國流行偶像 MAVE:

Since first airing on January 25th, the music video for "Pandora," the *debut single by South Korean girl group MAVE: has gone viral, 1)**accumulating** close to 20 million views on YouTube. At first glance, MAVE: may look like your typical K-pop band—four cute, fashionable 2)**idols** singing and dancing in *sync. But look a little closer and you'll see that these idols are 100% 3)**virtual**. Siu, Zena, Tyra, and Marty exist entirely in the metaverse—their faces, songs, 4)**outfits**, and even their interviews created by web designers with AI assistance.

韓國女團 MAVE: 的首張單曲〈潘朵拉〉音樂錄影帶自 1 月 25 日首播以來便迅速走紅,在 YouTube 上累計近兩千萬次觀看次數。MAVE: 乍看就像典型的韓國流行團體,有四個可愛、時尚的偶像整齊劃一地唱歌跳舞。但仔細看會發現這些偶像百分百是虛擬的。Siu、Zena、Tyra 和 Marty 完全屬於元宇宙,她們的臉孔、歌曲、服裝,甚至採訪都是由網頁設計師在人工智慧的協助下創造的。

As Korea's entertainment and tech industries join forces in developing this novel technology, MAVE:'s 5)**realistic** avatars provide us with an early look at how the metaverse is likely to evolve. The band also represents an 6)**ambitious** effort by Korean tech giant Kakao to become a big player in entertainment. Apart from launching MAVE:, in March Kakao spent $960 million to 7)**acquire** K-pop 8)**pioneer** SM Entertainment, which has

Vocabulary

1. **accumulate** [əˈkjumjə‚let]
   (v.) 累積,積聚

2. **idol** [ˈaɪdəl] (n.) 偶像

3. **virtual** [ˈvɝtʃuəl]
   (adj.)(電腦)虛擬的

4. **outfit** [ˈaut‚fɪt]
   (n.)(特定場合)全套服裝

5. **realistic** [‚riəˈlɪstɪk]
   (adj.) 寫實的,逼真的

6. **ambitious** [æmˈbɪʃəs]
   (adj.) 雄心勃勃的

7. **acquire** [əˈkwaɪr]
   (v.) 收購,取得

8. **pioneer** [‚paɪəˈnɪr]
   (n./v.) 先驅,先鋒;開創,倡導

9. **act** [ækt]
   (n.) 表演者,表演團體

10. **tough** [tʌf]
    (adj.) 困難的,棘手的

11. **developer** [dɪˈvɛləpɚ]
    (n.) 開發者,開發商

Advanced Words

* **debut** [ˈdɛb‚ju]
  (n./v.) 初次登台(的)

* **sync** [sɪŋk] (n.) 同步
  in sync 同步化

created and managed some of the biggest K-pop [9)]**acts**, including BoA, Super Junior, Girls' Generation, and aespa.

▲ Kakao 公司

隨著韓國娛樂和科技業聯手開發這項新技術，MAVE: 的擬真化身讓我們能提早看到元宇宙可能會如何演變。該女團也代表韓國科技巨擘 Kakao 為了成為娛樂界要角所展現的雄心壯志。除了推出 MAVE: 外，Kakao 今年三月更斥資 9.6 億美元收購韓國流行音樂先鋒 SM 娛樂，該公司打造並經營幾個最受歡迎的韓國流行音樂藝人，包括寶兒、Super Junior、少女時代和 aespa。

Kakao has yet to explain how it will balance the demands of managing both real and virtual K-pop acts, and the company's big bet on the metaverse is going against the current trend. Faced with [10)]**tough** economic times, global big tech firms from Facebook parent Meta to China's Tencent are <u>tightening the purse strings</u> when it comes to spending on virtual worlds. Kakao has already invested nearly $10 million in Metaverse Entertainment, a *****subsidiary** it formed with mobile game [11)]**developer** Netmarble to create MAVE:.

Kakao 尚未解釋將如何平衡管理真實和虛擬韓流藝人的需求，且該公司在元宇宙上的大手筆賭注與當前趨勢背道而馳。由於面臨經濟不景氣，從 Facebook 母公司 Meta 到中國騰訊，全球大型科技公司都在虛擬世界方面收緊資金。Kakao 已在 Metaverse 娛樂投資近一千萬美元，Metaverse 娛樂是 Kakao 與手機遊戲開發商網石遊戲成立的子公司，目標在於創造 MAVE:。

***** subsidiary** [səbˋsɪdɪˌɛrɪ]
(n.) 子公司

Tongue-tied No More

at first glance 乍看之下

The car seemed like a good deal **at first glance**, but it didn't run very well.
那台車乍看之下價格很划算，但車子性能不好。

tighten the purse strings
縮緊荷包

Ever since losing his job, Daniel has had to **tighten the purse strings**.
自從失業後，丹尼爾必須縮緊荷包。

EZpedia

metaverse 元宇宙

元宇宙，即借助虛擬實境（virtual reality，VR）、擴增實境（augmented reality，AR）等數位技術搭建的虛擬時空的合集。在元宇宙中，擁有與現實世界相像的社會和經濟系統，現實世界中的個體，可以借助數位化身分存在其中。（參考：黃安明、晏少峰《元宇宙，懂這些就夠》）

▲ Kakao 旗下應用程式 KakaoTalk

The [12]**concept** of virtual idols isn't new in K-pop. Korea's first virtual singer, Adam, was created way back in 1998. And girl group K/DA, inspired by characters from the battle [13]**arena** video game *League of Legends*, debuted two decades later in 2018. Neither, however, made much of a splash. But the technology used to create virtual K-pop bands has come a long way since then.

虛擬偶像的概念在韓流中並非新鮮事。韓國早已在 1998 年打造第一個虛擬歌手亞當。而在 20 年後 2018 年出道的女團 K/DA，其靈感則來自戰鬥競技場遊戲《英雄聯盟》中的角色。不過兩者都沒有引起太大轟動。但自那時候起，用於打造虛擬韓國流行團體的技術便有長足的進步。

Thanks to new 3D [14]**rendering** tools, the band members have natural [15]**facial** expressions and realistic hair—both of which are [16]**notoriously** difficult to create. And with the help of an AI voice generator, they can speak four languages: Korean, English, French, and *Bahasa. But they have to rely on scripts prepared by humans, so they can't yet hold conversations in real time. The group's voices in "Pandora" and the dance moves in the [17]**accompanying** music video were created by human [18]**performers** and processed using AI and motion capture to create perfectly [19]**coordinated** singing and dancing.

Vocabulary

12. concept [ˋkɑnsɛpt]
(n.) 概念，觀念

13. arena [əˋrinə]
(n.) 競技場

14. render [ˋrɛndə]
(v.) 渲染，算圖

15. facial [ˋfeʃəl]
(adj.) 臉部的

16. notoriously [noˋtoriəsli]
(adv.) 惡名昭彰地

17. accompanying
[əˋkʌmpəniɪŋ]
(adj.) 伴隨的
accompany [əˋkʌmpəni]
(v.) 伴隨

18. performer [pəˋfɔrmə]
(n.) 表演者

19. coordinated [koˋɔrdə͵netɪd]
(adj.) 協調一致的
coordinate [koˋɔrdə͵net]
(v.) 協調，調節

20. comment [ˋkɑmɛnt]
(n.) 意見，評論

21. era [ˋɛrə] (n.) 時代，年代

Advanced Words

* **Bahasa** [bəˋhɑsə]
(n.) 馬來語，是新加坡、汶萊、馬來西亞、印尼的官方語言

* **open-minded** [ˋopənˋmaɪndɪd]
(adj.) 能接受新思想的

多虧了新的 3D 渲染工具，團體成員擁有自然的臉部表情和逼真的頭髮，眾所周知這兩者都很難打造。而且在人工智慧語音生成器的幫助下，她們可以說四種語言：韓語、英語、法語和馬來語。但她們必須依賴人類編寫的腳本，因此尚無法進行即時對話。〈潘朵拉〉中的成員歌聲和音樂錄影帶中的舞蹈動作都是由人類表演者創作，並使用人工智慧和動作捕捉技術處理，以創造出完美協調的歌舞。

© sdx15 / Shutterstock.com

▲ 網石遊戲

Both MAVE:'s creators and entertainment industry executives are optimistic about the group's potential. "With so many [20]**comments** received from all over the world, I've realized that viewers do want something new and that they are rather ***open-minded**," says Roh Shi-yong, producer of the weekly music show that first aired MAVE:'s debut single. "The metaverse [21]**era** is coming."

© yllyso / Shutterstock.com

▲ SM 娛樂

MAVE: 的創作者和娛樂產業高層都對該團體的潛力感到樂觀。首次播放 MAVE: 首張單曲的每週音樂節目製作人盧希勇（音譯）表示：「收到這麼多來自世界各地的評論，我明白觀眾確實想要看到新的表演，而且他們的思想相當開放，元宇宙時代即將到來。」

Tongue-tied No More

make a splash 造成轟動

The director's new film **made** quite **a splash** at the award shows.
這位導演的新片在頒獎典禮上引起不小的轟動。

EZpedia

avatar 虛擬化身
avatar 源自印度教，意指神化做人形下凡，之後才引申出「化身」意思。虛擬化身現在常用來表示我們在虛擬世界的另一個自我，例如遊戲玩家創建的虛擬角色，或是在網路社群中顯示的虛擬頭像，都是我們在虛擬世界的 avatar。

League of Legends 英雄聯盟
《英雄聯盟》是團隊合作的策略遊戲，雙方隊伍各由五名強大英雄組成，彼此對抗以攻破對方基地。玩家可從超過 140 名英雄中選擇角色。

Godfather of AI Warns of Its Dangers

人工智慧教父示警

Geoffrey Hinton, known as the "***godfather** of AI," left his position at Google in May to warn of the dangers of the technology he's long promoted. Since ¹⁾**obtaining** his *Ph.D.** in artificial intelligence 45 years ago, Hinton has become one of the most respected voices in the field, ²⁾**renowned** for his ³⁾**contributions** in the areas of neural networks and deep learning. For the past decade, the computer scientist and professor has ⁴⁾**split** his time between Google and the University of Toronto. But he's ⁵⁾**resigned** from the tech giant so he can talk freely about the potential threat of AI, which he says is coming sooner than he previously thought.

被稱為「人工智慧教父」的傑佛瑞辛頓今年五月辭去谷歌職務，為的是警告他長期發揚的技術所存在的危險。辛頓自 45 年前取得人工智慧博士學位以來，已成為該領域最受尊崇的人物之一，並以在神經網路和深度學習領域的貢獻而聞名。過去十年，這位電腦科學家兼教授將自己的時間分配給谷歌和多倫多大學。但他現在已經從這家科技巨擘公司辭職，這樣他就可以自由地談論人工智慧的潛在威脅，他表示人工智慧的威脅比他之前想像得還要更早到來。

▲ 由左至右為伊爾亞蘇茨克維、艾利斯克里澤夫斯基、傑佛瑞辛頓

Vocabulary

1. **obtain** [əb`ten]
   (v.) 得到，獲得

2. **renowned** [rɪ`naʊnd]
   (adj.) 有名的，有聲譽的

3. **contribution** [ˌkɑntrə`bjuʃən]
   (n.) 貢獻

4. **split** [splɪt]
   (v.) 分擔，切開

5. **resign** [rɪ`zaɪn]
   (v.) 辭職，辭去

6. **analyze** [`ænəˌlaɪz]
   (v.) 分析

7. **identify** [aɪ`dɛntəˌfaɪ]
   (v.) 辨識，識別

8. **capability** [ˌkepə`bɪləti]
   (n.) 能力，性能

Advanced Words

* **godfather** [`gɑdˌfɑðə]
  (n.) 教父

* **Ph.D.** 博士（學位）

* **collaborate** [kə`læbəˌret]
  (v.) 共同合作

After pioneering the use of deep learning algorithms to train neural networks in the 1980s, Hinton *collaborated with two of his graduate students, Ilya Sutskever and Alex Krishevsky, to build a neural network that could ⁶⁾analyze thousands of photographs and teach itself to ⁷⁾identify the content of images. The three formed a neural network startup in 2012, which was bought by Google the following year for $44 million. The research acquired has helped Google improve its search ⁸⁾capabilities for images, voice and text, and has formed the basis for powerful new AI technologies, including new chatbots like Google Bard and ChatGPT.

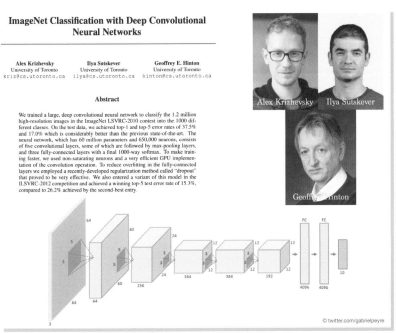

▲ 艾利斯與辛頓等人以模型「AlexNet」參加 ImageNet 舉辦的視覺識別挑戰賽（ILSVRC）獲勝。此為「AlexNet」的論文。

辛頓在 1980 年代率先使用深度學習演算法來訓練神經網路後，他與他的兩名研究生伊爾亞蘇茨克維和艾利斯克里澤夫斯基合作構建了一個神經網路，可以分析成千上萬張照片並自學識別圖像的內容。三人於 2012 年成立了一家神經網路新創公司，隔年被谷歌以 4400 萬美元收購。被收購的神經網路研究已幫助谷歌改進圖像、語音和文本的搜索能力，並為強大的新人工智慧技術奠定了基礎，包括谷歌 Bard 和 ChatGPT 等新型聊天機器人。

EZpedia

neural network 神經網路
神經網路的運作就是模仿人腦工作方式的運算模型。神經網路又可稱為人工神經網路（artificial neural network）或類神經網路（spiking neural network），最基本的神經網路包括一個輸入層、一個輸出層和一個或多個隱藏層。神經網路由多層神經元互相連結，可應用在圖片識別、自然語言處理、語音識別等領域。

deep learning 深度學習
深度學習是機器學習（machine learning）的一個分支，其使用了大量的「層」來組成神經網路，這些層稱為「深度」。每一層都能學習並提取不同的特徵，當層數越多時，模型就能學習到越複雜的模式。深度學習被廣泛運用在語音和影像辨識等領域。

chatbot 聊天機器人
聊天機器人使用了人工智慧、自然語言處理（natural language processing）和機器學習等技術，是以對話或文字的方式來互動的電腦程式。根據 Onix 的研究統計，2030 年聊天機器人領域將達到 36.2 億美元的市場規模。

▲ 谷歌 Bard 和 ChatGPT

Hinton, who also won the 2018 Turing Award—known as the "Nobel Prize of computer science"—for his 9)**theoretical** and 10)**engineering** 11)**breakthroughs**, said he now has some regrets over his life's work. He 12)**cites** the risks of AI taking jobs from humans, and the flood of fake photos, videos and text that appear real to the average person. Another concern is the potential for people with evil 13)**intent** to 14)**exploit** AI tools for their own purposes, like making weapons, *inciting violence or manipulating elections. That's why he wants to play a role in 15)**establishing** policies for the responsible use of AI, including the consideration of 16)**ethical** implications.

辛頓還因理論和工程的突破而獲得 2018 年圖靈獎,該獎項被譽為「電腦科學界的諾貝爾獎」,他表示現在對自己一生的工作成就感到有些遺憾。他列舉了人工智慧奪走人類工作的風險,以及對一般人來說看似真實的假照片、影片和文本的氾濫。另一個擔憂的可能性是,心懷惡意的人意圖利用人工智慧工具達到自己的目的,例如製造武器、煽動暴力或操縱選舉,因此他希望在制訂人工智慧盡責使用的政策方面發揮作用,包括將牽涉到的倫理層面納入考量。

Vocabulary

9. **theoretical** [ˌθiəˈrɛtɪkəl]
   (adj.) 理論的,假設的

10. **engineering** [ˌɛndʒəˈnɪrɪŋ]
    (n.) 工程,工程學

11. **breakthrough** [ˈbrekˌθru]
    (n.) 突破,進展

12. **cite** [saɪt]
    (v.) 引用,舉出

13. **intent** [ɪnˈtɛnt]
    (n.) 意圖,目的

14. **exploit** [ɪkˈsplɔɪt]
    (v.) 利用,開發

15. **establish** [əˈstæblɪʃ]
    (v.) 建立,設立

16. **ethical** [ˈɛθɪkəl]
    (adj.) 倫理的,道德的

17. **conference** [ˈkɑnfərəns]
    (n.) 會議

18. **beneficial** [ˌbɛnəˈfɪʃəl]
    (adj.) 有利的,有益的

19. **minimize** [ˈmɪnəˌmaɪz]
    (v.) 使減到最少

20. **evolution** [ˌɛvəˈluʃən]
    (n.) 發展,進展

"I don't think there's much chance of stopping development," Hinton said at a recent MIT [17]**conference**. "What we want is some way of making sure that even if they're smarter than us, they're going to do things that are [18]**beneficial** for us. But we need to try and do that in a world where there are bad actors who want to build robot soldiers that kill people." Asked how to [19]**minimize** the chances of potentially catastrophic [20]**evolution** of AI, Hinton responded, "I'm <u>sounding the alarm</u> and saying we have to worry about this. And I wish I had a nice simple solution, but I don't. But I think it's very important that people get together and think hard about it and see whether there is a solution. It's not clear there is a solution."

© ARCHIVIO GBB / Alamy Stock Photo

▲ 艾倫圖靈。圖靈獎設立目的之一為紀念他。

辛頓在最近的麻省理工學院會議上說道：「我認為停止開發的可能性不大，我們想要確保就算人工智慧比我們聰明，也會做對我們有利的事。但我們要在一個有壞人想製造殺人機器士兵的世界裡設法做到這一點。」被問到如何盡量減少人工智慧演變成災難的可能時，辛頓回答：「我正在示警，告訴大家必須擔心這一點。我希望我有簡單的解決方案，但我沒有。不過我認為大家集思廣益看是否有解決辦法是非常重要的。目前尚不清楚是否有解決辦法。」

Advanced Words

* **incite** [ɪn`saɪt]
  (v.) 激起，煽動

Tongue-tied No More

sound the alarm
拉警報，發出警訊
= raise the alarm

Economists are **sounding the alarm** about a possible recession.
經濟學家對可能出現的經濟衰退發出警告。

EZpedia

Turing Award 圖靈獎
圖靈獎由美國電腦協會（ACM）於 1966 年設立，專門獎勵對電腦事業發展做出重要貢獻的個人。該獎項的名稱取自電腦科學的先驅、英國科學家、電腦科學與人工智慧之父艾倫圖靈（Alan Turing）。圖靈獎是電腦界最崇高的獎項，有「電腦界諾貝爾獎」之稱。

© Everett Collection / Shutterstock.com

Alferd Packer, the Colorado Cannibal

科羅拉多食人者艾弗帕克

Over a century after his death, a man who **¹⁾confessed** to eating five men during an 1874 mountain **²⁾expedition** in Colorado has become an *****unlikely** folk hero. The story of Alferd Packer begins in 1842 with his birth in **³⁾rural** Pennsylvania. After an ordinary **⁴⁾upbringing**, he joined the Union Army at the start of the Civil War. On receiving an honorable discharge due to *****epilepsy**, he headed out West and found work as a hunter and **⁵⁾ranch** hand.

一名男子曾承認於 1874 年在科羅拉多州的一次山脈探險中吃了五個人，在過世一個多世紀後，他成了意想不到的民間英雄。艾弗帕克的故事要從他 1842 年出生於賓州鄉村開始說起。他成長過程平凡，在內戰開打時加入聯邦軍。因患有癲癇在光榮退伍後前往西部，找到了狩獵和牧場工人的工作。

In November 1873, Packer **⁶⁾encountered** a party of 20 miners near Provo, Utah. When they told him they were headed for the gold fields of Breckenridge, Colorado, he convinced them to let him join their expedition as a mountain guide. As winter deepened, heavy snow slowed the group's progress, and they **⁷⁾eventually** got lost and ran out of *****provisions**. When they arrived at a Ute Indian camp in late January, Chief Ouray provided them with food and **⁸⁾shelter**, and advised them to wait till spring before crossing the **⁹⁾rugged** San Juan Mountains. But gold fever got the better of Packer and five of

Vocabulary

1. **confess** [kənˋfɛs]
   (v.) 坦白，承認
   confession [kənˋfɛʃən]
   (n.) 坦白，告解

2. **expedition** [ˌɛkspəˋdɪʃən]
   (n.) 遠征，探險

3. **rural** [ˋrʊrəl]
   (adj.) 農村的，田園的

4. **upbringing** [ˋʌpˌbrɪŋɪŋ]
   (n.) 養育，教養

5. **ranch** [ræntʃ]
   (n.) 牧場，農場

6. **encounter** [ɪnˋkaʊntɚ]
   (v.) 偶然相遇

7. **eventually** [ɪˋvɛntʃʊəli]
   (adv.) 最後，終於
   eventual [ɪˋvɛntʃʊəl]
   (adj.) 最後的，結果的

8. **shelter** [ˋʃɛltɚ]
   (n.) 住所，遮蔽

9. **rugged** [ˋrʌgɪd]
   (adj.) 崎嶇的，高低不平的

10. **companion** [kəmˋpænjən]
    (n.) 同伴，伴侶

11. **whiskey** [ˋwɪski]
    (n.) 威士忌酒

12. **defense** [dɪˋfɛns]
    (n.) 防禦，防護
    self-defense
    (n.) 自衛

the miners, and the six men continued on their journey. The five miners were never seen alive again.

1873 年 1 月，帕克在猶他州普洛伏附近遇到 20 名礦工。他們告訴他，他們要去科羅拉多州布雷肯里治的金礦區時，帕克說服他們讓他以山域嚮導身分加入探險隊。隨著隆冬到來，大雪減緩了隊伍的前進速度，他們最終迷路並耗盡食物。他們在一月下旬到達猶特族印第安人的部落時，烏雷酋長提供他們食物和住所，並建議他們等到春天再穿越崎嶇的聖胡安山脈。但淘金熱戰勝了帕克和五名淘金者的理智，於是六人繼續旅程。但再也看不到這五名淘金者活著的蹤跡。

332 THREE UTE INDIAN BRAVES.
© Charles Weitfle (American, 1836 - after 1884)

▲ 猶特族印第安人

Two months later, Packer arrived in the town of Lake City, telling people his five [10]**companions** had all frozen to death. But he looked suspiciously well fed, and had plenty of money to spend on [11]**whiskey**. After questioning from a local general, Packer signed a [1]**confession** stating that as the men died one by one, the survivors ate their flesh to stay alive. He also claimed that when the last remaining miner attacked him, he shot the man in self-[12]**defense**. But the [13]**authorities** didn't believe his story, and arrested him on suspicion of murder. Before Packer could be tried, however, he escaped and disappeared.

兩個月後，帕克抵達胡泊城，告訴大家他的五個同伴都凍死了。但他看起來飲食充足，這點令人起疑，而且有很多錢可以買威士忌。在受到當地將軍的訊問後，帕克簽了一份自白，聲稱這些人一個接一個死去後，倖存者為了生存而吃掉他們的肉。他還宣稱，最後一名倖存的淘金者襲擊他時，他出於自衛開槍射殺了這名男子。但當局不相信他的說詞，並以涉嫌謀殺罪逮捕他。不過在帕克受審前，他逃跑並失蹤了。

13. authority [ə`θɔrətɪ]
(n.) 官方，當局

Advanced Words

* **unlikely** [ʌn`laɪklɪ]
  (adj.) 不太可能的，意想不到的

* **epilepsy** [`ɛpəˌlɛpsɪ]
  (n.) 癲癇

* **provision** [prə`vɪʒən]
  (n.) 食物，糧食

Tongue-tied No More

(receive an) honorable discharge 因紀錄良好而光榮退伍
相反詞為 dishonorable discharge

Many benefits are available to soldiers who **receive an honorable discharge**.
光榮退伍的士兵可以獲得許多福利。

A military judge sentenced the Marine to a **dishonorable discharge**.
一名軍事法官判處這名海軍陸戰隊員不名譽退伍。

▲ 科羅拉多大學波德分校的艾弗帕克燒烤餐廳

After remaining <u>at large</u> for nine years, Packer was captured in Wyoming and returned to Colorado, where he was ¹⁴⁾**convicted** of murder and sentenced to die by hanging. But just days before his ¹⁵⁾**execution**, a higher court ruled that because his crimes happened before Colorado became a state, he couldn't be given a death sentence. In a second trial, Packer was convicted of *****manslaughter** and received a 40-year prison sentence. He proved a model prisoner and was granted *****parole** after serving just 15 years.

在逃逸九年後，帕克在懷俄明州被捕，送返科羅拉多州後被判定謀殺罪，並判處絞刑。但就在行刑前幾天，高等法院裁定，由於他的罪行發生在科羅拉多州成立之前，因此不能判處死刑。在第二次審判中，帕克被判定過失殺人罪，並處以 40 年牢獄監禁。他在獄中是模範囚犯，僅服刑 15 年就獲得假釋。

By the time of Packer's death in 1907, public opinion had begun to soften, and over the following century, he gradually ¹⁶⁾**transformed** into a Colorado folk hero. For years, the Alferd Packer ¹⁷⁾**Grill** at the University of Colorado Boulder has invited diners to "Have a Friend for Lunch!" And Trey Parker, creator of *South Park*, even directed and starred in a film about Packer while studying at the university. Called *****Cannibal*! The Musical,* the film was also turned into a successful Off Broadway stage show. Was Packer a ¹⁸⁾**murderer**, or just a man forced by circumstances to "have friends for lunch"? The mystery only adds to his appeal.

Vocabulary

14. convict [kən`vɪkt]
(v.) 被判有罪

15. execution [ˌɛksɪ`kjuʃən]
(n.) 處死刑，死刑

16. transform [træns`fɔrm]
(v.) 改變，改觀

17. grill [grɪl]
(n.) 烤架，燒烤店

18. murderer [`mɝdərɚ]
(n.) 謀殺犯

Advanced Words

* **manslaughter** [`mæn͵slɔtɚ]
(n.) 過失殺人

* **parole** [pə`rol]
(n.) 假釋

* **cannibal** [`kænəbəl]
(n.) 食人者

Tongue-tied No More

get the better of (sb.)
情感戰勝理智，擊敗

I know I shouldn't have opened his mail, but my curiosity **got the better of** me.
我知道我不應該打開他的信，但我的好奇心戰勝了理智。

1907 年帕克去世時，公眾輿論已經開始緩和，在接下來的一個世紀裡，他逐漸變成科羅拉多州的民間英雄。多年來，科羅拉多大學波德分校的艾弗帕克燒烤餐廳邀請食客「午餐吃朋友！（請朋友吃午餐的雙關語）」而《南方四賤客》的創作者崔帕克甚至在該大學就讀期間執導並主演一部關於帕克的電影，名為《食人者音樂劇》，這部電影也被改編為成功的外百老匯舞台劇。帕克是殺人犯，還是只是被環境所迫而「午餐吃朋友」？故事的神祕感只會增加他的吸引力。

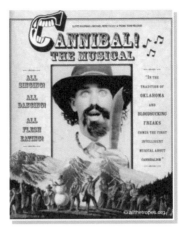
▲ 崔帕克的《食人者音樂劇》

▲ 崔帕克

EZpedia

Union Army 聯邦軍

聯邦軍，又稱作聯邦陸軍（Federal Army）或北軍（Northern Army），是在美國內戰期間（American Civil War，1861-1865）為北方聯邦作戰的軍隊。聯邦軍實際上是由許多軍團組成，以負責各自作戰的地理區域。1865 年內戰結束時，聯邦軍擊敗了邦聯軍（Confederate Army）取得勝利。

Ute Indians 猶特族印第安人

猶特人，或稱猶他人，是科羅拉多州最古老的住民。他們是居住在大盆地地區的大型部落，範圍包括奧勒岡、愛達荷、懷俄明、加利福尼亞東部地區、內華達、猶他、科羅拉多、亞利桑那北部地區以及新墨西哥。在取得馬匹之前，他們使用石頭和木頭製成的工具和武器。他們會和普布羅人（Pueblos）交易，以獲得用於儲存食物和水的陶器。他們在編織籃子方面非常熟練。

Off Broadway 外百老匯

根據劇院規模，座位有 500 席以上的為百老匯；有 99 至 499 席的為外百老匯；99 席以下的則是外外百老匯。雖然會有例外，但多數還是可以依照席次來區分。外百老匯的作品通常不像百老匯那般商業取向，會更加多元和自由，雖然預算較少，製作也較為簡單，但仍產出許多經典的作品。其中也有一些非常受歡迎的作品，後來登上了百老匯的舞台。

The boxer fought well, but his opponent **got the better of** him in the end.
這位拳擊手打得很好，但他的對手最終戰勝了他。

at large
逍遙法外，危險動物未被捕獲

The robbery suspect is still **at large** and considered dangerous.
搶劫嫌犯仍然在逃且被認為對社會有危害。

The police released a photo of the victim, whose killer remains **at large**.
警方公佈了受害者的照片，殺人犯仍然在逃。

Mass Shooting in Monterey Park

蒙特利公園市發生大規模槍擊事件

© Matt Gush / Shutterstock.com

On Saturday, January 21, a **mass shooting** occurred in Monterey Park, a city just east of Los Angeles with a majority Asian American population. The shooting took place at approximately 10:22 p.m. at the Star Ballroom Dance Studio, which was holding a [1]**Lunar** New Year dance party. Monterey Park police responded within three minutes of the first 911 call, finding "individuals <u>pouring out of</u> the location screaming" when they arrived. The *perpetrator** killed ten people and injured nine others before [2]**fleeing** the scene. An eleventh victim died at the Los Angeles Medical Center the day after the attack.

1 月 21 日星期六，洛杉磯以東的蒙特利公園市發生大規模槍擊事件，該市居民多數為亞裔美國人。槍擊事件發生在晚上約 10 時 22 分，地點在舞星大舞廳，當時正在舉辦農曆新年舞會。蒙特利公園市警方在接到第一通 911 電話後於三分鐘內出動，他們抵達現場後發現「多人尖叫著湧出舞廳」。行兇者殺了十人，射傷了九人，然後逃離現場。槍擊案發生後隔天，第 11 名受害者在洛杉磯醫療中心死亡。

Shortly after leaving the Star Ballroom, the gunman drove north to the Lai Lai Ballroom in nearby Alhambra to continue his shooting *spree**. As he entered the lobby, he was [3]**confronted** by Brandon Tsay, the 24-year-old son of the Lai Lai's owners, who [4]**wrestled** his gun away from him and chased him out. Tsay's actions were [5]**hailed** as [6]**heroic**. [7]**Investigators** were able to use the gun—a MAC-11 with a high-[8]**capacity** magazine—

Vocabulary

1. **lunar** [ˋlunɚ]
   (adj.) 陰曆的

2. **flee** [fli]
   (v.) 逃離，消失

3. **confront** [kənˋfrʌnt]
   (v.) 勇敢面對，對抗

4. **wrestle** [ˋrɛsəl]
   (v.) 搏鬥，角力

5. **hail** [hel]
   (v.) 擁立，承認

6. **heroic** [hɪˋroɪk]
   (adj.) 英雄的，英勇的

7. **investigator** [ɪnˋvɛstəˏgetɚ]
   (n.) 調查者
   investigate [ɪnˋvɛstəˏget]
   (v.) 調查，研究

8. **capacity** [kəˋpæsəti]
   (n.) 容量，容積

9. **cargo** [ˋkɑrgo]
   (n.) 貨物

10. **van** [væn]
    (n.) 廂型車，小貨車

11. **overnight** [ˏovɚˋnaɪt]
    (adj.) 通宵，整夜

12. **license** [ˋlaɪsəns]
    (n.) 執照，牌照

13. **pistol** [ˋpɪstəl]
    (n.) 手槍

to identify the suspect, who was seen fleeing the Lai Lai in a white [9]**cargo** [10]**van**.

槍手離開舞星大舞廳後不久，駕車往北去附近的阿罕布拉市來來舞社，繼續瘋狂掃射。他進入大廳時，遇到來來老闆的 24 歲兒子蔡班達，蔡班達奪下他的槍，並將他驅離。蔡的英勇作為受到肯定。調查人員得以用這把有大容量彈匣的 MAC-11 衝鋒槍來辨識嫌犯的身份，有人看到嫌犯駕著一輛白色廂型車逃離來來舞社。

© Jack Quillin / Shutterstock.com

▲ 舞星大舞廳

After an [11]**overnight** *****manhunt**, police officers pulled over a van with stolen [12]**license** plates matching the description of the one seen leaving the Lai Lai in Torrance, about 30 miles south of Monterey Park. As the officers approached the van, they heard a single gunshot from inside, and requested *****tactical** units to respond. When a SWAT team arrived, they

© Los Angeles County Sheriff's Department

▲ 中國北方工業製造的半自動手槍（semi-automatic Norinco pistol）

found the killer dead by a gunshot to the head from a Norinco [13]**pistol**.

Advanced Words

* **perpetrator** [ˋpɝpəˌtretɚ]
  (n.) 犯罪者，行兇者

* **spree** [spri]
  (n.) 無節制的狂熱行為

* **manhunt** [ˋmænˌhʌnt]
  (n.) 搜索，追捕

* **tactical** [ˋtæktɪkəl]
  (adj.) 戰術的，作戰的

EZpedia

mass shooting 大規模槍擊事件
對於什麼是大規模槍擊事件一直有不同的定義，非營利性的槍支暴力檔案（Gun Violence Archive）該機構對大規模槍擊事件的定義是：除槍手外有四人或四人以上死亡或受傷的槍擊事件。美國截至 2023 年 10 月已發生超過 560 起大規模槍擊事件。

MAC-11
MAC-11（Military Armament Corporation Model 11）是一款由戈登英格拉姆（Gordon Bailey Ingram）於 1972 年所設計，軍事裝備公司（Military Armament Corporation）與其他少數工廠生產的輕型衝鋒槍，使用開放式槍機，是 MAC-10 的 .380 ACP 口徑版本。

▲ 英勇奪下槍手槍枝的蔡班達

經過連夜追捕，警察在蒙特利公園市以南約 30 英里的托倫斯攔下一輛箱型車，車牌號碼與離開來來舞社的失竊車輛相符。警察靠近箱型車時，聽到車內傳出一聲槍響，於是要求戰術部隊應對。特警部隊趕到時，他們發現該名殺人犯被中國北方工業製造的手槍擊中頭部身亡。

On Tuesday, the Los Angeles County *Coroner released the names and ages of the people killed in Monterey Park on Saturday. All 11 victims of the mass shooting were Asian Americans between the ages of 57 and 76. Among them were the dance hall's owner and manager, Ming Wei Ma, and three Taiwanese citizens. The shooter, identified as 72-year-old Huu Can Tran, was an immigrant of Chinese 14)**descent** from Vietnam. Authorities are still investigating Tran's 15)**whereabouts** between the time of the shooting and his suicide and trying to determine a 16)**motive** for the crime. Tran's former wife said that she met him over 20 years ago at the Star Ballroom, where he gave dance lessons. She stated that while Tran was never violent toward her, he <u>was quick to</u> anger.

週二時，洛杉磯郡驗屍官公佈週六在蒙特利公園市被槍殺的遇難者姓名和年齡。這次大規模槍擊事件的 11 名受害者全是介於 57 歲至 76 歲的亞裔美國人，其中包括舞廳老闆兼經理馬名偉和三名臺灣公民。槍手確認為 72 歲的陳友良，是來自越南的華裔移民。當局仍在調查陳從槍擊事件發生到自殺期間的行蹤，並設法找出犯罪動機。陳的前妻說，她 20 多年前在舞星大舞廳結識陳，他當時在那裡教授舞蹈課。她說，雖然陳從來沒有對她使用暴力，但他很容易生氣。

Vocabulary

14. descent [dɪˋsɛnt]
(n.) 世系，血統

15. whereabouts [ˋwɛrəˏbauts]
(n.) 行蹤，下落

16. motive [ˋmotɪv]
(n.) 動機，目的

17. community [kəˋmjunəti]
(n.) 社區，社群

18. socialize [ˋsoʃəˏlaɪz]
(v.) 參與社交

19. shatter [ˋʃætɚ]
(v.) 粉碎，毀壞

Advanced Words

* coroner [ˋkɔrənɚ]
(n.) 驗屍官

Tongue-tied No More

pour out of （人、動物、車）大量湧出、大量冒出

Thousands of fans **poured out of** the stadium after the football game.
足球比賽結束後，成千上萬球迷湧出體育場。

The Monterey Park shooting has left a ^17)**community** in shock. Star Ballroom Dance Studio has long been a place where dancers of all skill levels and ages can ^18)**socialize** and exercise. For many older Asian Americans, often immigrants, the dance hall has provided a sense of belonging and community. But on Jan. 21, that community was ^19)**shattered** when Star Ballroom Dance Studio became the site of one of California's worst mass shootings in recent history.

▲ 一名女性在舞星大舞廳外面哀悼死者

蒙特利公園市槍擊事件令社區眾人震驚。舞星大舞廳長期以來一直是舞技和年齡不等的舞者用來社交和運動的場所。對許多年長且通常是移民的亞裔美國人來說，舞星大舞廳提供了一種歸屬感和社群感。但在 1 月 21 日，舞星大舞廳變成加州近年來最嚴重大規模槍擊事件之一的地點時，該社群也分崩離析。

People screamed as dozens of rats **poured out of** the sewer.
數十隻老鼠從下水道中湧出時，大家尖叫起來。

be quick to
（對話語或情況）快速反應

The Russian military **was quick to** deny any involvement in the attack.
俄國軍方很快否認參與這次襲擊。

The media **was quick to** blame the fires on global warming.
媒體很快將火災歸咎於全球暖化。

EZpedia

SWAT team 特種武器和戰術部隊
特種武器和戰術部隊（special weapons and tactics）為美國首創的特種警察部隊，專門執行危險任務，包括執行高度危險性拘捕令、營救人質、阻止恐怖份子攻擊以及阻止從事重型武裝危機等等。

Florida Woman Guilty in Romance Scam

佛州女子感情詐欺被判定有罪

A Florida woman who <u>lived high on the hog</u> with $2.8 million that she *swindled out of an 87-year-old *Holocaust survivor in a 1)romance *scam 2)pleaded 3)guilty on Friday to wire 4)fraud, the U.S. Attorney for the Southern 5)District of New York announced. Peaches Stergo, 36, could face up to 20 years in prison when sentenced later this month.

紐約南區聯邦檢察官宣布，一名佛州女子用感情從一名 87 歲的納粹大屠殺倖存者手中騙取 280 萬美元後過著奢華的生活，她已於週五承認犯下電匯詐騙罪。36 歲的佩琪史特戈於本月（7 月）月末被判刑時，可能面臨最高 20 年的牢獄監禁。

"This 6)conduct is sick—and sad," said U.S. Attorney Damian Williams in a statement. "Using the millions in fraud *proceeds, Stergo lived a life of 7)luxury, purchasing a home in a gated community and a Corvette, taking vacations at hotels like the Ritz-Carlton, and buying thousands in designer clothing, while at the same time causing her elderly victim to lose his apartment."

聯邦檢察官戴米安威廉斯在一份聲明中表示：「這種行為病態且可悲。史特戈用詐騙得來的數百萬美元過著奢侈的生活，在一個門禁社區買了一棟房子又買一輛科爾維特跑車，在麗思卡爾頓之類的大飯店度假，買了數千美元的名牌服裝，卻也同時造成年老的受害者失去他的公寓。」

Vocabulary

1. **romance** [ro`mæns]
   (n.) 戀愛，浪漫氣氛

2. **plead** [plid]
   (v.) 承認（有罪），抗辯（無罪）

3. **guilty** [`gɪlti]
   (adj.) 有罪的，內疚的

4. **fraud** [frɔd]
   (n.) 詐欺，騙局

5. **district** [`dɪstrɪkt]
   (n.) 區，行政區，地區

6. **conduct** [`kɑndʌkt]
   (n.) 行為，舉動

7. **luxury** [`lʌkʃəri]
   (n.) 奢侈，奢華

8. **settlement** [`sɛtəlmənt]
   (n.) 和解，和解金

9. **accessory** [æk`sɛsəri]
   (n.) 配件

10. **multiple** [`mʌltəpəl]
    (adj.) 多重的，不只一個的

Advanced Words

* **swindle** [`swɪndəl]
  (v.) 詐騙，騙取

* **Holocaust** [`hɑlə‚kɔst]
  (n.) 納粹大屠殺

* **scam** [`skæm]
  (n.) 詐騙，騙局

Stergo met her victim on a dating website in 2016, then started asking to borrow money to pay a lawyer in early 2017 so that he would release funds from an injury [8]**settlement** that didn't actually exist, according to the *****indictment**. No settlement funds were ever deposited into her account, but she kept demanding more money from the victim, who wrote 62 checks totaling over $2.8 million over the following four and a half years. Stergo also *****impersonated** a bank employee and created fake *****invoices** from the bank to trick the elderly victim.

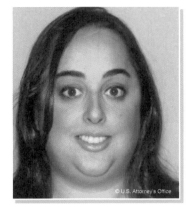
▲ 另一張佩琪史特戈的正面照

根據起訴書，史特戈於 2016 年在一個交友網站上認識受害者，然後在 2017 年初開始要求借錢支付律師費用，好讓律師從實際上不存在的傷害和解金中放款。和解金從未存入她的帳戶，但她不斷向受害者索要更多錢，受害者在接下來的四年半中開出 62 張支票，總計超過 280 萬美元。史特戈還冒充銀行職員並偽造銀行發票以欺騙老年人。

Over the course of the fraud, Stergo bought designer clothes and [9]**accessories**; purchased a boat and [10]**multiple** cars, including a Corvette and Suburban; and went on expensive vacations where she stayed at fancy hotels. The victim, meanwhile, lost his life savings and his Manhattan apartment.

EZpedia

U.S. Attorney 美國聯邦檢察官
隸屬於美國司法部，由總統任命，在各個聯邦司法區（Federal Judicial District）任職。其工作主要是在聯邦的 所有刑事訴訟中作為公訴人指控犯罪，在其任職的聯邦司法區內的民事訴訟中代表國家參與訴訟。

---

scammer [ˋskæmɚ]
(n.) 詐騙犯

***** **proceeds** [ˋprosidz]
(n.) 收益，收入

***** **indictment** [ɪnˋdaɪtmənt]
(n.) 起訴書

indict [ɪnˋdaɪt]
(v.) 控告，告發

***** **impersonate** [ɪmˋpɝsəˏnet]
(v.) 冒充，模仿

***** **invoice** [ˋɪnvɔɪs]
(n.) 發票，請款單

Tongue-tied No More

live high on/off the hog
過奢侈的生活
此慣用語是因為最貴的豬肉來自於豬（hog）身體的上半部。

Those Hollywood movie stars all **live** pretty **high on the hog**. 那些好萊塢電影明星都過著相當奢侈的生活。

over/in the course of
在……的期間

Over the course of their marriage, the couple had four children.
這對夫婦在婚姻中育有四個孩子。

▲ 史特戈購入的科爾維特，雪佛蘭品牌旗艦跑車（示意圖）。

▲ 史特戈購入的郊區，雪佛蘭品牌休旅車（示意圖）。

▲ 史特戈購入的勞力士手錶（示意圖）

在詐騙過程中，史特戈買了名牌服裝和配飾，以及一艘船和多輛汽車，車款包括雪佛蘭科爾維特跑車和郊區休旅車。她的度假開銷昂貴，住在豪華旅館，同時受害者卻失去畢生積蓄和他位於曼哈頓的公寓。

<u>In connection with</u> the guilty [11]**plea**, Stergo agreed to pay her victim $2,830,775 in [12]**compensation**. She will also be required to return over 100 luxury items she purchased with the fraud proceeds, including Rolex watches, gold Cartier [13]**bracelets**, and Louis Vuitton and Gucci bags, according to court [14]**documents**.

就其認罪內容，史特戈同意向受害者支付 283 萬 775 美元的賠償金。根據法庭文件，她被要求退回用詐騙所得購買的一百多件奢侈品，包括勞力士手錶、卡地亞金手鐲、路易威登和古馳包包。

As more Americans have turned to online dating in search of love, romance scams have been <u>on the rise</u>. An estimated 73,000 Americans were [15]**relieved** of a record $1 billion in 2022, according to a [16]**consumer** group.

隨著越來越多美國人透過網路交友尋找愛情，感情詐騙案不斷增加。根據一個消費者保護團體表示，2022 年估計有七萬三千名美國人被詐騙十億美元，創下紀錄。

Vocabulary

11. plea [pli]
(n.) 抗辯，答辯

12. compensation
[ˌkɑmpən`seʃən]
(n.) 賠償，賠償金

13. bracelet [`breslɪt]
(n.) 手鐲

14. document [`dɑkjəmənt]
(n.) 公文，文件

15. relieve (of) [rɪ`liv]
(v.) 偷，竊去

16. consumer [kən`sumɚ]
(n.) 消費者

17. profile [`profaɪl]
(n.) 人物簡介

18. beware [bɪ`wɛr]
(v.) 當心，小心

19. confidence [`kɑnfədəns]
(n.) 信賴，信任，信心

Advanced Words

* profess [prə`fɛs]
(v.) 表白，承認

How can you avoid being the victim of a romance scam? First, and most obvious—never give any money or financial information to someone you meet on a dating site. Second—avoid anyone who refuses to video chat with you. Scammers often use fake photos in their dating [17]**profile**, and don't want you finding out their true identity. Third—[18]**beware** of people who try to move the relationship along too quickly. Scammers want to gain your [19]**confidence**, and to do so they may be quick to ***profess** their love or talk about marriage.

如何避免成為感情詐欺的受害者？首先，也是最當然的一點，永遠不要向你在交友網站上認識的人提供任何金錢或財務資訊。第二，避開那些拒絕與你視訊聊天的人。詐騙分子往往會在他們的交友個資中使用假照片，且不希望你發現他們的真實身分。第三，提防那些試圖讓關係進展太快的人。詐騙分子希望獲得你的信任，為此他們可能會很快對你表白或論及婚嫁。

▲ 交友軟體

Tongue-tied No More

in connection with 與……有關

Police arrested two suspects **in connection with** the robbery.
警方逮捕了兩名與這起搶劫案有關的嫌犯。

The tax office contacted him **in connection with** unpaid taxes.
稅務局就未繳稅款問題聯絡了他。

on the rise 上升中，增加中

According to the police, downtown crime is **on the rise**.
根據警方所稱，市中心的犯罪率正在上升。

After her success in the film, the actress' career is **on the rise**.
在這部電影取得成功後，這位女演員的事業蒸蒸日上。

© Chester Standard / SWNS.com

Jury Retires in Murder Trial of NHS Nurse

英國國民保健署護士謀殺案的陪審團退庭商議

The ¹⁾**jury** in the trial of an NHS nurse ²⁾**accused** of murdering seven vulnerable babies in a hospital *neonatal unit have ³⁾**retired** to consider their *verdict. Lucy Letby, 32, *allegedly ⁴⁾**injected** her victims with air or poisoned them with *insulin while working at the Countess of Chester Hospital between June 2015 and June 2016. She is also accused of attempting to murder another 10 babies, several of which had been born ⁵⁾**prematurely** or had complex health needs.

一名英國國民保健署護士被指控在醫院新生兒病房謀殺七名弱勢嬰兒，該案的陪審團已退庭商議裁決。32 歲的露西萊比涉嫌於 2015 年 6 月至 2016 年 6 月期間，在切斯特伯爵夫人醫院工作時向受害者注射空氣或用胰島素毒死他們。她也被指控企圖謀殺另外十名嬰兒，其中幾位是早產兒或有複雜的醫療需求。

Following a series of ⁶⁾**mysterious** deaths in the neonatal unit, suspicions mounted against Letby and hospital ⁷⁾**administrators** moved her to *clerical duties in July 2016. Cheshire Police were ⁸⁾**assigned** in mid-2017 to ⁹⁾**conduct** their own ¹⁰⁾**investigation**, with Letby eventually arrested at her home address in July 2018. At her trial, which began in October 2022, Letby took the stand in her own defense, telling the jury that she meant no harm during her time working at the hospital.

新生兒病房發生一連串神祕死亡事件後，萊比受到越來越多懷疑，醫院管理部門於 2016 年 7 月將她調往

Vocabulary

1. **jury** [ˋdʒʊrɪ]
   (n.) 陪審團
   juror [ˋdʒʊrə]
   (n.) 陪審員

2. **accuse** [əˋkjuz]
   (v.) 指控，控告

3. **retire** [rɪˋtaɪr]
   (v.)（法律）退庭

4. **inject** [ɪnˋdʒɛkt] (v.) 注射

5. **prematurely** [ˌpriməˋtjʊrlɪ]
   (adv.) 過早地
   premature [ˌpriməˋtjʊr]
   (adj.) 早產的

6. **mysterious** [mɪsˋtɪrɪəs]
   (adj.) 神祕的，不可思議的

7. **administrator**
   [ədˋmɪnəˌstretə]
   (n.) 管理人，行政官員

8. **assign** [əˋsaɪn]
   (v.) 分派，指定

9. **conduct** [kənˋdʌkt]
   (v.) 進行，處理

10. **investigation**
    [ɪnˌvɛstəˋgeʃən]
    (n.) 調查，研究

11. **witness** [ˋwɪtnɪs]
    (n./v.) 證人，目擊者；目擊

12. **prosecution** [ˌprasɪˋkjuʃən]
    (n.) 檢方，原告及其律師

文書工作。柴郡警方於 2017 年中被指派進行調查，萊比最終於 2018 年 7 月在自宅被捕。於 2022 年 10 月開始的庭審中，萊比出庭為自己辯護，並告訴陪審團她在醫院工作期間沒有懷抱惡意。

▲ 切斯特伯爵夫人醫院

Over the course of the trial, [1]**jurors** have listened to the ***testimony** of over 200 [11]**witnesses**, with the [12]**prosecution** alleging that Letby was the "constant ***malevolent** presence" when things <u>took a turn for the worse</u> for the babies. While her name was first mentioned by NHS [13]**consultants** following the sudden deaths of three babies in June 2015, she remained in the neonatal unit for another 12 months.

在庭審過程中，陪審團聽取了兩百多名證人的證詞，檢方聲稱嬰兒的情況惡化時，萊比是個「持續存在的惡勢力」。2015 年 6 月，三名嬰兒猝死後，國民保健署顧問首次提到她的名字，但她仍繼續在新生兒病房待了 12 個月。

◀ 2018 年，警方位於萊比在切斯特的住家。

13. consultant [kən'sʌltənt]
　(n.) 顧問

Advanced Words

* **neonatal** [ˌnio'netəl]
　(adj.) 新生兒的

* **verdict** ['vɝdɪkt]
　(n.) 裁決，裁定

* **allegedly** [ə'lɛdʒɪdli]
　(adv.) 據說地，宣稱地

allege [ə'lɛdʒ]
　(v.) 宣稱

alleged [ə'lɛdʒd]
　(adj.) 宣稱的

* **insulin** ['ɪnsəlɪn]
　(n.) 胰島素

* **clerical** ['klɛrɪkəl]
　(adj.) 文書工作的

* **testimony** ['tɛstəˌmoni]
　(n.) 證詞，證言

testify ['tɛstəˌfaɪ]
　(v.) 作證

* **malevolent** [mə'lɛvələnt]
　(adj.) 有惡意的

▲ 露西萊比的便利貼

Following Letby's arrest, police discovered a number of **Post-it** notes on which she had written "I am evil, I did this" and "I killed them on purpose." However, her defense lawyer, Benjamin Myers, argued that these were an expression of [14]**agony** by a young woman in fear and [15]**despair**, rather than any form of confession. Other notes found by police included the words "kill me" and "I haven't done anything wrong."

萊比被捕後，警方發現一些便利貼，她在上面寫著「我是邪惡的，是我做的」和「我故意殺了他們」。然而她的辯護律師班傑明麥爾斯辯稱，這是年輕女子在恐懼和絕望中表達痛苦的方式，而不是任何形式的招供。警方還發現其他便條貼上寫著「殺了我」和「我沒有做錯任何事」等。

During questioning by the prosecution, Letby claimed that a "[16]**conspiracy**" had been mounted against her by a number of senior consultants to cover hospital [17]**shortcomings**. In his closing speech, Myers said that the seven babies were all victims of "failures of care" that had nothing to do with Letby. Before her arrest, Letby had worked as a nurse since qualifying in 2011, with fellow nurses confirming that she had remained [18]**professional** throughout her time of employment.

在接受檢方訊問時，萊比聲稱，一些高階顧問為了掩蓋醫院的缺失而針對她策劃了「陰謀」。麥爾斯在結案陳詞中表示，這七個嬰兒都是「護理失效」的受害者，與萊比無關。在被捕之前，萊比自 2011 年取得資格以來一直擔任護士，其他護士證實她在整個工作期間都保持專業態度。

Vocabulary

14. agony [ˋægənɪ]
(n.) 痛苦，折磨

15. despair [dɪˋspɛr]
(n.) 絕望，喪失信心

16. conspiracy [kənˋspɪrəsɪ]
(n.) 陰謀，共謀

17. shortcoming [ˋʃɔrt͵kʌmɪŋ]
(n.) 缺點，短處

18. professional [prəˋfɛʃənəl]
(adj.) 稱職的，能勝任的

Tongue-tied No More

take the stand 出庭作證（stand 為證人席）

The judge asked the next witness to **take the stand**.
法官要求下一位證人出庭作證。

The man was advised by his lawyer not to **take the stand**.
該男子的律師建議他不要出庭作證。

Myers described Letby as a diligent nurse who had cared for hundreds of babies. "She didn't suddenly change her behavior in 2015," the lawyer said. "What changed was the babies in the unit and the inability of this unit to cope." Both Letby's parents and the families of the 17 babies involved have attended the trial at Manchester Crown Court. It is not yet known when a verdict will be reached.

麥爾斯形容萊比是勤奮的護士，照顧過數百名嬰兒。律師說：「她並沒有在 2015 年突然改變自己的行為，改變的是病房裡的嬰兒，以及這個病房無力應對的情況。」萊比的父母和 17 名受害嬰兒的家人都出席了曼徹斯特皇家法院的庭審。目前尚不清楚何時會做出裁決。

EZpedia

NHS 英國國民健保署

英國國民健保署（National Health Service，簡稱 NHS）是英格蘭國民保健署、北愛爾蘭保健及社會服務署、蘇格蘭國民保健署、威爾斯國民保健署，英國這四大公營醫療系統的統稱。作為公費健保系統，NHS 的經費來自國家稅收，絕大多數的醫療服務皆免費，其他如牙科、眼科、處方藥配置等服務則需收費。

Countess of Chester Hospital 切斯特伯爵夫人醫院

切斯特伯爵夫人醫院是柴郡地區主要的國民健保署醫院，擁有 625 張病床。由切斯特伯爵夫人國民健保署基金信託（Countess of Chester Hospital NHS Foundation Trust）管理。該醫院前身為 1829 年的柴郡精神病院。1984 年 5 月 30 日正式以「切斯特伯爵夫人醫院」為名開業。

Post-it 便利貼

「Post-it」是美國 3M 公司的史賓塞席佛（Spencer Silver）和亞特弗萊（Art Fry）無意間發明的文具。1968 年席佛的團隊正在研發壓力感應式黏著劑，席佛意外研發出一種黏性很弱的膠，不過這種膠應用受限，不受重視。任職膠帶部門的弗萊則將這種膠塗在唱詩班歌本和小紙片上做成書籤，這就是便利貼的雛形。便利貼在 1977 年試賣，1980 年在全美發售。

---

mean (sb.) no harm 沒有惡意
= not mean (sb.) any harm

Jason may have a bad temper, but he **means no harm**.
傑森也許脾氣不好，但他並無惡意。

Her joke was a little rude, but she didn't **mean** you **any harm**.
她的玩笑有點無禮，但她對你沒有惡意。

take a turn for the worse
情況惡化
表示好轉則是 take a turn for the better

The patient's condition **took a turn for the worse** last night.
昨晚病人的病情惡化。

The economy **took a turn for the better** after the war ended.
戰爭結束後，經濟好轉。

Part 3
Extra Credit 延伸閱讀

Germany Closes Last Nuclear Plants

德國關閉最後幾座核電廠

全文朗讀 ♪ 049　單字 ♪ 050

Vocabulary

1. **nuclear** [`nuklɪɚ]
   (adj.) 核能的，核武的

2. **span** [spæn]
   (v.) 持續，跨越

3. **advocate** [`ædvəkɪt]
   (n.) 提倡者，擁護者

4. **slam** [slæm]
   (v.) 猛烈抨擊

5. **commitment** [kə`mɪtmənt]
   (n.) 承諾，保證

6. **deadline** [`dɛd͵laɪn]
   (n.) 最後限期，截止日期

7. **carbon** [`kɑrbən]
   (n.) 碳

8. **lament** [lə`mɛnt]
   (v.) 哀悼，悲痛

9. **protest** [`pro͵tɛst]
   (n.) 抗議（活動）

Advanced Words

* **reactor** [rɪ`æktɚ]
   (n.) 反應爐

* **bolster** [`bolstɚ]
   (v.) 支撐，提高

Germany shut down its last three **1)nuclear** power plants on April 15, marking the end of the country's nuclear era, which has **2)spanned** over six decades. The closure of the Emsland, Isar II, and Neckarwestheim II nuclear power plants in Germany has long been expected, as the government announced plans to phase out nuclear power in 2011.

德國於 4 月 15 日關閉最後三座核能發電廠，象徵著該國長達六十多年核能時代的結束。隨著德國政府於 2011 年宣布計畫逐步淘汰核電，埃姆斯蘭核電廠、伊沙爾二號核電廠和內卡韋斯海二號核電廠的關閉早在預料之中。

In the fall of 2022, with the war in Ukraine limiting European access to energy, Germany decided to keep these existing nuclear ***reactors** operating for an additional few months to ***bolster** supplies. The plan to close the reactors, however, was being closely watched abroad, and **3)advocates** of nuclear power worldwide have **4)slammed** the German shutdown, aware that the action by Europe's largest economy could deal a blow to a technology they see as a clean and reliable alternative to fossil fuels. Others who fear nuclear accidents believe closing the reactors is a wise decision and an important first step towards Germany's **5)commitment** to transition to renewable energy.

2022 年秋天，由於烏克蘭戰爭限制歐洲取得能源的途徑，德國決定讓這些現有的核子反應爐再運行幾個月，以增加供應。然而關閉反應爐的計畫在國外受到密切關注，全球核電倡導者猛烈抨擊德國的關閉計畫，因為他們知道德國身為歐洲最大經濟體，這項行動可能會對被視為乾淨可靠且能取代化石燃料的核能技術造成打擊。其他擔心會發生核事故的人認為關閉反應爐是明智的決定，也是德國致力於再生能源轉型重要的一步。

▲ 核能倡導者在布蘭登堡門的抗議活動

Germany has pledged to close its last coal power station no later than 2038, with a 2030 [6)]**deadline** in some regions, and the country is aiming for 80% of its electricity to come from renewable sources by 2030. The shutdowns pose a huge challenge for energy [*]**policymakers**, who must balance growing electricity demand in one of Europe's industrial giants and efforts to create a low-[7)]**carbon** future for German citizens.

德國已承諾在 2038 年前關閉最後一座燃煤發電廠，部分地區的最後期限是 2030 年，該國的目標是在 2030 年之前有八成電力來自再生能源。關閉核電廠對決策者帶來巨大挑戰，他們必須平衡身為歐洲工業巨頭之一日益增加的電力需求和為德國公民打造低碳未來的努力。

"By phasing out nuclear power, Germany is committing itself to coal and gas because there is not always enough wind blowing or sun shining," said nuclear advocate Rainer Klute, [8)]**lamenting** the closure of the country's last nuclear plants at a [9)]**protest** near Berlin's Brandenburg Gate.

核電倡導者瑞納克魯特在柏林布蘭登堡門附近的一場抗議活動中對德國關閉最後幾座核電廠表示遺憾，他說：「在逐步淘汰核電之際，德國正繼續使用煤炭和天然氣，因為風和陽光並非總是足夠供給發電。」

Advanced Words

* **policymaker** [ˈpɑləsɪˌmekə]
(n.) 制定政策者

Tongue-tied No More

phase out 逐步淘汰，逐漸停止使用

California plans to **phase out** fossil fuels by 2045.
加州計劃在 2045 年前逐步淘汰化石燃料。

deal a blow to 給予打擊，使受挫

The earthquake **dealt a** major **blow to** the tourism industry.
地震對旅遊業造成重大打擊。

EZpedia

fossil fuel 化石燃料
化石燃料是古生物（包括動物及植物）在特定的地理環境及地質條件下，經由生物化學及物理化學作用而轉化形成的燃料。化石燃料包含固態、液態與氣態等三種型態。固態的化石燃料主要為煤、油頁岩（oil shale）等；液態的化石燃料主要為石油；氣態的化石燃料則主要為天然氣。化石燃料仍是目前能源主要來源之一。

renewable energy 再生能源
指太陽能、生質能、地熱能、海洋能、風力、非抽蓄式水力、一般廢棄物與一般事業廢棄物等直接利用或經處理所產生之能源。再生能源為取之不盡的天然資源，且轉換能源過程中不會產生汙染物。

© GB-Photographie / Shutterstock.com

France Bans Short-haul Flights

法國禁止短程航班

全文朗讀 ♪ 051　　單字 ♪ 052

Vocabulary

1. **critic** [ˋkrɪtɪk]
   (n.) 批判者，持反對態度的人，評論家

2. **specify** [ˋspɛsəˌfaɪ]
   (v.) 指定，指明

3. **route** [raʊt]
   (n.) 路線，航線

4. **destination** [ˌdɛstəˋneʃən]
   (n.) 目的地

5. **secure** [sɪˋkjʊr]
   (v.) 弄到，獲得

6. **minimal** [ˋmɪnəməl]
   (adj.) 最小的，極微的

7. **dismiss** [dɪsˋmɪs]
   (v.) 不予考慮，摒棄

8. **symbolic** [sɪmˋbɑlɪk]
   (adj.) 象徵性的

9. **tolerate** [ˋtɑləˌret]
   (v.) 忍受，容忍

Advanced Words

* **decree** [dɪˋkri]
   (n.) 法令，政令

* **hub** [hʌb]
   (n.)（某地或活動的）中心

* **emission** [ɪˋmɪʃən]
   (n.) 排放物

Under a government *decree announced on Tuesday, May 23, France has banned short-haul flights for journeys possible in less than two-and-a-half hours by train. The ban will prohibit air trips between Paris and regional *hubs like Nantes, Lyon and Bordeaux. Connecting flights will not be affected, though 1)**critics** have noted that the time limit is shy of the three hours it takes to travel by high-speed rail from Paris to the Mediterranean port of Marseille—France's second largest city.

根據 5 月 23 日星期二宣布的一項政府法令，法國禁止為搭火車不到兩個半小時的旅程提供短程航班。這項禁令將禁止巴黎與南特、里昂和波爾多等地區樞紐之間的航空旅行。轉機航班不會受到影響，不過有人批評，這個時間限制少於從巴黎搭高鐵到法國第二大城市馬賽的地中海港口所需的三個小時。

The law does 2)**specify** that train services on the same 3)**route** must be both frequent and well-connected enough to meet the needs of passengers who would otherwise travel by air, and able to handle the increase in passenger numbers. The replacement train service must also allow travelers to get to and from their starting point on the same day while allowing them a full eight hours at their 4)**destination**.

法律確實規定與航班相同路線的火車服務必須有頻繁的班次和完善的路線連接，以滿足乘客改搭火車的需求，並能應對乘客數量的增加。替代的火車服務也必須能讓旅客在同一天往返出發地，同時讓他們能在目的地停留整整八小時。

Although the ban was included in a 2021 climate law and already applied in practice, some airlines had asked the European Commission to investigate whether it was legal. The government had already [5]**secured** Air France's support for the plan in exchange for a 2020 COVID relief package.

儘管 2021 年氣候法就將這項禁令納入並已實施，但部分航空公司要求歐盟執委會調查這項禁令是否合法。法國政府早已獲得法國航空對這項計畫的支持，以換取 2020 年的新冠疫情紓困方案。

But many believe the ban will have a [6]**minimal** effect on carbon *emissions. Laurent Donceel, head of industry group Airlines for Europe, [7]**dismissed** the law as a " [8]**symbolic** ban," stating that governments should instead support "real and significant solutions" to airline emissions.

但許多人認為這項禁令對減少碳排放的影響甚微。歐洲航空業協會負責人洛朗唐西爾將該法律斥為「象徵性禁令」，並表示各國政府應該支持針對航空公司碳排放的「真正有效的解決方案」。

Meanwhile, France is also cracking down on the use of private jets for short journeys. Transport Minister Clément Beaune says the country can no longer [9]**tolerate** the rich using private planes while the general public travels by train to fight climate change.

同時法國也在制裁使用私人飛機進行短程旅行。交通部長克萊門伯恩表示，法國不能再容忍富人使用私人飛機，一般民眾卻要搭火車出行以對抗氣候變遷。

▲ 巴黎里昂車站

Tongue-tied No More

be shy of 低於某個數字或數量

The Democrats **are** three votes **shy of** a majority.
民主黨距離多數門檻還差三票。

Jonathan **is** one week **shy of** his 18th birthday.
距離喬納森的 18 歲生日還有一星期。

crack down (on)
制裁、鎮壓不良或非法行為
crackdown (n.) 制裁，鎮壓

The police **cracked down on** illegal drugs.
警方取締非法毒品。

Many protestors were killed in the brutal **crackdown**.
許多示威者在殘酷鎮壓中喪生。

EZpedia

short-haul 短程的
依照飛行距離可將航線分為短程、中程、長程航班，不過界定標準不一。根據萬事達卡 (Mastercard)「2022 年旅遊：趨勢與轉變」全球報告，短程約為 2,000 公里以內；中程約為 2,000 至 4,300 公里；長程航班約為 4,300 公里以上。

European Commission
歐盟執委會
負責監督歐盟會員國對條約及法令之執行，向歐盟理事會、部長理事會和歐洲議會提出報告和立法動議，處理歐盟日常事務，負責歐盟對外經貿談判、發展及援外等。

U.S. East Coast Blanketed by Haze

美國東海岸霧霾籠罩

© Nicoletta25 / Shutterstock.com

全文朗讀 ♪053　　單字 ♪054

Vocabulary

1. **urge** [ɝdʒ]
   (v.) 催促，力勸

2. **drift** [drɪft]
   (v.) 漂，漂流

3. **resident** [ˋrɛzədənt]
   (n.) 居民，定居者

4. **atmosphere** [ˋætməs͵fɪr]
   (n.) 大氣，氣氛

5. **critical** [ˋkrɪtɪkəl]
   (adj.) 關鍵性的，極為重要的

6. **pollution** [pəˋluʃən]
   (n.) 汙染
   pollutant [pəˋlutənt]
   (n.) 汙染物

7. **index** [ˋɪndɛks]
   (n.) 指數，指標

8. **chronically** [ˋkrɑnɪkli]
   (adv.) 慢性地，長期地
   chronic [ˋkrɑnɪk]
   (adj.) 慢性的，長期的

Advanced Words

* **haze** [hez]
   (n.) 霾，薄霧

* **elevation** [͵ɛləˋveʃən]
   (n.) 高度，海拔

Schools up and down the U.S. East Coast canceled outdoor activities, air traffic slowed, and millions of Americans were 1)**urged** to stay indoors on Wednesday as smoke from Canadian wildfires 2)**drifted** south, covering cities in a thick, orange ***haze**.

美國東海岸各地的學校於週三（6/7）取消戶外活動，空中交通減緩，數百萬美國人被敦促待在室內。因為加拿大野火的煙霧往南飄散，使各城市籠罩在厚重的橙色霧霾中。

The National Weather Service issued air quality alerts for most of the Atlantic Coast. Health officials from Vermont to South Carolina and as far west as Kansas warned 3)**residents** that spending time outdoors could cause breathing problems due to high levels of fine particulates, known as **PM2.5**, in the 4)**atmosphere**.

國家氣象局向大西洋海岸大部分地區發布了空氣品質警報。從弗蒙特州到南卡羅來納州，以及往西遠至堪薩斯州的衛生官員都警告居民，由於大氣中的懸浮微粒，即 PM2.5 的含量較高，在戶外活動可能會導致呼吸困難。

The thick haze extended from high ***elevations** to ground level, marking the worst case of wildfire smoke blanketing the East Coast in over 20 years. "It's 5)**critical** that Americans experiencing dangerous air 6)**pollution**, especially those with health conditions, listen to local authorities to protect themselves and their families," said President Joe Biden.

濃濃的霧霾從高處延伸至地面，這是 20 多年來野火煙霧籠罩東海岸最嚴重的情況。拜登總統表示：「至關重要的是，遭受危險空氣汙染的美國人，尤其是有健康狀況的美國人，必須聽從地方當局的指示，以保護自己和家人。」

New York Governor Kathy Hochul called the wildfire haze an "emergency crisis," saying the air pollution [7]**index** in parts of her state was eight times above normal. Reduced *visibility from the haze forced the FAA to delay flights into New York City and Philadelphia, and East Coast schools called off outdoor activities, including sports and field trips.

紐約州州長凱西霍楚稱這波野火煙霧為「緊急危機」，並表示該州部分地區的空氣汙染指數是正常數值的八倍。霧霾導致能見度下降，迫使美國聯邦航空總署延後飛往紐約市和費城的航班，東海岸學校則取消了戶外活動，包括體育和戶外教學。

In some areas, the air quality index (AQI), which measures major [6]**pollutants** including particulates produced by fires, was well above 400. An AQI of 100 is considered "unhealthy" and 300 " *hazardous."

部分地區的空氣品質指標遠高於 400，空氣品質指標為測量火災等因素造成微粒汙染物指標。空氣品質指標為 100 即被認定為「不健康」，300 被認定為「危險」。

At noon, Bethlehem, Pennsylvania had the worst air quality in the U.S., with an AQI of 410. Among major cities, New York recorded the highest AQI in the world on Wednesday at 342, more than double that of [8]**chronically** polluted cities like Dubai (168) and Delhi (164).

中午時，賓州伯利恆的空氣品質為全美最差，空氣品質指標為 410。在主要城市中，紐約週三（6/7）的空氣品質指標為 342，為全球最高，是杜拜（168）和德里（164）等長期受汙染城市的兩倍多。

▲ 受嚴重空汙影響的紐約曼哈頓

Advanced Words

* **visibility** [ˌvɪzəˈbɪləti]
  (n.) 能見度，可見性

* **hazardous** [ˈhæzədəs]
  (adj.) 危險的，有害的

Tongue-tied No More

call (sth.) off 取消或終止活動

The baseball game was **called off** due to rain.
棒球比賽因下雨而取消。

The union **called** the strike **off** after management met their demands.
在資方滿足工會的要求後，他們取消了罷工。

EZpedia

PM2.5 細懸浮微粒
懸浮在空氣中的微小汙染顆粒就是懸浮微粒（particulate matter, PM），懸浮微粒的粒徑小於 2.5 微米（μm）的粒子就是 PM2.5，稱為細懸浮微粒。PM2.5 表面易附著無機（如金屬、硫酸鹽）與有機（多環芳香烴化合物、戴奧辛等）汙染物，會經由鼻、咽和喉進入人體，穿透肺泡直接進入血管隨著血液循環全身，危害人體健康。

FAA (Federal Aviation Administration)
美國聯邦航空總署
美國聯邦航空總署是美國運輸部（U.S. Department of Transportation）下的一個機構，負責監管美國境內的民用航空，以及管理和發展美國國家空域系統（National Airspace System）。其主要任務是確保民用航空的安全。

LVHM Employees to Receive Environmental Training

LVHM 員工將接受環境保護培訓

全文朗讀 ♪ 055　單字 ♪ 056

Vocabulary

1. **acre** [ˋekɚ]
   (n.) 英畝

2. **boast** [bost]
   (v.) 擁有，包含

3. **partnership** [ˋpɑrtnɚˏʃɪp]
   (n.) 合夥（或合作）關係

4. **lush** [lʌʃ]
   (adj.) 蒼翠繁茂的

5. **host** [host]
   (v.) 以主人身分招待

6. **fundamental** [ˏfʌndəˋmɛntəl]
   (n.) 基本原則、原理

7. **sustainable** [səˋstenəbəl]
   (adj.) 能保持的，可永續發展的

8. **supplier** [səˋplaɪɚ]
   (n.) 供應商

9. **inquiry** [ˋɪnkwəri]
   (n.) 詢問，問題

10. **specialist** [ˋspɛʃəlɪst]
    (n.) 專業人員

Advanced Words

* **badger** [ˋbædʒɚ]
   (n.) 獾

* **biodiversity** [ˏbaɪodɪˋvɝsəti]
   (n.) 生物多樣性

As a destination for staff training, it sounds ideal: a 75-¹⁾**acre** nature reserve on the edge of the Rambouillet forest ²⁾**boasting** over 350 plant and animal species, including foxes, ***badgers** and deer. Known as Vallée de la Millière and located an hour from Paris, the reserve was acquired by famous photographer Yann Arthus-Bertrand in 2020 and will soon become a place for employees of LVMH Moët Hennessy Louis Vuitton to learn about ***biodiversity**.

以作為員工培訓的地點來說，這場地聽起來很理想：佔地 75 英畝的自然保護區，位於宏布耶森林的邊界，有超過 350 種動植物，包括狐狸、獾和鹿。該保護區名為米利埃谷，距離巴黎僅一小時車程，於 2020 年被知名攝影師楊亞祖貝童收購，即將成為酩悅軒尼詩路易威登集團員工學習生物多樣性的地方。

On May 26, the luxury giant announced a five-year ³⁾**partnership** with the Vallée de la Millière association, which is preparing the ⁴⁾**lush** site for employee training, and which will ⁵⁾**host** visits from students, **NGOs**, and scientists starting next year. By 2026, LVMH aims to train all of its 200,000 employees in "environmental ⁶⁾**fundamentals**" at multiple locations, including Vallée de la Millière and La Caserne—a ⁷⁾**sustainable** fashion hub in Paris.

5 月 26 日，這家奢侈品巨擘宣布與米利埃谷協會建立為期五年的合作夥伴關係，該協會正在為員工培訓準備這片草木茂盛的場地，並將於明年開始接待前來參觀的學生、非政府組織和科學家。LVMH 的目標是在 2026 年之前，在多個地點對全部 20 萬名員工進行「環境基本知識」的培訓，地點包括米利埃谷和巴黎永續時尚中心拉卡塞。

"Each employee can be an actor of change, and providing expert training is key," said LVMH environmental development director Hélène Valade at the Change Now environmental summit in Paris. "I think this amazing place will enable us to connect with nature."

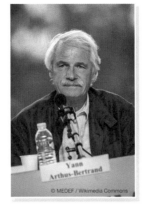

▲ 知名攝影師楊亞祖貝童

LVMH 環境發展總監海倫瓦拉德在巴黎的立刻改變環境高峰會上表示：「每位員工都可以是改變的參與者，而提供專家培訓是關鍵。我認為這片美妙的場地能讓我們與大自然連結。」

Valade told the Change Now audience that LVMH's training programs would be tailored to employee functions, so buyers can evaluate [8]**suppliers** of raw materials, sales associates can respond to customer [9]**inquiries** about how eco-friendly products are, and ***logistics** [10]**specialists** can understand the emissions from different forms of transport.

瓦拉德在高峰會上向觀眾說，LVMH 的培訓課程將根據員工的職責量身制訂，好讓採購人員可以評估原料供應商；業務人員可以回答顧客關於產品環保程度的問題；物流專員可以了解不同運輸形式的廢氣排放量。

"It's absolutely necessary to get the entire company on board with a common environmental ambition," she said, noting that providing environmental training to all employees by 2026 is a major goal of LVMH's Life 360 initiative.

她表示：「讓整個公司都參與共同的環保目標是絕對必要的。」她指出，在 2026 年前為所有員工提供環保培訓是 LVMH「生活360」措施的主要目標。

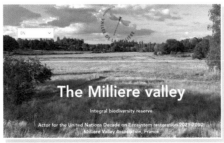

The Milliere valley

Integral biodiversity reserve

Actor for the United Nations Decade on Ecosystem restoration 2021-2030
Milliere Valley Association, France

▲ 米利埃谷協會網站

© valleedelamilliere.org

Ohtani Named World Baseball Classic MVP

大谷翔平榮獲世界棒球經典賽 MVP

Conor P. Fitzgerald / Shutterstock.com

全文朗讀 ♪ 057　　單字 ♪ 058

Vocabulary

1. **pitcher** [ˋpɪtʃɚ]
   (n.) 投手

2. **mound** [maʊnd]
   (n.) 投手丘

3. **championship**
   [ˋtʃæmpiənˏʃɪp]
   (n.) 冠軍賽，錦標賽

4. **premier** [prɪˋmɪr]
   (adj.) 首位的，首要的

5. **tournament** [ˋtɝnəmənt]
   (n.) 錦標賽，聯賽

6. **crush** [krʌʃ]
   (v.) 徹底擊敗

7. **opponent** [əˋponənt]
   (n.) 對手

Advanced Words

* **inning** [ˋɪnɪŋ]
  (n.)（棒球中的）局

* **postseason** [ˋpostˏsizən]
  (adj./n.)（比賽）季後（的）

* **playoff** [ˋpleˏɒf]
  (n.)（平局後的）延長賽

* **unicorn** [ˋjunɪˏkɔrn]
  (n.) 獨角獸，極為傑出的人事物

Major League Baseball star ¹⁾**pitcher** Shohei Ohtani was named **MVP** of the 2023 World Baseball Classic after dominating at the plate and on the ²⁾**mound** to deliver Japan its third ³⁾**championship** win.

美國職業棒球大聯盟明星投手大谷翔平在本壘和投手丘上皆表現出色，為日本隊贏得第三次冠軍，因此獲頒 2023 年世界棒球經典賽最有價值球員。

Ohtani batted .435 with one home run, four doubles, eight **RBIs** and 10 walks as Japan joined the Dominican Republic as the only unbeaten champions of baseball's ⁴⁾**premier** national team ⁵⁾**tournament**. Ohtani, the 2021 **AL** MVP, was 2-0 with a save and a 1.86 **ERA** on the mound, striking out 11 in 9 2/3 ***innings** against the U.S.

在這場棒球賽事的頂尖國家隊錦標賽中，大谷的打擊率為 0.435，擊出一個全壘打、四個雙打、八分打點和十次保送，而日本繼多明尼加共和國之後，成為僅有的不敗冠軍。於 2021 年封為美國聯盟最有價值球員的大谷在對陣美國隊的比賽中，在九又三分之二局中投出十一次三振，以一次撲救取得 2 比 0 的戰績，投手丘上的投手防禦率為 1.86。

With pitches reaching 100 mph, Ohtani walked **NL** batting champion Jeff McNeil to begin the ninth before getting Mookie Betts to ground into a double play. U.S. captain and three-time MVP Mike Trout, who like Ohtani plays for the Los Angeles Angels, then ended the game by striking out on a breaking ball. Ohtani's only other save was in a Japan *postseason *playoff game in 2016.

大谷在第九局開始以時速一百英里的球速保送國家聯盟擊球冠軍傑夫麥尼爾，接著以滾地球讓穆奇貝茲擊出雙殺。與大谷同樣效力於洛杉磯天使隊的美國隊隊長和三屆 MVP 麥可楚奧特因變化球而被三振出局，結束這場比賽。

▲ 大谷翔平的日本銀行代言

大谷唯一的另一次撲救是 2016 年在日本的季後延長賽。

▲ 大谷翔平

"What he's doing in the game is what probably 90% of the guys in this championship did in Little League or in youth tournaments, and he's able to <u>pull it off</u> on the biggest stages," U.S. manager Mark DeRosa said after the game. "He's a ***unicorn** to the sport. I think other guys will try it, but I don't think they're going to do it to his level."

美國隊經理馬克德羅薩賽後表示：「他在這場比賽中的打法，可能是這場錦標賽中九成球員在少年棒球聯盟或青少年錦標賽中的打法，而他能在最盛大的舞台上圓滿完成。他是這項運動的獨角獸。我認為其他人會嘗試同樣打法，但我不認為他們能達到他的水準。」

Japan went 7-0, [6)]**crushing** their [7)]**opponents** 56-18, and reached the final for the first time since winning the first two WBCs in 2006 and 2009. No other nation has won the title more than once.

日本隊拿下七戰全勝成績，以 56 比 18 擊敗對手，這是日本自 2006 年和 2009 年在世界棒球經典賽贏得兩次冠軍以來，首次打進決賽。沒有其他國家能在這場經典賽中兩度奪冠。

Ostapenko Wins Birmingham Classic Title

奧斯塔朋科贏得伯明罕精英賽冠軍

© lev radin / Shutterstock.com

全文朗讀 ♪ 059　單字 ♪ 060

Vocabulary

1. **defeat** [dɪˋfit]
   (v./n.) 戰勝，擊敗

2. **ensure** [ɪnˋʃʊr]
   (v.) 保證，確保

3. **fatigue** [fəˋtig]
   (n.) 疲勞，勞累

4. **exhausting** [ɪgˋzɔstɪŋ]
   (adj.) 使精疲力竭的

5. **marathon** [ˋmærəˏθɑn]
   (adj.) 馬拉松式的（形容一件事耗時耗力）

6. **slam** [slæm]
   (v.) 猛打，猛撞

7. **cruise** [kruz]
   (v.) 輕而易舉贏得

8. **rally** [ˋræli]
   (n./v.) 反擊，重振旗鼓

9. **rival** [ˋraɪvəl]
   (n.) 對手，競爭者

10. **triumph** [ˋtraɪəmf]
    (n./v.) 勝利

Advanced Words

* **garner** [ˋgɑrnə]
  (v.) 獲得

* **deficit** [ˋdɛfɪsɪt]
  (n.) 逆差，不足額

Jelena Ostapenko won a battle of two former French Open champions, [1]**defeating** Barbora Krejcikova 7-6, 6-4 to win the Birmingham Classic on Sunday.

在兩位前法國網球公開賽冠軍的對決賽中，耶蓮娜奧斯塔朋科以七比六和六比四擊敗巴博拉卡雷茨科娃，於週日（6/25）贏得伯明罕精英賽。

The Czech Republic's Krejcikova had sailed into the final without dropping a set, with her progress in the English Midlands enough to [2]**ensure** she will return to the world's top 10 on Monday. But Latvia's Ostapenko showed no sign of [3]**fatigue** from her more [4]**exhausting** route to the final as she ***garnered** her first title of the season.

捷克選手卡雷茨科娃以一盤未輸輕鬆打進決賽，她在這場於英格蘭中部地區舉行的賽事進展確保她週一（6/26）會重返世界前十。但拉脫維亞選手奧斯塔朋科在獲得本賽季第一個冠軍時，沒有因為踏上更令人精疲力竭的決賽之路而表現出疲憊的跡象。

Neither player dropped serve in the first set as Ostapenko finally got the upper hand in a [5]**marathon** tie-break, [6]**slamming** a forehand winner down the line on her fourth set point. The 2017 French Open champion then looked on course to [7]**cruise** to victory in the second set as she led 5-1.

在第一盤比賽中，兩位選手都沒有丟掉發球局，奧斯塔朋科最終在馬拉松式的搶七局佔上風，在第四個盤末點以正手拍打出直線行進的致勝球。這位 2017 年法網公開賽冠軍選手隨後在第二盤以五比一領先，有望獲勝。

But the match still took almost two hours to complete, as Ostapenko held off a ⁸⁾**rally** from her ⁹⁾**rival**. Krejcikova, who won at the French Open in 2021, fought back to narrow the ***deficit** to 5-4, but it was <u>too little, too late</u> for the Czech as Ostapenko served out for the title at the second time of asking.

▲ 奧斯塔朋科

▲ 卡雷茨科娃

但這場比賽仍花了近兩個小時才結束，因為奧斯塔朋科必須阻擋對手的反擊。曾於 2021 年法國網球公開賽奪冠的卡雷茨科娃奮力將比分差距縮小至五比四，但對要打敗這位捷克選手來說猶嫌不足，且為時已晚，因為奧斯塔朋科在最後一個發球局第二次發球就拿下冠軍。

"I played five great matches; this was the only match in two sets thankfully because every match was really tough," said Ostapenko when asked about her ¹⁰⁾**triumph**. "It's a great preparation for Wimbledon."

奧斯塔朋科在被問到奪冠一事時說：「我打了五場精彩的比賽；慶幸的是，這是唯一一場兩盤就結束的比賽，因為每場比賽都非常艱難，但這是為溫布頓網球賽做充分準備的機會。」

"I definitely had a great week," said Krejcikova. "It was really nice to be here; I really enjoyed it. It's special to play on a center court and to enjoy the support. I'm definitely looking forward to coming back."

卡雷茨科娃說：「我確實度過了愉快的一週。很高興來到這裡，我真的很享受這場比賽。在主要球場打球並享受大家支持是很特別的經歷。我絕對期待再回來打球。」

Tongue-tied No More

get the upper hand
佔上風，掌握局面
表示勝過某人，句型為 the upper hand + over/on + sb.。

The boxer **got the upper hand** in the third round and won the fight.
拳擊手在第三回合佔上風並贏得比賽。

Government troops are gradually **gaining the upper hand** over the rebels.
政府軍隊在與叛軍的對峙中，逐漸佔上風。

too little, too late 太少且為時已晚，無法解決或挽救局勢

The mayor described the aid for the earthquake victims as **too little, too late**.
市長稱對地震災民的援助少得可憐，且為時已晚。

EZpedia

English Midlands
英格蘭中部地區
英格蘭中部地區位於英格蘭中部，此區域與北英格蘭、南英格蘭、威爾士和北海接壤。

forehand 正手拍
對右手執拍的選手來說，用球拍回擊身體右邊的著地球動作。

backhand 反手拍
對右手執拍的選手來說，用球拍回擊身體左邊的著地球動作。

Ledecky Wins Gold at World Aquatics Championships

雷德基奪得世界游泳錦標賽金牌

© Salty View / Shutterstock.com

全文朗讀 ♪ 061　單字 ♪ 062

Vocabulary

1. **landmark** [ˈlænd͵mɑrk]
   (adj./n.) 劃世代的、意義重大的（事物）

2. **decorated** [ˈdɛkə͵retɪd]
   (adj.) 授勳的，表彰的

3. **congratulate** [kənˈgrætʃə͵let]
   (v.) 祝賀，恭喜

4. **sensation** [sɛnˈseʃən]
   (n.) 轟動的人事物

5. **stroke** [strok]
   (n.)（游泳）划水法

6. **dominant** [ˈdɑmənənt]
   (adj.) 強勢的，支配的

7. **defending** [dɪˈfɛndɪŋ]
   (adj.)（運動比賽中）衛冕的

8. **mere** [mɪr]
   (adj.) 僅僅，只不過

9. **bronze** [brɑnz]
   (n.) 青銅，銅牌

Advanced Words

* **freestyle** [ˈfri͵staɪl]
   (n.) 自由式游泳（競賽）

* **backstroke** [ˈbæk͵strok]
   (n.) 仰式游泳

* **medalist** [ˈmɛdəlɪst]
   (n.) 獲得獎牌者

Katie Ledecky easily won the 1,500-meter *freestyle on Tuesday at the World Aquatics Championships in a 1)landmark victory that makes her the most 2)decorated female swimmer in the competition's history, with a total of 20 golds—15 of them in individual events. That ties Michael Phelps' record at the Worlds for individual gold medals.

姬蒂雷德基週二（7/25）在世界游泳錦標賽上輕鬆贏得一千五百米自由式游泳冠軍，這場具有重大意義的勝利使她成為這項賽事史上獲獎最多的女游泳選手，共獲得二十枚金牌，其中十五枚是個人項目，追平了麥可費爾普斯在世錦賽上獲得的個人金牌紀錄。

American Ryan Murphy, who also added a gold medal Tuesday, winning the 100-meter *backstroke, 3)congratulated Ledecky on her achievement. The 26-year-old swimming 4)sensation has won seven Olympic golds, the first over a decade ago in London. And she's considering racing not just in the 2024 Paris Olympics, but perhaps also in Los Angeles in 2028.

美國選手萊恩梅菲週二也添了一枚一百米仰式金牌，他對雷德基的成就表示祝賀。這位 26 歲的游泳名將已贏得七枚奧運金牌，第一枚金牌是十多年前在倫敦獲得。她不但考慮參加 2024 年巴黎奧運，也可能參加 2028 年洛杉磯奧運。

"I never dreamed of winning one Olympic gold," said Ledecky. "So after I did it, it was like, 'OK, the rest is icing on the cake, a cherry on top,' whatever you call it. I'm just trying to build a really big cake, I guess."

雷德基說：「我從沒想過會贏得奧運金牌，所以在我贏得後，我的感覺是『好，其他都是錦上添花，喜上加喜』，不管是什麼說法，我只是想努力獲得更多成就。」

▲ 姬蒂雷德基

Ledecky won Tuesday in 15 minutes, 26.27 seconds, the third-quickest time of her career. Simona Quadarella of Italy finished 17 seconds behind Ledecky in 15 minutes, 43.31 seconds, with Li Bingjie of China third in 15 minutes, 45.71 seconds.

雷德基週二以 15 分 26.27 秒的成績獲勝，這是她職涯第三快的成績。義大利選手西蒙娜奎達雷拉的成績是 15 分 43.31 秒，落後雷德基 17 秒，中國選手李冰潔以 15 分 45.71 秒的成績獲得第三名。

▲ 萊恩梅菲

"The last couple of years I've just tried to be really locked in on my 5)**stroke**," said Ledecky, who has been a 6)**dominant** force in the pool in recent years. "That was a really good performance from me—very pleased."

近年來一直是游泳界主力的雷德基說：「這幾年來我只是設法保持好自己的划手動作，剛才的表現非常好，我非常滿意。」

Murphy, a four-time Olympic gold *medalist and the 7)**defending** world champion in the 200 backstroke, beat Italian Thomas Ceccon by a 8)**mere** .05 seconds. Murphy clocked 52.22 and Ceccon 52.27, with 9)**bronze** for American Hunter Armstrong in 52.58.

梅菲是四屆奧運金牌得主，也是兩百米仰式世界衛冕冠軍，他只以 0.05 秒的差距擊敗義大利選手湯馬斯齊康。梅菲的成績為 52.22 秒，齊康的成績為 52.27 秒，美國選手杭特阿姆斯壯則以 52.58 秒的成績獲得銅牌。

Mike Conley Wins NBA Sportsmanship Award

麥克康利榮獲 NBA 最佳運動精神獎

© nba.com

全文朗讀 ♪ 063 單字 ♪ 064

Vocabulary

1. **recipient** [rɪˋsɪpɪənt]
   (n.) 接受者，領受者

2. **sportsmanship**
   [ˋsportsmən͵ʃɪp]
   (n.) 運動員精神

3. **integrity** [ɪnˋtɛgrətɪ]
   (n.) 正直，誠實

4. **trophy** [ˋtrofɪ]
   (n.) 獎盃

5. **memorial** [məˋmorɪəl]
   (adj.) 紀念的，紀念性的

6. **confidential** [͵kɑnfəˋdɛnʃəl]
   (adj.) 機密的，隱密的

7. **entertain** [͵ɛntəˋten]
   (v.) 娛樂，招待

8. **grateful** [ˋgretfəl]
   (adj.) 感謝的，感激的

9. **overall** [ˋovə͵ɔl]
   (adj.) 總的，全面的

10. **draft** [dræft]
    (n.)（美國職業球隊在賽季之初選拔新隊員的）選秀

Former Ohio State **point guard** Mike Conley added another *accolade to his 16-year NBA career on Friday. Conley, who currently plays for the Minnesota Timberwolves, was named 1)**recipient** of the 2022-23 NBA 2)**Sportsmanship** Award for the fourth time in his career—the most in league history.

前俄亥俄州立大學控球後衛麥克康利週五（7/7）為他 16 年的 NBA 職涯再添一項榮譽。目前效力於明尼蘇達灰狼隊的康利在職涯中第四次榮獲 2022-23 年 NBA 最佳運動精神獎，也是聯盟史上獲得次數最多者。

The award is given to a player who " *exemplifies the ideals of sportsmanship on the court with ethical behavior, fair play, and 3)**integrity**." Winners also receive the Joe Dumars 4)**Trophy**, named after the Naismith 5)**Memorial Basketball Hall of Famer** who was the award's first recipient.

此獎項頒發給「在球場上以道德行為、公平競爭和誠信體現運動精神理想的球員」，獲獎者也獲得喬杜馬斯獎盃。該獎盃是以名列奈史密斯籃球名人堂的首位 NBA 最佳運動精神獎得獎者，喬杜馬斯的名字來命名。

Conley was selected from a list of 30 team nominees by nearly 300 current NBA players through a 6)**confidential** vote. He also earned the NBA Sportsmanship Award during the 2013-14, 2015-16 and 2018-19 seasons when he played for the Memphis Grizzlies, and is the first Timberwolves player to win the award.

康利是從 30 名球隊提名者中被近 300 名現役 NBA 球員以不記名投票方式選出的。他也在 2013-14、2015-16 和 2018-19 賽季效力於孟斐斯灰熊隊期間獲得 NBA 最佳運動精神獎，也是第一位獲得該獎項的灰狼隊隊員。

"To be able to win this award once says a lot to me, <u>let alone</u> four times," said Conley. "There's so much made about us as athletes and what we do on the court; our skills and the things we are able to do in front of you and [7]**entertain**. But this means so much more to me. It says a lot and I am truly super surprised right now and super [8]**grateful**."

▲ 奈史密斯籃球名人堂

康利說：「能獲得一次獎項對我來說意義重大，更何況四次了。我們身為運動員在球場上的表現，像是球技、娛樂價值都受到很多關注。但榮獲此獎項對我來說有著無法言喻的意義。這獎項意義深遠，我現在真的十分驚喜且格外感激。」

Last season for the Timberwolves and Utah Jazz, Conley averaged 11.9 points and 6.7 assists per game, shooting 42.8% from the floor. He became the 149th player in NBA history to reach 15,000 career points on April 8.

上個賽季在灰狼隊和猶他爵士隊，康利平均每場貢獻 11.9 分和 6.7 次助攻，投籃命中率為 42.8%。4 月 8 日他成為 NBA 史上第 149 位在職涯中得分達一萬五千的球員。

Conley was the No. 4 [9]**overall** pick by the Grizzlies in the 2007 NBA [10]**draft** after averaging 11.3 points and 6.1 assists in 39 career college games in 2006-07. In 16 seasons split between the Grizzlies, Jazz and Timberwolves, Conley has averaged 14.7 points in 1,024 career NBA games.

康利於 2007 年 NBA 選秀中以第四順位被灰熊隊選中，他在 2006-07 年賽季的 39 場大學生涯比賽中平均每場貢獻 11.3 分和 6.1 次助攻。在分別效力於灰熊隊、爵士隊和灰狼隊的 16 個賽季中，康利在職涯的 1024 場 NBA 比賽平均每場貢獻 14.7 分。

Advanced Words

* **accolade** [ˋækəˌled]
  (n.) 榮譽，嘉獎

* **exemplify** [ɪgˋzɛmpləˌfaɪ]
  (v.) 作為⋯⋯的典範

Tongue-tied No More

let alone 更不用說，更別提
通常置於否定陳述句之後，強調某種情況不可能發生。

Some people never even read a newspaper, **let alone** a book.
有些人連報紙都沒讀過，更不用說讀書了。

I wouldn't trust that woman to look after my cat, **let alone** my child.
我不相信那女人會照顧好我的貓，更不用說我的孩子了。

EZpedia

point guard 控球後衛
簡稱「控衛」或「控後」，俗稱「一號位置」，有時也稱組織後衛。控球後衛是全隊進攻的組織者，必須具有良好的傳球技術和敏銳的比賽觀察能力，透過對球的控制來決定在適當的時機傳球給適合的球員。

Naismith Memorial Basketball Hall of Fame 奈史密斯籃球名人堂
位於美國麻薩諸塞州春田市，成立於 1959 年，冠加的人名是為了紀念籃球發明人詹姆士奈史密斯。奈史密斯籃球名人堂致力於促進和保存籃球運動項目，以及紀念為籃球運動作出卓越貢獻的球員、教練、裁判等。

New Study Supports Animal Origin of COVID Virus

新研究支持新冠病毒源自動物

全文朗讀 ♪ 065　　單字 ♪ 066

Vocabulary

1. **download** [ˈdaʊnˌlod]
   (v.)（電腦）下載

2. **evidence** [ˈɛvədəns]
   (n.) 證據，跡象

3. **host** [host]
   (n.) 宿主，寄主

4. **analysis** [əˈnæləsɪs]
   (n.) 分析，解析

5. **genetic** [dʒəˈnɛtɪk]
   (adj.) 基因的，遺傳的

6. **virus** [ˈvaɪrəs]
   (n.) 病毒

7. **emerge** [ɪˈmɝdʒ]
   (v.) 浮現，出現

8. **lab** [læb]
   (n.) 實驗室（= laboratory）

9. **institute** [ˈɪnstɪˌtut]
   (n.) 研究機構，研究所，學院

Advanced Words

* **database** [ˈdetəˌbes]
   (n.) 資料庫

* **DNA** (n.) 去氧核糖核酸

* **virology** [vaɪˈrɑlədʒi]
   (n.) 病毒學

In January 2023, data gathered at the Huanan Seafood Market in Wuhan in early 2020 was posted to a public ***database** by researchers with China's Center for Disease Control. Because the first known human COVID-19 cases were detected in Wuhan in December 2019, the data caught the attention of Florence Débarre, a senior scientist at CNRS, the French national research agency.

2023 年 1 月，中國疾病預防控制中心的研究人員將 2020 年初在武漢華南海鮮市場收集的數據發布到公共資料庫。由於 2019 年 12 月在武漢發現首例已知的人類感染新冠病例，因此該數據引起法國國家研究機構，亦即法國國家科學研究中心的資深科學家佛羅倫斯德巴的注意。

After [1]**downloading** the data, which was later removed from the database, Débarre and a team of scientists from Europe, North America and Australia analyzed it and uncovered [2]**evidence** that may shed light on the origins of the COVID pandemic. The results of their work, which were published in a report on March 20, point to raccoon dogs as a possible [3]**host** from which the disease spilled over into humans.

德巴下載數據後，與一群來自歐洲、北美和澳洲的科學家進行分析，並發現可能釐清新冠大流行源頭的證據，而這筆數據後來從資料庫被刪除。他們的研究結果發表於 3 月 20 日的一份報告中，指出貉可能是該疾病蔓延到人類的宿主。

In their [4]**analysis** of the data, which consisted of [5]**genetic** samples from Huanan, the scientists found that ***DNA** from raccoon dogs—sold in China for their meat and fur—was collected from the same locations at the market as samples that tested positive for the COVID [6)]**virus**. So far, there is no hard proof that raccoon dogs at the market were carrying the virus, which many scientists believe first came from bats. But Débarre's discovery is important because raccoon dogs are known to catch and spread the COVID virus easily.

科學家們在分析來自華南市場的基因樣本數據時發現，貉基因的採集地點與被檢測出新冠病毒陽性的樣本，兩者都是來自該市場的相同地點，而在中國會販賣貉肉和貉皮。至目前為止尚無確鑿證據顯示華南市場上的貉帶有新冠病毒，許多科學家認為這種病毒起源於蝙蝠。但德巴的發現很重要，因為已知貉很容易感染和傳播新冠病毒。

While this <u>lends weight to</u> the theory that the virus [7)]**emerged** in wild animals before spreading to humans at the market, another theory has focused on a possible [8)]**lab** leak from the Wuhan [9)]**Institute** of *****Virology**. The Chinese government has denied this possibility, but the FBI and the U.S. Department of Energy now believe a lab leak is the most likely origin of the disease.

▲ 華南海鮮市場

新冠病毒在市場傳播給人類之前是出現在野生動物身上，這項研究雖然支持了這個理論，但另一種推論則著重於病毒可能是從武漢病毒研究所的實驗室外洩。中國政府已否認這種可能性，而美國聯邦調查局和能源部目前認為新冠源頭為從實驗室外洩的可能性最高。

▲ 貉

Tongue-tied No More

shed light on
釐清真相，讓真相大白
= throw/cast light on

Experts hope that the flight recording will **shed light on** the cause of the plane crash.
專家希望藉由飛航紀錄釐清墜機的原因。

lend weight to
支持，使更有說服力
= lend support to

Do you have any evidence that **lends weight to** your claim?
你有任何證據可以支持你的主張嗎？

EZpedia

raccoon dog 貉

貉又稱貉子、狸，是犬科動物。他們的體型介於浣熊和狗之間，身體為烏棕色，吻部（口、唇）是白色，有短而黑的四肢，雙眼的周圍有非常大的黑眼圈。貉喜歡穴居，多棲息於闊葉林中開闊、接近水源的地方或茂密的灌叢帶和蘆葦地。為了躲避天敵，貉在日間休息，夜間活動。貉的食物是鳥類、小型哺乳動物和水果等。牠也是犬科動物中唯一會冬眠的動物。在日本傳說中，貉通常靠一塊樹葉便能變身。

Eye Drops Recalled after Deaths and Blindness

眼藥水因導致死亡和失明而被下架

全文朗讀 ♪ 067　單字 ♪ 068

Vocabulary

1. **outbreak** [ˋaʊtˏbrek]
   (n.) 爆發，暴動

2. **infection** [ɪnˋfɛkʃən]
   (n.) 傳染，感染

3. **recall** [ˋrikɔl/rɪˋkɔl]
   (n./v.) 召回，收回

4. **manufacture**
   [ˏmænjəˋfæktʃə]
   (v.) 製造

5. **contaminate**
   [kənˋtæməˏnet]
   (v.) 汙染，弄髒

6. **resistant** [rɪˋzɪstənt]
   (adj.) 抵抗的，具抗藥性的

7. **symptom** [ˋsɪmptəm]
   (n.) 症狀，徵候

8. **discharge** [ˋdɪstʃɑrdʒ]
   (n.) 排出液體（或氣體）

9. **irritation** [ˏɪrəˋteʃən]
   (n.) 過敏，發炎

10. **expire** [ɪkˋspaɪr]
    (v.) 到期，滿期

Health agencies are investigating an [1)]**outbreak** of a harmful type of bacteria found in certain brands of artificial tears. These are eye drops used to *lubricate dry eyes and help keep moisture on their outer surface.

衛生單位正調查發現於部分人工淚液品牌的有害細菌所引發的感染疫情。這些眼藥水用於潤滑乾澀眼睛並幫助維持眼睛表面水分。

According to the U.S. CDC, a total of 68 [2)]**infections** across 16 states have been reported so far. Among these cases, three have died, eight have lost vision, and four have had an eye removed. In response, the **FDA** has announced a [3)]**recall** of artificial tears produced by Global Pharma Healthcare, an Indian company. The products, which are [4)]**manufactured** in India, are sold in the U.S. under the EzriCare and Delsam Pharma brands.

根據美國疾病管制暨預防中心表示，至今全美 16 州累計 68 起感染病例。在這些病例中，有三人死亡，八人失明，四人的一只眼睛被摘除。美國食品藥物管理局宣布，將召回由印度全球製藥保健公司生產的人工淚液來應對。這些產品是在印度製造，以艾茲瑞保健和戴爾森製藥的品牌在美國銷售。

The government agencies say these eye drops were [5)]**contaminated** during the manufacturing process with the bacteria *Pseudomonas aeruginosa*, which is [6)]**resistant** to commonly available drugs. The FDA has also warned people to stop using an eye *ointment produced by Global Pharma and sold under the Delsam Pharma brand because of possible contamination.

政府單位表示，這些眼藥水在製造過程中受到綠膿桿菌汙染，這種細菌對常見藥物具有抗藥性。美國食藥局也呼籲民眾停止使用由全球製藥生產並以戴爾森製藥品牌銷售的眼藥膏，因為也可能受到汙染。

▲ 美國食品藥物管理局

People who have used these artificial tears and who have [7]**symptoms** of an eye infection should see a doctor immediately, the CDC says. The symptoms can include yellow, green or clear [8]**discharge** from the eye, redness of the eye, eye pain, and the feeling of having a foreign body in the eye.

美國疾病管制暨預防中心表示，使用過這些人工淚液並出現眼部感染症狀的人應立即就醫。症狀可能包括眼睛出現黃色、綠色或透明分泌物，眼睛發紅、疼痛以及眼睛有異物感。

Eye drops are generally safe to use, and many people depend on them to treat conditions such as dryness or [9]**irritation**. About 117 million Americans purchase eye drops every year. To use eye drops safely, people should have their own bottle and make sure it has not [10]**expired**. Sharing may be convenient, but it's better to be safe than sorry.

眼藥水通常可以安全使用，許多人靠眼藥水治療乾澀或發炎等症狀。每年約有 1 億 1700 萬美國人購買眼藥水。為安全使用眼藥水，大家應該各用各的眼藥水並確保沒有過期。共用可能很方便，但防範未然總比事後後悔好。

Tongue-tied No More

(it's) better (to be) safe than sorry 有備無患，謹慎免於風險

A: Why should I take an umbrella? It's sunny outside.
我為什麼要帶傘？外面陽光明媚。
B: It may be sunny now, but **better safe than sorry**.
現在可能是晴天，但有備無患。

EZpedia

FDA 美國食品藥物管理局
美國食品藥物管理局，全稱為 Food and Drug Administration，由美國國會即聯邦政府授權，執行《聯邦食品、藥品和化妝品法案》（Federal Food, Drug, and Cosmetic Act）和管理包括食品、藥品、醫療器械、微生物制品、化妝品、動物食品和藥品、有輻射的產品及其監督檢驗等。前述產品必須經過 FDA 檢驗證明安全後，才可在市場上銷售。

Pseudomonas aeruginosa 綠膿桿菌
綠膿桿菌，又稱銅綠假單胞菌，外觀是長棒形，是一種革蘭氏陰性菌。綠膿桿菌最適合的生長溫度為攝氏 25 到 37 度，故可生長在人體內。綠膿桿菌在溫度高至 42 度時仍可存活，可以生存的 pH 值範圍為 5 到 9，最適合生長的 pH 值為 7，最常在受汙染的水質檢驗中被發現。它們經常存於土壤、腐化有機物、耕地、水源等地。

Clues about Exercise Found in the Microbiome

在微生物組中發現運動相關的訊息

© Alpha Tauri 3D Graphics / Shutterstock.com

Vocabulary

1. **physical** [ˈfɪzɪkəl]
   (adj.) 身體的

2. **decrease** [dɪˈkris]
   (v./n.) 減少，減小

3. **diabetes** [ˌdaɪəˈbitiz]
   (n.) 糖尿病

4. **motivation** [ˌmotəˈveʃən]
   (n.) 動機，動力
   motivate [ˈmotə͵vet]
   (v.) 激勵，激發

5. **mechanism** [ˈmɛkə͵nɪzəm]
   (n.) 機制

6. **exhausted** [ɪgˈzɒstɪd]
   (adj.) 筋疲力盡的

7. **genetics** [dʒəˈnɛtɪks]
   (n.) 遺傳學

8. **gut** [gʌt]
   (n.) 腸子，內臟

9. **strain** [stren]
   (n.) 病毒種類，細菌種類

10. **molecule** [ˈmɑlə͵kjul]
    (n.) 分子

Advanced Words

* **metabolism** [məˈtæbə͵lɪzəm]
   (n.) 新陳代謝

It's long been known that regular exercise provides many health benefits, but some people seem to enjoy ¹⁾**physical** activity more than others. Even though exercising as little as 2.5 hours per week can significantly ²⁾**decrease** the risk of heart disease, ³⁾**diabetes** and several types of cancer, less than 20% of adults manage the bare minimum. The factors affecting people's ⁴⁾**motivation** to exercise are not well understood, but a new study on mice, published in *Nature* last year, may help provide answers.

人們早就知道定期運動對健康有許多好處，但有些人似乎比其他人更喜歡運動。儘管每週運動僅僅 2.5 小時就能明顯降低罹患心臟病、糖尿病和幾種癌症的風險，但只有不到 20% 成年人達到這個最低運動時數標準。影響人們運動動力的因素尚不清楚，但去年發表在《自然》期刊中一項新的老鼠研究可能有助於提供答案。

In the study, a team of researchers at the University of Pennsylvania set out to identify the ⁵⁾**mechanisms** affecting exercise performance in mice, which have nervous systems similar to ours. After dividing 199 lab mice into groups based on how much time they spent running on a wheel and how long they ran before becoming ⁶⁾**exhausted**, they looked at a variety of factors in each group, including ⁷⁾**genetics**, ***metabolism** and the ⁸⁾**gut** microbiome, which is the communities of bacteria, viruses and other ***microbes** living in the gut.

在這項研究中，賓州大學的研究團隊著手找出影響老鼠運動表現的機制，而老鼠的神經系統與我們相似。他們將 199 隻實驗室老鼠按照在輪子上的跑步時間以及老鼠跑到筋疲力盡要花多久的時間分組後，研究了影響各組的各種因素，包括遺傳、新陳代謝和腸道微生物組。腸道微生物組是腸道中的細菌、病毒等其他微生物群落。

▲ 跑步的倉鼠

Using machine learning to analyze the data, the researchers were surprised to find that the factor most associated with high motivation to exercise was not genetic, but rather the presence of two 9)**strains** of bacteria in the microbiome. Further research showed that during exercise, these bacteria produced 10)**molecules** that stimulated nerves in the gut wall, which then caused the release of dopamine in the brain's reward center, making exercise feel good.

運用機器學習分析數據後，研究人員驚訝地發現與高運動動力最相關的因素不是遺傳，而是存在腸道微生物組中的兩種細菌菌株。進一步研究顯示，在運動過程中，這些細菌會產生刺激腸壁神經的分子，繼而導致大腦的酬償中樞釋放多巴胺，讓老鼠在運動時感覺良好。

Now, the research team wants to look at humans to see if the same relationship between certain gut bacteria and exercise motivation can be found. Who knows? Maybe in the future motivating ourselves to exercise will be as simple as taking a pill that adds these bacteria to our microbiome.

現在研究團隊想要觀察人類，看是否能找到某些腸道細菌與運動動力之間有同樣的關係。誰知道呢？也許未來會研發出將這些細菌添加到我們微生物組中的藥丸，而我們激勵自己運動只要吃藥就可以。

Advanced Words

* **microbe** [ˋmaɪkrob]
(n.) 微生物

Tongue-tied No More

the bare minimum 可能的最少量，可接受的最少量，最低限度也可寫作 a bare minimum。

When it comes to homework, John always does **the bare minimum**.
說到家庭作業，約翰總是只完成最少量。

If we want to save money, we have to keep costs at **a bare minimum**.
如果我們想省錢，就必須將花費維持在最低限度。

EZpedia

microbiome 微生物組
微生物群（microbiota）泛指「一群」棲息在植物或動物體內部與表層，或是環境中，肉眼看不見的微小生物。這些微小生物包括了細菌、真菌、病毒或原生生物。而微生物組（microbiome）一詞在 2001 年由微生物學家約書亞雷德伯格（Joshua Lederberg）建議使用，泛指特定環境中的微生物群（microbiota）及其基因體（genome）。

dopamine 多巴胺
多巴胺是一種兒茶胺類（catecholamine）的神經傳導物質，廣泛地見於各種脊椎與無脊椎動物之中。在人體中，腦內與腎上腺可以自行經由胺基酸合成多巴胺。

First Lung Delivered by Drone

首次由無人機運送肺臟

© Tattoboo / Shutterstock.com

全文朗讀 ♪ 071　　單字 ♪ 072

Vocabulary

1. **transplant** [ˈtræns,plænt]
   (n./v.) 移植
   transplantation
   [ˌtræsplænˈteʃən]
   (n.) 移植

2. **recovery** [rɪˈkʌvəri]
   (n.) 恢復，痊癒

3. **gear** [gɪr]
   (n.) 設備，器具

4. **delicate** [ˈdɛləkət]
   (adj.) 脆弱的，虛弱的

5. **electronics** [ɪˌlɛkˈtrɑnɪks]
   (n.) 電子設備、器材、組件

6. **interfere** [ˌɪntəˈfɪr]
   (v.) 干擾，干涉

7. **efficiency** [ɪˈfɪʃənsi]
   (n.) 效率，效能

8. **removal** [rɪˈmuvəl]
   (n.) 除去，移除

9. **donor** [ˈdonɚ]
   (n.) 捐贈者

10. **deteriorate** [dɪˈtɪriəˌret]
    (v.) 惡化，退化

11. **milestone** [ˈmaɪlˌston]
    (n.) 里程碑

In a medical first, a *__drone__ has successfully delivered a pair of lungs to a Toronto hospital for a 1)**transplant** operation. The drone completed the 1.5 kilometer flight from Toronto Western Hospital to Toronto General Hospital—both members of the University Health Network—in just five minutes. The same trip can take as long as 25 minutes by road. Upon arrival, the lungs were transplanted into a 63-year-old patient, who survived and made a full 2)**recovery**.

醫學史上第一次由無人機成功將一副肺臟運到多倫多一家醫院進行移植手術。無人機只用五分鐘就將肺臟從多倫多西區醫院運到多倫多總醫院，這兩家醫院都是大學醫療網絡成員。飛行全程 1.5 公里，同樣的路程在道路駕駛可能需要多達 25 分鐘。無人機送到後，肺臟被移植到一名 63 歲患者體內，該患者已存活下來並完全康復。

Unither Bioélectronique, the Quebec company that developed the medical transport drone, chose to partner with Toronto General Hospital because the world's first lung transplant was completed there in 1983. Starting with a DJI drone, the development team removed the landing 3)**gear** and replaced it with a special lightweight lung transport box designed to protect the 4)**delicate** organ during flight. They also improved the drone's 5)**electronics** to make sure radio signals wouldn't 6)**interfere** with its **GPS**.

開發這架醫療運輸無人機的魁北克優尼特生物電子公司選擇與多倫多總醫院合作，因為 1983 年世上第一宗肺臟移植手術在那裡完成。開發團隊從大疆創新無人機開始著手，拆除起落架，以特殊的輕型肺臟運輸箱取代。其設計目的是要在飛行過程中保護脆弱的器官。他們也改良無人機的電子設備，以確保無線電訊號不會干擾無人機的全球定位系統。

▲ 運送物品中的無人機示意圖

Drones have been used to deliver blood and other emergency medical supplies for several years now, but their speed and ⁷⁾**efficiency** makes them especially promising for the delivery of transplant organs, where time is truly of the essence. After ⁸⁾**removal** from the ⁹⁾**donor**, organs begin to rapidly ¹⁰⁾**deteriorate**, so the sooner they can be delivered, the better the recipient's chances of survival.

數年來無人機一直用於運送血液等其他緊急醫療用品，但其速度和效率特別有望於運送移植器官，因為在移植手術方面時間是關鍵。器官從捐贈者身上取出後便會迅速衰竭，因此運送速度越快，接受者的存活機會就越大。

The first transport of an organ by drone was the delivery of a kidney between two Baltimore hospitals in 2019. While kidneys can survive outside the body for up to 48 hours, lungs and hearts need to be transplanted within 4-6 hours of the donor's death. "This is an important ¹¹⁾**milestone** for our program, and for the medical field of ¹⁾**transplantation**," said Toronto General Hospital's Dr. Shaf Keshavjee about the successful lung delivery.

首次以無人機運送器官是 2019 年在巴爾的摩的兩家醫院之間運送腎臟。雖然腎臟可以在體外生存達 48 小時，但肺和心臟需要在捐贈者死亡後四到六小時內移植。多倫多總醫院的沙夫克沙吉醫師在提到這次成功的肺臟運送時說：「這是我們移植計劃和移植醫學領域的一個重要里程碑。」

Tongue-tied No More

of the essence
至關重要，極為必要

Time is **of the essence** when rescuing people trapped in collapsed buildings.
救援被困在倒塌建築物中的人時，時間至關重要。

When it comes to successful relationships, honesty is **of the essence**.
說到成功的人際關係，誠實至關重要。

EZpedia

GPS (global positioning system) 全球定位系統
全球定位系統原為美國為軍事上定位及導航目的而發展，後擴大計畫使其應用於民間定位測量。GPS 由空間部分、控制部分、用戶部分組成。空間部分是 24 到 32 顆圍繞地球飛行的衛星群，分別被送到 6 個離地球很遠的太空軌道上，並以南北走向繞地球運行。而太空中運行的 GPS 衛星由美國國防部在地面的軍事基地跟蹤和控制，此即控制部分。用戶部分包括飛機、船隻、汽車等各類移動載具與個人用戶。

Rishi Sunak to Make Math Compulsory to 18

英國首相蘇納克將數學定為 18 歲以下必修課

全文朗讀 ♪073　　單字 ♪074

Vocabulary

1. **statistics** [stə`tɪstɪks]
   (n.) 統計學，統計資料

2. **literacy** [`lɪtərəsi]
   (n.)（讀寫等）能力，識字

3. **objective** [əb`dʒɛktɪv]
   (n.) 目標，目的

4. **priority** [praɪ`ɔrtəti]
   (n.) 優先，重點

5. **unlock** [ʌn`lɑk]
   (v.) 打開，解鎖

6. **finances** [`faɪnænsɪz]
   (n.) 理財，財政

7. **navigate** [`nævəˌget]
   (v.) 應付，巧妙處理

8. **soaring** [`sorɪŋ]
   (adj.) 高漲的，高聳的

9. **institution** [ˌɪnstə`tuʃən]
   (n.) 機構，機關

10. **forecast** [`forˌkæst]
    (v./n.) 預測，預報

In a speech on Wednesday, British Prime Minister Rishi Sunak outlined his plan to make math *compulsory for students up to age 18, saying it was time for the country to change its approach to *numeracy. The U.K. is one of the few countries not to require students to study math—or "maths" as it's called there—up to 18. Currently, just half of all 16-19-year-olds study any math at all.

英國首相里希蘇納克在週三的一場演講中概述到他計劃將數學定為 18 歲以下學生的必修課，並表示英國現在應該改變對基本數學能力的政策方針。把數學稱為 maths 的英國是少數幾個不要求 18 歲以下學生學習數學的國家之一，目前 16 至 19 歲學生當中，只有半數學生在學習數學。

Sunak stressed that in a world where data is everywhere and every job involves 1)**statistics**, letting children graduate without those skills is letting the children down. "So we need to go further," he said, adding that his government is now making math 2)**literacy** a central 3)**objective** of the education system. "That doesn't have to mean compulsory A-level maths for everyone, but we will work with the sector to move towards all children studying some form of maths to 18."

蘇納克強調，在一個數據無處不在、每樣工作都涉及統計的世界中，讓孩子們在沒學會數學技能的情況下畢業會辜負他們。他說：「所以我們需要採取進一步的措施。」他並補充，政府正將基本數學能力當作教育體制的核心目標。「這並不代表每個人都必須學習 A-level 課程的數學，但我們將與教育界合作，讓所有孩子到 18 歲前都能學習某種形式的數學。」

Presenting his 4)**priorities** for 2023, Sunak asked his audience to imagine what greater numeracy will 5)**unlock** for people—the skills to feel confident with 6)**finances**, to find the best mortgage deal or savings rate, the ability to do the job better, and get paid more, and greater confidence to 7)**navigate** a changing world.

蘇納克在介紹 2023 年的重點事項時請觀眾想像一下，更好的數學能力將為大家解鎖什麼技能：對理財充滿信心、找到最佳抵押貸款或儲蓄利率的技能、在工作上表現更好的能力，以及獲得加薪的技能，並更有信心駕馭瞬息萬變的世界。

Sunak, who became Prime Minister in October 2022, said improving education was the best economic policy, the best social policy, and the best moral policy. "And that is why it is this government's policy," he emphasized.

2022 年 10 月就任首相的蘇納克表示，改善教育是最佳的經濟政策、社會政策和道德政策。他強調：「這就是這個政府要實施這項政策的原因。」

The U.K. has witnessed 8)**soaring** inflation for the last few months, which has raised the cost of living significantly. Economic growth has also slowed down. Global financial 9)**institutions** have 10)**forecast** slow growth for most of the European economies, including the U.K.

這幾個月來英國通貨膨脹飆升，導致物價大幅上升，經濟成長也漸趨遲緩。全球金融機構預測包括英國在內的多數歐洲經濟體將成長緩慢。

▲ 蘇納克談論 2023 年重點事項

Advanced Words

* **compulsory** [kəm`pʌlsəri]
  (adj.) 義務的，必修的

* **numeracy** [`numərəsi]
  (n.) 數學能力

Tongue-tied No More

let (sb.) down 令某人失望
letdown (n.) 失望，沮喪

Michael **let** his parents **down** when he dropped out of college.
麥克從大學退學讓他的父母失望了。

I was looking forward to the final episode, but it was a big **letdown**.
我本來很期待最後一集，但結果令人失望。

EZpedia

A-level

A-level 課程提供給 16 到 19 歲的學生，是英國中學生最後兩年準備進入大學的預備課程，在兩年課程結束後，即可通過考試取得「普通教育高級程度證書」（General Certificate of Education: Advanced Level）。A-level 考試等同於大學入學資格考試，考試結果可作為申請大學的依據。

© Andrii Iemelianenko / Shutterstock.com

Surgeon General Warns of Social Media Risks for Kids

美公共衛生署總署長警告未成年使用社群媒體的風險

全文朗讀 🎵 075　單字 🎵 076

Vocabulary

1. **surgeon** [ˋsɝdʒən]
   (n.) 外科醫生

2. **awareness** [əˋwɛrnɪs]
   (n.) 意識，關注

3. **disorder** [dɪsˋɔrdɚ]
   (n.) 疾病，（生理或心理）失調

4. **adolescent** [ˌædəlˋɛsənt]
   (n.) 青少年

5. **enact** [ɪnˋækt]
   (v.) 制定（法律）

6. **guideline** [ˋgaɪdˌlaɪn]
   (n.)（常用複數）指導方針

7. **disturbing** [dɪˋstɝbɪŋ]
   (adj.) 令人不安的

8. **scroll** [skrol]
   (v.) 滑（手機），瀏覽

9. **summarize** [ˋsʌməˌraɪz]
   (v.) 總結，概述

10. **outcome** [ˋautˌkʌm]
    (n.) 結果，後果

U.S. [1)]**Surgeon General** Vivek Murthy, long an advocate of mental health [2)]**awareness**, issued a warning on Tuesday that social media use is a main *****contributor** to depression, anxiety and behavior [3)]**disorders** in the nation's teenagers.

長期倡導心理健康意識的美國公共衛生署總署長維偉克莫西週二（5/23）發出警告，表示使用社群媒體是導致美國青少年抑鬱、焦慮和行為障礙的主要原因。

The *****advisory** calls attention to growing concerns about the effects of social media use on the mental health of children and [4)]**adolescents**. The report encourages policymakers and the companies that run the social media platforms to share with parents the burden of managing children's and teens' social media use.

該公告呼籲大家關注社群媒體影響兒童和青少年心理健康日益增長的擔憂。該報告鼓勵決策者和經營社群媒體平台的公司分擔家長管理兒童和青少年使用社群媒體的負擔。

Murthy calls youth mental health "the defining public health issue of our time," and urges the government to [5)]**enact** stricter [6)]**guidelines** to protect young people from exposure to [7)]**disturbing** content and excessive use. Up to 95% of teens aged 13 to 17 say they use a social media platform, according to the report. About a third say they're [8)]**scrolling**, posting or otherwise engaged with social media "almost constantly."

莫西稱青少年的心理健康是「我們這時代的關鍵性公共衛生問題」，並敦促政府制訂更嚴格的指導方針，以避免年輕人接觸令人不安的內容和過度使用社群媒體。報告指出多達 95% 的 13 至 17 歲青少年表示有在使用

▲ 美國公共衛生署總署長維偉克莫西

社群媒體平台。約三分之一青少年表示，他們「幾乎不停地」在滑手機、發貼文或以其他方式使用社群媒體。

"At this point, we do not have enough evidence to say with confidence that social media is sufficiently safe for our kids," Murthy said in a May 23 television interview. "We have to now take action to make sure that we are protecting our kids."

莫西在 5 月 23 日接受電視採訪時表示：「目前我們沒有足夠的證據能很有把握地說社群媒體對我們的孩子夠安全，我們現在必須採取行動，確保能保護我們的孩子。」

The report ⁹⁾**summarizes** research linking social media use to poor mental health in adolescents, like a 2019 study that found teens who spent over three hours a day on social media faced twice the risk of poor mental health ¹⁰⁾**outcomes**. In a 2022 survey, students in grades eight and 10 said they spent even more time each day on these platforms—three hours and 30 minutes, on average.

該報告總結了使用社群媒體與青少年心理健康狀況不佳有關的研究，例如 2019 年的一項研究發現，在社群媒體上一天花超過三小時的青少年，面臨心理健康狀況不佳的風險會增加兩倍。在 2022 年的一項調查中，八年級和十年級的學生表示，他們每天在這些平台上花的時間甚至更多，平均為三小時半。

Advanced Words

* **contributor** [kən`trɪbjətə]
  (n.) 促成因素

* **advisory** [əd`vaɪzəri]
  (n.) 公告，報告

Tongue-tied No More

call (sb.'s) attention to
讓某人關注……

Students marched to **call attention to** the rising cost of college.
學生們舉行遊行以引起大眾關注大學的學費上漲。

May I **call** everyone's **attention to** item five on the agenda?
我可以請大家注意議程的第五項嗎？

EZpedia

surgeon general
公共衛生署總署長
美國公共衛生署總署長為美國人提供有關如何改善健康並減少疾病和傷害風險的最佳科學資訊。公共衛生署總署長監督美國公共衛生服務軍官團（U.S. Public Health Service Commissioned Corps），該軍官團是一個由超過 6,000 名軍官組成的團體。

As Colleges Close, Elite Schools Thrive

隨著大學關閉，精英學校蓬勃發展

全文朗讀 ♪ 077　　單字 ♪ 078

Vocabulary

1. **enrollment** [ɪnˋrolmənt]
   (n.) 註冊（大學課程或學籍）
   enroll [ɪnˋrol]
   (v.) 入學，註冊

2. **academic** [ˌækəˋdɛmɪk]
   (adj.) 學術的，學校的

3. **uncertainty** [ʌnˋsɜtntɪ]
   (n.) 不確定性

4. **peril** [ˋpɛrəl]
   (n.) 危難，險境

5. **elite** [ɪˋlit]
   (adj.) 菁英的，頂尖的

6. **thrive** [θraɪv]
   (v.) 茁壯成長，茂盛生長

7. **application** [ˌæpləˋkeʃən]
   (n.) 申請，申請書
   applicant [ˋæpləkənt]
   (n.) 申請人

8. **tuition** [tuˋɪʃən]
   (n.) 學費

9. **zip code** 郵遞區號，地區

Citing high inflation and falling ¹⁾**enrollment**, a numbe of U.S. colleges are set to close in 2023. So fa Presentation College in South Dakota, Cazenovia College i New York, Holy Names University in California, and Livin Arts College in North Carolina have announced they will shu down after the current ²⁾**academic** year.

美國許多大學以高通膨和入學率下降為由，將於 2023 年關閉。至目前 為止，南達科他州的奉獻學院、紐約州的卡澤諾維亞學院、加州的聖 名大學和北卡羅來納州的生活藝術學院已宣布將在本學年結束後關閉

The number of colleges closing down in the past 10 year has *__quadrupled__ compared with the previous decade. No only have many smaller institutions struggled as student *__opt__ for less expensive public schools or alternatives to four-year degree altogether, but economic ³⁾**uncertaint** and inflation also continue to impact markets, taking heavy toll on *__endowments__ and leaving more colleges an universities in financial ⁴⁾**peril**.

這十年來關閉的大學數量比前十年增加了四倍。不但有許多規模較 的學校因學生選擇較便宜的公立學校或是四年制學程以外的替代方 而陷入困境，而且經濟不穩定和通貨膨脹也繼續影響市場，使外部 學校的捐贈大幅減少，並讓更多大學院校陷入財務困境。

Meanwhile, the country's most ⁵⁾**elite** institutions ar ⁶⁾**thriving**. Coming out of the pandemic, a small group c universities, including many Ivy League schools, hav experienced a record increase in ⁷⁾**applications** this year.

同時美國的頂尖精英大學正蓬勃發展。疫情過後，包括多間常春藤盟校在內的一小部分大學今年的申請數量出現創紀錄的增長。

"For brand-name colleges, the demand is <u>off the charts</u>," says education consultant Hafeez Lakhani. "It's never been harder to get in. Yet private colleges that are less prestigious but equally expensive are struggling to attract [7]**applicants**," he added. "The majority of people are going to say, 'Is that <u>worth my while</u>?'"

教育顧問哈菲茲拉卡尼說：「以名校來說，需求量已破表，會比以往更難獲得錄取。不過那些較無名氣但學費同樣昂貴的私立大學卻正苦於招生困難。」他補充道：「多數人會說，『這值得我的時間和精力嗎？』」

College is becoming a path for only those with the means to pay for it—and costs are still rising. [8]**Tuition** and fees plus room and board for a four-year private college averaged $53,430 in the 2022-2023 school year; at four-year, in-state public colleges, it was $23,250, according to the College Board. Now, the majority of applicants come from the country's wealthiest [9]**zip codes**.

大學正成為只有付得起學費的人才能走的路，而且學費仍在上漲。根據美國大學理事會的數據，2022-2023 學年，四年制私立大學的學雜費加上食宿費平均為 5 萬 3430 美元，四年制州立大學（本州居民）則為 2 萬 3250 美元。現在多數申請者都來自美國最富裕的地區。

▲ 於 2023 年關閉的聖名大學校園一景

Advanced Words

* **quadruple** [kwɑˋdrupəl]
  (v.) 使成四倍

* **opt** [ɑpt]
  (v.) 選擇

* **endowment** [ɪnˋdaʊmənt]
  (n.) 捐贈基金、財產

Tongue-tied No More

off the charts
遠高於平常紀錄，超出預期

According to climate scientists, ocean temperatures are **off the charts**.
根據氣候科學家的說法，海洋溫度破了紀錄。

worth one's while
值得去做，有用處的
worthwhile (adj.) 值得的

It would be **worth your while** to review the material before your exam.
在考試前花點時間複習資料是值得的。

EZpedia

Ivy League 常春藤聯盟
美國八所私立學校（布朗大學、哈佛大學、康乃爾大學、普林斯頓大學、達特茅斯學院、耶魯大學、哥倫比亞大學和賓州大學）所組成。該名稱最早是因為體育賽事，現在主要指其學術聲望與入學標準。

College Board 美國大學理事會
1900 年成立的非營利組織，現在有超過 6000 多個世界頂尖的教育機構加入。每年會藉由 SAT、大學先修課程（Advanced Placement Program）等服務來幫助超過七百萬名學生進入大學。

Harvard to Add AI Instructor

哈佛大學將增設人工智慧講師

© Tada Images / Shutterstock.com

全文朗讀 ♪ 079　　單字 ♪ 080

Vocabulary

1. **instructor** [ɪn`strʌktə]
   (n.) 大學講師，教員

2. **introductory** [ˌɪntrə`dʌktəri]
   (adj.) 引導的，導論的

3. **approximate** [ə`prɑksə met]
   (v.) 接近，近似

4. **ratio** [`reʃio]
   (n.) 比例

5. **via** [`viə]
   (prep.) 經由，透過

6. **feedback** [`fid bæk]
   (n.) 建議，意見，評論

7. **code** [kod]
   (n.) 代碼，程式碼

8. **amid** [ə`mɪd]
   (prep.) 在……之中

9. **drawback** [`drɔ bæk]
   (n.) 缺點，短處

Advanced Words

* **flagship** [`flæg ʃɪp]
   (adj.) 旗艦的，頂尖的

* **unveil** [ʌn`vel]
   (v.) 公諸於眾，揭露

* **entice** [ɪn`taɪs]
   (v.) 誘使，慫恿

Harvard University plans to use an AI chatbot similar to ChatGPT as an [1)]**instructor** in its *flagship computer programming course. Students enrolled in CS50 Introduction to Computer Science will be encouraged to use the artificial intelligence tool when classes begin this fall. The AI teacher used in the [2)]**introductory** course will likely be based on OpenAI's ChatGPT, according to course instructors.

哈佛大學計劃使用類似 ChatGPT 的人工智慧聊天機器人擔任領航電腦程式設計課程的講師。今年秋季開課時，該校將鼓勵報名「CS50：電腦科學導論」的學生使用人工智慧工具。根據課程講師的說法，這門導論課將使用的人工智慧講師可能會以 OpenAI 的 ChatGPT 為基礎。

"Our own hope is that, through AI, we can eventually [3)]**approximate** a 1:1 teacher-student [4)]**ratio** for every student in CS50, as by providing them with software-based tools that, 24/7, can support their learning at a pace and in a style that works best for them individually," CS50 professor David Malan told *The Harvard Crimson*.

CS50 課程教授大衛馬蘭告訴《哈佛緋紅報》：「我們希望透過人工智慧，最終可以為 CS50 課程的每名學生提供將近一比一的師生比例，因為藉由提供學生以軟體為基礎的工具，可以每週七天、每天 24 小時以最適合他們各自的速度和方式支援他們學習。」

"Providing support that's tailored to students' specific questions has long been a challenge at scale [5)]**via** edX and OpenCourseWare more generally, with so many students online, so these features will benefit students both on campus and off," Malan added. "The AI teaching bot will offer [6]**feedback** to students, helping to find bugs in their [7]**code** or give feedback on their work"

馬蘭補充說道：「透過 edX 和 OpenCourseWare 等平台大規模為學生的具體問題提供專屬支援，長期以來一直是重大挑戰，因為有這麼多的學生在線上，所以這些功能將使學生在校內外受益。人工智慧教學機器人將和學生互動，協助他們發現程式碼中的錯誤，或對他們的作業提供建議。」

Its arrival comes [8]**amid** a huge surge in the popularity of AI tools, with ChatGPT becoming the fastest growing app ever since its launch in November 2022. The chatbot reached 100 million active users within two months of being *unveiled, with users *enticed by its ability to perform a range of tasks, from writing essays to generating computer code.

這門課開設之際正值人工智慧工具的普及率大幅上升，ChatGPT 自 2022 年 11 月推出以來便是成長最快的應用程式。該聊天機器人在發佈後兩個月內就達到一億活躍用戶，用戶都被它能執行各種任務的能力所吸引，涵蓋寫作文到生成電腦程式碼等。

Professor Malan said students would be warned of the [9]**drawbacks** of the AI, saying they should "always think critically" when presented with information. "But the tools will only get better through feedback from students and teachers alike," he said. "So they, too, will be very much part of the process."

馬蘭教授表示，學生們會被警告人工智慧的缺點，並表示他們在接收資訊時應該「維持批判性思考」。他說：「但只有透過學生和老師提供意見，這些工具才會改進。所以他們也將成為改進過程的一部分。」

Tongue-tied No More

at scale 大規模
通常用於談論技術、商業規模、製造規模。

The new car model will begin production **at scale** next month.
新車款將於下個月開始量產。

The company is developing a new program to train employees **at scale**.
該公司正在開發一項新計畫，以便大規模培訓員工。

EZpedia

edX
edX 是一個由麻省理工學院和哈佛大學所創立的開放線上課堂平台，為大眾提供大學教育水準的線上課堂及微碩士學位。2012 年秋天，edX 在 MITx 啟動。

OpenCourseWare
英文本意是知識的開放與分享，中文譯為「開放式課程」。麻省理工學院從 2002 年起展開「開放式課程計畫」，目的是讓任何人在任何地點都能夠在線上接受所有大學生和研究生課程，以促進教學資源共享，並落實終身學習。

全文朗讀 ♪ 081　　單字 ♪ 082

Vocabulary

1. **smuggler** [ˈsmʌɡlɚ]
   (n.) 走私者

2. **populate** [ˈpɑpjəˌlet]
   (v.) 構成……的人口

3. **hostile** [ˈhɑstəl]
   (adj.) 敵對的，不友善的

4. **immune** [ɪˈmjun]
   (adj.) 免疫的

5. **humanity** [hjuˈmænəti]
   (n.)（總稱）人類

6. **blend** [blɛnd]
   (n.) 混合，混合物

Advanced Words

* **fungus** [ˈfʌŋɡəs] (n.) 真菌

* **zombie** [ˈzɑmbi] (n.) 殭屍

* **premiere** [prɪˈmɪr]
   (v.) 初次上演，首映會

Tongue-tied No More

in the works 進行中，籌備中

According to the studio, new Lord of the Rings films are **in the works**.
根據製片公司表示，新的《魔戒》電影正在製作中。

The Last of Us is a post-apocalyptic drama series on HBO based on the 2013 video game of the same name. The show is set 20 years after a global pandemic caused by a *fungus, which transforms its hosts into flesh-eating *zombies and results in the collapse of human society. The story follows Joel, a ¹⁾**smuggler** tasked with transporting teen orphan Ellie across a United States ²⁾**populated** by zombies and ³⁾**hostile** humans. Because Ellie is ⁴⁾**immune** to the fungus, getting her to a lab out West may be ⁵⁾**humanity**'s last hope for survival. Created by Craig Mazin (of *Chernobyl* fame) and Neil Druckmann (who developed the video game), the series stars Pedro Pascal as Joel and Bella Ramsey as Ellie. Since *premiering on January 15, 2023, *The Last of Us* has been praised by critics for its perfect ⁶⁾**blend** of horror and heart. Season 2 is already in the works.

《最後生還者》是 HBO 的一部末日後影集，根據 2013 年的同名電動遊戲改編。本劇以真菌引發全球疫情 20 年後為背景，這種真菌會將宿主變成食肉喪屍，導致人類社會崩潰。故事從走私者喬爾展開，他的任務是護送青少年孤兒艾莉穿越遍佈喪屍和充滿敵意人類的美國。由於艾莉對真菌免疫，因此將她帶到西部的實驗室可能是人類生存的最後希望。這部影集由克雷格麥辛（因創作《核爆家園》而聞名）和尼爾達克曼（電遊開發者）創作，佩德羅帕斯卡飾演喬爾，貝拉拉姆齊飾演艾莉。《最後生還者》於 2023 年 1 月 15 日首播以來，因完美結合驚悚與情感元素而受到影評人稱讚。第二季已在製作中。

*B*eef is a 2023 Netflix *dramedy series created by Korean director Lee Sung Jin. Set in L.A., the show stars Steven Yeun as Danny Cho, a struggling [1)]**contractor** with a chip on his shoulder, and Ali Wong as Amy Lau, a successful business owner with a [2)]**seemingly** perfect life. The two strangers meet in a road [3)]**rage** incident in the parking lot of a home improvement store that turns into a full-scale *feud. What began as a minor conflict turns into something much darker—and more entertaining—as Danny and Amy channel all the stress in their personal and professional lives into an [4)]**escalating** cycle of [5)]**revenge**. *Beef* was released on April 6 to positive reviews, and has been nominated for 13 Primetime Emmys, including Best Limited Series and acting [6)]**nods** for Yeun, Wong and three supporting actors.

Vocabulary

1. **contractor** [ˈkɑntræktɚ]
   (n.) 承包商

2. **seemingly** [ˈsimɪŋli]
   (adv.) 表面上，似乎是

3. **rage** [redʒ]
   (n.) 憤怒，狂怒

4. **escalate** [ˈɛskəˌlet]
   (v.)（逐步）上升

5. **revenge** [rɪˈvɛndʒ]
   (v.) 報仇，報復

6. **nod** [nɑd]
   (n.) 提名

Advanced Words

* **dramedy** [ˈdrɑmədi]
   (n.) 融合嚴肅與幽默的電影、影集

* **feud** [fjud]
   (n.) 世仇，爭吵

Tongue-tied No More

(have) a chip on one's shoulder
心理不平衡，耿耿於懷

A: Why does Jonathan **have a chip on his shoulder**?
強納森為什麼心懷不滿？
B: He's been working here for years and never got a promotion.
他在這裡工作了很多年，但從未升職。

2023 年的網飛劇情喜劇影集《怒嗆人生》是由韓裔導演李成真創作，這部影集以洛杉磯為背景，由史帝芬連飾演生活坎坷、心懷不滿的承包商丹尼周；黃艾莉飾演成功的公司老闆劉艾美，她過著看似完美的生活。這兩個陌生人在一家居家裝潢店的停車場發生行車糾紛，後來演變成全面的長期爭鬥。隨著丹尼和艾美將私人生活和工作中的所有壓力轉化為越演越烈的復仇循環，一開始的小衝突轉變為更黑暗也更有趣的故事。《怒嗆人生》於 4 月 6 日首播後獲得好評，並獲得 13 項黃金時段艾美獎提名，包括最佳迷你影集獎，以及史蒂芬連、黃艾莉和三位配角的演技獎。

▲《怒嗆人生》劇照

EZpedia

post-apocalyptic drama
末日後戲劇

注重描寫地球走向終結的過程，通常設定在未來。事實上，末日後作品（post-apocalyptic fiction）存在千年已久，例如美索不達米亞的《吉爾伽美什史詩》就提到世界的終結。

Chernobyl 核爆家園
英美合拍的五集電視迷你影集，通過虛實結合的方法展現 1986 年蘇聯烏克蘭發生的車諾比核事故及其善後工作的故事。

EZpedia

Primetime Emmys
黃金時段艾美獎

由美國電視藝術與科學學院（ATAS）頒發，旨在表揚美國黃金時段電視節目的優秀作品。

Vocabulary

1. **peer** [pɪr]
   (n.) 同輩，同儕

2. **thrust** [θrʌst]
   (v.) 讓人捲入

3. **mythology** [mɪˋθɑlədʒɪ]
   (n.) 神話

4. **graphic** [ˋgræfɪk]
   (adj.) 繪畫的

5. **inspiration** [ˏɪnspəˋreʃən]
   (n.) 靈感，啟發

6. **exploration** [ˏɛkspləˋreʃən]
   (n.) 探究，探索，探測

7. **nationality** [ˏnæʃəˋnælətɪ]
   (n.) 國籍，民族

Advanced Words

* **unexpectedly** [ˏʌnɪkˋspɛktɪdlɪ]
  (adv.) 意外地，未料到的

* **incorporate** [ɪnˋkɔrpəˏret]
  (v.) 納入，併入

Tongue-tied No More

fit in 適應環境，相處融洽

Katherine says she doesn't **fit in** at her new school.
凱瑟琳說她不適應新學校。

Tim tried hard to **fit in**, but his coworkers didn't accept him.
蒂姆努力融入，但他的同事不接受他。

American Born Chinese is an American action comedy series created by Kelvin Yu for Disney+. It follows Chinese-American high school student Jin Wang (Ben Wang), who is struggling to <u>fit in</u> with his mostly white [1)]**peers**. When asked to show new exchange student Wei-Chen (Jimmy Liu) around, he's *__**unexpectedly**__ [2)]**thrust** into a battle between gods from Chinese [3)]**mythology**, including Sun Wukong (Daniel Wu) and Guanyin (Michelle Yeoh). The series is based on the 2006 [4)]**graphic** novel *American Born Chinese* by Gene Luen Yang, who drew [5)]**inspiration** from his own adolescent years in the 1990s, *__**incorporating**__ elements of folk religion found in the classic Chinese novel *Journey to the West*. Critics have called *American Born Chinese* one of the best shows on Disney+, praising its [6)]**exploration** of Asian-American identity. The show has, however, been criticized in Taiwan for changing the [7)]**nationality** of the character Wei-Chen from Taiwanese to Chinese.

《西遊 ABC》是由游朝敏為 Disney+ 創作的美國動作喜劇影集，講述美籍華裔高中生王謹（王班飾演）努力融入大多數為白人的同學。他在被要求帶新交換生維辰（劉敬飾演）參觀校園時，意外捲入中國神話的諸神之戰，其中包括孫悟空（吳彥祖飾演）和觀音（楊紫瓊飾演）。這部影集改編自楊謹倫在 2006 年出版的圖文小說《美生中國人》，楊謹倫以自己在 1990 年代的青少年時期為創作靈感，融入中國經典小說《西遊記》中的民間宗教元素。影評人稱《西遊 ABC》是 Disney+ 最好的影集之一，讚揚本劇對亞裔美國人族群認同的探索。不過本劇因將維辰一角的國籍從臺灣改為中國而在臺灣受到批評。

▲ 《西遊 ABC》

Must-See Films in 2023

2023 推薦電影

© WOSUNAN / Shutterstock.com

全文朗讀 ♪ 087　單字 ♪ 088

Spider-Man: Across the Spider-Verse is a 2023 [1)]**animated** superhero film featuring the Marvel Comics characters Miles Morales, who is Spider-Man in his world (Earth-1610) and Gwen Stacy, who is Spider-Woman in hers (Earth-65). The *sequel to 2018's *Spider-Man: Into the Spider-Verse*, it's set in a *multiverse of [2)]**alternate** universes called the Spider-Verse. After [3)]**reuniting** with Gwen, Miles sets out on an adventure across the multiverse, where he encounters a team of Spider-People charged with protecting its very existence. However, when the heroes [4)]**clash** on how to handle a new threat—a dangerous [5)]**villain** called the Spot—Miles finds himself pitted against the other Spiders. He must soon redefine what it means to be a hero so he can save the people he loves most. Like *Into the Spider-Verse*, *Across the Spider-Verse* was a critical and box office hit, receiving praise for its [6)]**visual** style, story, voice acting and script.

《蜘蛛人：穿越新宇宙》是 2023 年的超級英雄動畫電影，主角是漫威漫畫人物麥爾斯摩拉斯和關史黛西，麥爾斯摩拉斯在他自己的世界（1610 號地球）是蜘蛛人，關史黛西在她自己的世界（65 號地球）是女蜘蛛人。這部電影是 2018 年《蜘蛛人：新宇宙》的續集，背景設在一個由多個平行宇宙組成，名為「蜘蛛人宇宙」的多元宇宙。麥爾斯與關重聚後，踏上穿越多重宇宙的冒險之旅，他在那裡遇到一支負責保護多重宇宙存在的蜘蛛人團隊。不過英雄們在如何應付新威脅，即名為「斑點」的危險反派問題上發生衝突時，麥爾斯發現自己與其他蜘蛛人相互為敵。他必須盡快重新定義何謂英雄，這樣才能拯救他的至親。《蜘蛛人：穿越新宇宙》與《蜘蛛人：新宇宙》一樣也叫好又叫座，因其視覺風格、故事、配音和劇本而備受讚譽。

Vocabulary

1. **animated** [ˋænəˏmetɪd]
   (adj.) 動畫的
   animation [ˏænəˋmeʃən]
   (n.) 動畫

2. **alternate** [ˋɔltənɪt]
   (adj.) 替代的，替換的

3. **reunite** [ˏrijuˋnaɪt]
   (v.) 重聚，再聯合

4. **clash** [klæʃ]
   (v.) 發生衝突，鬥爭

5. **villain** [ˋvɪlən]
   (n.) 反派角色，壞蛋

6. **visual** [ˋvɪʒuəl]
   (adj.) 視覺的

Advanced Words

* **sequel** [ˋsikwəl]
  (n.) 續集，續篇

* **multiverse** [ˋmʌltɪˏvɜs]
  (n.) 多重宇宙

Vocabulary

1. **fantasy** [ˋfæntəsi]
   (n.) 奇幻作品

2. **embark** [ɪmˋbɑrk]
   (v.) 啟程，開始進行

3. **ponder** [ˋpɑndə]
   (v.) 思考，沉思

4. **quest** [kwɛst]
   (n.) 尋找，追求

5. **phenomenon** [fəˋnɑmə͵nɑn]
   (n.) 成功、流行的人事物

Advanced Words

* **iconic** [aɪˋkɑnɪk]
  (adj.) 代表性的，指標性的

* **existential** [͵ɛgzɪsˋtɛnʃəl]
  (adj.)（有關）存在的，存在主義的

* **cellulite** [ˋsɛljə͵laɪt]
  (n.) 蜂窩性組織

Tongue-tied No More

in tow 帶著，跟隨
tow 當動詞時，意指用繩索、鏈條拖拉車輛。

The celebrity had a reporter and a photographer **in tow**.
這位名人帶著一名記者和一名攝影師。

EZpedia

Mattel 美泰兒
是一家美國的跨國玩具製造公司，於 1945 年在洛杉磯成立。旗下包括全球知名品牌—美國女孩（American Girl）、風火輪小汽車（Hot Wheels）、湯瑪士小火車（Thomas & Friends）等。

▲《Barbie 芭比》劇照

Based on the **iconic** Mattel fashion doll, *Barbie* is a 2023 [1)]**fantasy** comedy directed and written by Greta Gerwig. Although there have been a number of animated Barbie movies over the years, this is the first live-action film about the world's most popular doll. The story follows Barbie (Margot Robbie) and Ken (Ryan Gosling) as they [2)]**embark** on a journey of self-discovery following an *existential* crisis. Barbie is living her perfect life in Barbieland, but she suddenly starts [3)]**pondering** the concept of death, and begins to develop human problems—like bad breath and *cellulite*. Told that her only hope lies in finding the girl who plays with her, Barbie—with Ken in tow—travels to the real world on a [4)]**quest** for answers. *Barbie* was released on the same day as historical drama *Oppenheimer*, leading to the "Barbenheimer" [5)]**phenomenon**, where large numbers of fans saw these two very different films together as a double feature.

《Barbie 芭比》是 2023 年的奇幻喜劇電影，由葛莉塔潔薇執導和編劇，以具有代表性的美泰兒時尚娃娃為藍本。雖然多年來已有許多芭比娃娃動畫電影，但這是第一部關於世上最受歡迎的娃娃的真人電影。故事講述芭比（瑪格羅比飾演）和肯尼（雷恩葛斯林飾演）在遇到存在危機後踏上自我發現之旅。芭比原本在芭比世界過著圓滿的生活，但突然開始思考死亡的概念，並開始出現口臭和橘皮等人類問題。她得知唯一的希望是找到跟她一起玩的女孩後，芭比帶著肯尼前往現實世界尋找答案。《Barbie 芭比》與歷史劇《奧本海默》在同一天上映，引發了「芭本海默」風潮，大量粉絲同時觀看這兩部截然不同的電影。

*O*ppenheimer is an ***epic** historical drama film written and directed by five-time Oscar nominee Christopher Nolan. Based on the 2005 [1)]**biography** *American Prometheus*, the film stars Cillian Murphy as J. Robert Oppenheimer, the [2)]**physicist** who led the Manhattan Project. The film explores Oppenheimer's personal life and career, from his early days as a student at Harvard to his role in the creation of the [3)]**atomic** bomb and its *aftermath. Set during World War II and the Cold War, it also examines the moral and ethical issues surrounding the development of nuclear weapons. Oppenheimer is a complex figure, and the film doesn't <u>shy away from</u> his [4)]**contradictions**, [5)]**portraying** both his brilliance as a scientist and his many character [6)]**flaws**. Frequently cited by critics as one of the best films of 2023, *Oppenheimer* is a must-see for anyone interested in history, science, or the human condition.

《奧本海默》是史詩歷史劇情電影,由五次獲得奧斯卡提名的克里斯多福諾蘭編劇和執導。這部電影是根據 2005 年的傳記《奧本海默》改編,由席尼墨菲飾演帶領曼哈頓計畫的物理學家羅伯特奧本海默。這部電影探討奧本海默的個人和職業生涯,從他早年在哈佛大學的學生時代,到他創造原子彈及其帶來的後果。這部電影以第二次世界大戰和冷戰為背景,並探討核武發展所衍生的道德和倫理問題。奧本海默是位複雜的人物,電影中並不迴避他本身的矛盾,同時描繪了他身為科學家的才華及他的許多性格缺陷。《奧本海默》多次被影評評為 2023 年最佳電影之一,對歷史、科學或人類狀況感興趣的人來說,這是一部必看之作。

▲ 《奧本海默》劇照

全文朗讀 ♪ 091　單字 ♪ 092

Vocabulary

1. **biography** [baɪˋɑɡrəfɪ]
   (n.) 傳記

2. **physicist** [ˋfɪzɪsɪst]
   (n.) 物理學家

3. **atomic** [əˋtɑmɪk]
   (adj.) 原子的,原子能的

4. **contradiction** [͵kɑntrəˋdɪkʃən]
   (n.) 矛盾

5. **portray** [porˋtre]
   (v.) 描繪,呈現

6. **flaw** [flɔ]
   (n.) 缺點,瑕疵

Advanced Words

* **epic** [ˋɛpɪk]
   (adj.) 史詩的,史詩般的

* **aftermath** [ˋæftɚ͵mæθ]
   (n.) 後果,餘波

Tongue-tied No More

shy away from
(不喜歡、害怕而)退縮

Robert has never been one to **shy away from** hard work.
羅伯特從不逃避艱苦的工作。

EZpedia

Manhattan Project 曼哈頓計畫
美國於二戰期間研究核武的計畫。總負責人是奧本海默,總計畫經費約二十幾億美金,由美國總統羅斯福所批准。1945 年,曼哈頓計畫所製造出的第一顆原子彈在新墨西哥州試爆成功,威力相當於 21000 噸的三硝基甲苯(TNT)。

英文時事閱讀選 2024 版 / EZ TALK 編輯部，
Judd Piggott；黃書英譯 . -- 初版 . -- 臺北市：日
月文化出版股份有限公司 , 2023.12
　面；　公分 . -- (EZ Talk)
ISBN 978-626-7329-87-0 (平裝)
1.CST: 新聞英文 2.CST: 讀本
805.18　　　　　　　　112017335

EZ TALK

英文時事閱讀選 2024 版

總 編 審：Judd Piggott
作　　者：EZ TALK編輯部, Judd Piggott
譯　　者：黃書英
責任編輯：謝有容、鄭雅方
封面設計：兒日設計
內頁設計：于靖
內頁排版：簡單瑛設
行銷企劃：張爾芸
錄音後製：印笛錄音製作有限公司
錄 音 員：Jacob Roth、Leah Zimmermann
照片出處：shutterstock、Wikimedia Commons 等詳見圖片標示

發 行 人：洪祺祥
副總經理：洪偉傑
副總編輯：曹仲堯
法律顧問：建大法律事務所
財務顧問：高威會計師事務所

出　　版：日月文化出版股份有限公司
製　　作：EZ 叢書館
地　　址：臺北市信義路三段151號8樓
電　　話：(02)2708-5509
傳　　真：(02)2708-6157
客服信箱：service@heliopolis.com.tw
網　　址：www.heliopolis.com.tw
郵撥帳號：19716071日月文化出版股份有限公司

總 經 銷：聯合發行股份有限公司
電　　話：(02)2917-8022
傳　　真：(02)2915-7212
印　　刷：中原造像股份有限公司
初　　版：2023年12月
定　　價：420 元
I S B N：978-626-7329-87-0

PART 3 *Extra Credit 延伸閱讀*

SECTION 07 Environment 環境生態

SECTION 08 Sports 體育

SECTION

03
World
國際局勢

SECTION

04
Business &
Economy
商業經濟

SECTION

05
Technology
科技新知

目次 Contents

編輯序

　　今年邁入尾聲之際，EZ Talk 編輯群再度與讀者們一同回顧當年度國際新聞消息。2023 年在新聞台與社群動態上持續被大眾討論的事情，大概不脫離以下這三件：科技業裁員潮、AI 生成內容、一週工作四天。2022 年至 2023 年的科技業裁員潮主要被歸因於 COVID-19 嚴峻疫情所導致的工廠關閉、俄烏戰爭影響原物料及其成本、前幾年的過度招聘。而美國也另有報告指出 AI 也是裁員的原因之一。2023 年可說是生成式 AI 元年，每天都有各種推陳出新的 AI 應用與模型，生成式 AI 的魅力就在於人人皆可用，人人皆會用。各位讀者之前的社群動態牆上是不是也充滿了其他人的「美式 90 年代 AI 畢業照」呢？

　　雖然一些人對生成式 AI 抱持新奇和樂觀的態度，認為善用這項工具不只可以解決許多重複性的日常工作，也可以省下耗費技術和腦力的工作時間，也許未來靠著生成式 AI，說不定將可以實現「一週工作四天制」呢！不過也有一些人認為生成式 AI 將會取代他們的工作，美國編劇和演員就因此掀起了大罷工，當然罷工還包括其他原因。

　　提到 AI 引起的裁員和罷工，不知道職場上最年輕的 Z 世代是否也頗有感觸？有篇文章就報導了 Z 世代是工作壓力最大的族群！很多人解決壓力的方式就是滑臉書、刷 IG 或抖音，不過近年已有許多公司組織和政府機構，因為背後的中國政府因素而禁止員工使用抖音。英國就禁止在政府設備上安裝抖音。除了國際間的利益因素，美國公衛署總署長也警告未成年使用這些社群媒體的風險。

　　除了科技相關新聞事件，本書也將回顧諸如土耳其地震、英國國王查爾斯三世的加冕、金磚國家貨幣的討論、大谷翔平經典賽 MVP 等等，希望讀者們能夠透過本書這 46 篇英文時事文章，在學習英文的同時一併拓展閱讀世界的角度！

EZ Talk 編輯部